HOME

REBEKAH LATTIN-RAWSTRONE

PRAISE FOR HOME

'Dark, perverse, convincing and compassionate –
Rebekah Lattin-Rawstrone's *Home* is an extremely
strong first novel' Toby Litt, author of *Hospital*

'Before you know it, Rebekah Lattin-Rawstrone's
acutely observed characters get under your skin and
you're living their lives. *Home* is magnetic,
claustrophobic and chilling – an exceptional
novel that will disturb and provoke me
for a long time to come'
Joseph D'Lacey, author of *Meat*

'A chilling depiction of evil made ordinary, *Home* is
a compelling vision of a world not too distant from
our own. The novel's rich everyday detail and
perfectly realised characters make the nightmare it
depicts even more disturbing. I am reminded of
Doris Lessing when I read Rebekah's work'
Paul Blaney, author of *The Anchoress*

'Exquisitely written, *Home* is a compelling, gut-
wrenching, raw novel. I loved this book and I can't
stop thinking about the questions
the novel asks of us all'
Dr Heidi James-Dunbar, author and lecturer in
creative writing at Kingston University

'*Home* is an unnerving novel that stays with you
long after you have finished reading it'
BookEmStevo

HOME

REBEKAH LATTIN-RAWSTRONE

Images by Katherine Jones

Red Button Publishing

Contents

For Helen and Joe

Woman – I

It would be hard to say how long I have been lying here. Time swims into itself, fluid, distanced. Every time I wake up, I see the same room, from the same angle. For a while, I was shocked by it. Its bland uniformity – the pebble-dash lino, the off-white walls – frightened me. I tried to mark time by the shadows on the ceiling. I followed the light as it rose from the bottom right of the window, over to the left. But the shadows, though shifting, were a constant presence. Even at night, darkness was never complete. Light filtered from under the door and the window cast a purple, orange haze across the sheets.

Slowly, as I swam on through the days, things took shape. I began to feel my body twitch and ache. Pins and needles seemed to course through my entire frame and the pain felt like a promise. I obsessed over every muscle twinge, waiting for it, anticipating it, following it in the hope of movement. The pain across my face and along my left arm was particularly strong. When I opened and closed my eyes, I could feel something tugging against the skin of my face. What I had taken for a sheet, bent along my line of sight, I recognised as a bandage, pressed hard across my nose, its edges scratching tape and plaster across the skin beneath my cheeks and by my ears. I strained my eyes along my aching arm to tubes at my wrist. I felt safe then. I knew I must be hurt or ill. I thought I was in a hospital and it comforted me. For a time I slept well, free of anxiety. I saw an end in sight.

But that sleeping freedom did not last. I woke thirsty and alone, the sheets wet with sweat, my silent limbs dragging me deeper into the centre of the bed. I was more than at sea, I was in space, floating endlessly: suspended. There was nothing for me to hold on to. The room was the only constant. I could remember nothing else. I did not know why I was there. It was as if I was being sucked into the bed, my body and mind pulled into a black hole where there was no time and so no memory.

I tried to scream. My lips were stiff and would not shape the breath that burst them apart. Though my jaw moved and my mouth was open, the sound that came out was a broken bleat. Thick and dull, my tongue slept in my mouth, breaking the sound. I made my throat raw with muffled screams, fear turning to tears that fell in the channels of my wrinkles and welled cold in my ears and along my bandage with all the force my body could not muster. This one release triggered another. An ugly squelching sound echoed through the room, stifling the tears. With shame I felt my bowel move. Unable to control it, I waited for the smell of acrid cabbage, a warmth under my thighs, but neither came. The gurgling did not stop, seeping silently into the sheets; instead it made the splashing, bubbling sound of water on plastic. I was spending pennies into bags. I lay awake then, feeling my tears dry. I can't be certain how much time passed, but I must have fallen asleep again. All I know is that I remember being woken by the sound of the door. I felt a surge of hope. There were people coming in. Though I knew someone must have come before, must have fitted me up with drips and bags, this was the first time I had been conscious of another person in the room.

The lady in front was a nurse. I could tell because she wore a uniform: light blue, pressed trousers and a shirt buttoned high at the collar.

'Well, hello there, Mrs Eames. You're awake. What a surprise.'

Her voice was unnecessarily loud and slow. It was the kind of voice people use when they speak to very small children.

Behind her, a woman and two young children straggled into the room. One of the children was carrying flowers.

'You've got visitors. Look who it is.'

She stood back a little, presenting the woman and the children to me, smiling insidiously. Then she stretched out an arm towards me.

'Here she is. Why don't you say hello.'

The child with the flowers, a young boy with messy brown hair sticking out at the crown, walked towards me and held out the flowers with one hand. He was still quite far away, at the foot of the bed. He didn't look like he wanted to be any closer.

He looked at me, then back at his mother and the nurse. They smiled him forwards.

'What's wrong with your face?' he said.

The woman's eyes and lips twitched at me rather desperately, as if apologising.

'Joe,' she said, under her breath, her teeth gritted. 'Remember what we talked about?'

Joe nodded and held the flowers out towards me.

'We brought you some flowers, Granny,' he said.

I stared at him. He wasn't looking at me, but at his feet. He was wearing combat trousers and trainers, camouflaged for somewhere else.

'Let's put those in some water, shall we?' the nurse said.

She took the flowers from the child and left the room. The boy looked up at me then and frowned. Behind him his mother shifted. The other child was clinging to her knees. She stroked this child's head.

'Sorry we haven't come before,' she said. 'This is Joseph, Joe, and this little one here is Amy. You remember? Josh's family.'

She paused, waiting for me to say something I suppose.

'I just thought you might want to see the kids,' she added, looking up from the little girl, searching my face. She looked tired and upset. 'Josh doesn't know we're here, but I know he'll be glad we came. He would want to know how you are. He misses you, I know he does. He … he misses you.'

I just stared at her, this woman, blinking into her hands as she stroked her child's head. I swear I didn't recognise her. I could tell she was lying about Josh wanting her to be there, but who was Josh? It was so confusing. Knowing I had found it hard to scream, I didn't expect to be able to speak, but I needed to try. I kept opening my mouth, scratching my upper lip on the plaster, but I could only manage a sort of gasping, guppy sound, my tongue paddling in saliva like a fish at low tide. I felt suddenly thirsty.

The nurse came back in with the flowers in a vase.

She set them down on the table on my right-hand side. She stood them next to a water jug and a glass. It was the first time I'd noticed them. I wanted to drink.

'There,' she said, 'doesn't that brighten up the place?' She smiled around at us.

I looked at her hopelessly and opened my mouth again making more incompetent noises as if I'd never been able to speak. It was so frustrating. I just wanted a sip of water.

'Can't she speak?' Joe asked the nurse. 'Do you want to say something, Granny?' And he turned to look right at me.

'She's crying,' the little girl said.

I wasn't crying, but I could feel that my bandage was still wet. It itched.

'Now, now,' her mother replied, 'this is a bit of a shock for Granny, isn't it? She didn't expect to see us. Look how happy she is.'

'Why doesn't she say something?' Joe asked the nurse again.

'Joe, darling, you know what Mummy said. Granny is very ill.'

'Your mummy is right, Joe. Granny might not be able to say anything. When you have a stroke, you can't always remember how to do things. You have to relearn. I can see your granny is very happy you're here, aren't you, Mrs Eames?' She looked at me, head on one side. Her hair was greasy and pinned up with those old-fashioned hairpins. She had a particularly nasty batch of raw pimples on her chin and forehead. They were covered in foundation, but you could see them anyway. Where she had picked them, the broken skin put cracks in the make-up, leaving her break-out more obvious than it might have been

11

otherwise. When she turned her face away from the others her smile soured, leaving fissures around the corners of her mouth. If I could, I would have punched her. I narrowed my eyes at her and summoning all my will, tried again to speak.

'hoo … iz mzuz eemz?' I said.

'What did she say?' Joe asked the nurse.

'hoo …' I started again.

'Now don't over-exert yourself, Mrs Eames,' the nurse said, leaning in over me, a piece of her foul hair falling into my face, 'there's plenty of time for talking.'

She turned back to the woman.

'She has a speech therapist every other afternoon. She's made a lot of progress.'

The woman nodded. She was trying not to cry. She held her daughter closer to her, stroking the child's hair through her fingers over and over again.

'Josh would be pleased,' she said. 'I wish he would come.'

The nurse moved around the bed and patted the woman on the shoulder.

'There, there,' she said, 'I'm sure it means the world to Mrs Eames. As soon as she's talking we'll never hear the end of it.'

'hoo …' I tried again. Joe was straining his ears and looking intently at me. He began to move closer to the bed. I needed him to listen. I needed someone to explain things. The name, the speech therapy, this was all new to me. Could I really have forgotten so much?

The nurse intervened.

'Right, Joe, do you want to hold your granny's hand? I just want to check her medication and then that's probably enough for today. We don't want to tire her out, do we?'

Joe looked very frightened. He turned to his mother, who was still stroking the little girl's hair. She smiled at him through her tears. Reluctantly – I could see it in the way his hands stretched well beyond his body – he reached out to take my hand. His fingers were warm and clammy.

'That's it,' the nurse said, 'you hold tight while I change this over.'

She added something to the drip, switching the bags, writing things down on my chart. It didn't hurt, but I liked holding Joe's hand. He didn't look like he felt similar pleasure. He was hardly touching me at all. Against his flesh, my hand looked old, the thick veins shining blue across the network of sinews, pushing against the paper of my skin. He looked terrified, staring at my hand, my arm, the flesh falling thin off the bones. He had such a pretty plump hand. I squeezed his fingers. But he pulled his hand free as if he had seen a corpse move. Only the nurse seemed to notice.

'There,' she said, flicking the drip to check the timings of its fall, 'see? She'll be much better now. All finished.' She put her hand on Joe's arm. 'Why don't you go and walk around the gardens with your sister while I talk to your mummy, hmm?'

Joe hung his head and let her lead him, Amy and Mummy towards the door.

'What happened to her face?' he asked, looking back at me over his shoulder.

The nurse pushed him out of the room, her hand firmly on his back, leaving the woman standing at the door.

'We'll come again, Diane,' she said, her little girl staring at me from among her skirts. 'I'm going to try and get Josh to come too. He'll be pleased, he really will, to know you're getting better.'

Pushing the girl in front of her, she left the room, firmly closing the door behind her.

'It's such a shame,' she said on the other side of the door. 'I don't know what I expected, but ...'

Her voice trailed off, growing smaller until all I could hear was the pounding in my head. They hadn't given me any water. I sank back into the pillows. Everything felt so heavy. There had clearly been some kind of mistake. I didn't recognise these people. If I could talk to someone I could explain that I was sure, whatever my name was, it wasn't Mrs Eames. Perhaps then they could tell me why I was here and what had happened to me. But I was so tired and my eyelids, battered by waves of exhaustion, wouldn't stay open.

'Mummy,' a high-pitched voice carried through the gap beneath the door, 'Mummy, why did Granny smell funny?'

I'm not your granny, I thought, and fell asleep.

When I woke, the room was darker. Apart from the drawn curtains, it was just as before. I wondered if I had dreamt up the family, the nurse. I strained my eyes around the room and, had it not been for the flowers, would have taken greater pleasure in the fact that I could move my neck, just enough to turn my head slightly, extending my vision. But there, on the side table, was the vase of flowers. They looked tired, their petals withered and drooping, but they were the same flowers the boy had brought.

I remembered the name they used, Diane Eames. Diane Eames. I repeated it over and again in my head, closing my eyes around the sound, trying to visualise the letters curved, hand-written on a page.

Could it be my name? I felt very certain that it could not. Did you forget everything when you had a stroke?

I tried to control the panic that began to creep over me. Could I remember nothing beyond this room? I tried to take comfort in the tightening of flesh I could feel all over my skin. Goosebumps were a good beginning. Perhaps in a few days, just as I could move my neck a little, I would be able to use my tongue. Perhaps I would be sitting up, reaching out for the water jug, or looking out of the window on to the street. Like my muscles, couldn't my mind slowly come back to itself? I looked up at the light shining through the drawn curtains and waited for something to change.

After that first visit, or what I remember as my first visit, they came and fitted me with another tube that goes right down my throat. It's a feeding tube. It hurt when they put it in place. There was no doctor, just the female nurse, her foul hair in my eyes and her breath like an armpit in my face as she pushed a thin plastic tube hard up one nostril. My nose, they say, was broken during the fall. She had the gall to say, 'There we are, much better,' when she'd done it. It made me want to vomit. I could taste blood. I don't know what they put down the tube, but even fed straight in I can smell it: it's like rancid steak and kidney pie, tripe, the scraps of skin and bone crushed into dog food. It's the same smell that lingers in my doorway. I hear them cleaning the floors, but no polish could cover it. It disgusts me. And of course, with this down my throat, there is even less chance of speaking.

I can feel my body bloating and when I do get a chance to try my muscles, when the drugs are down low, there's little movement. My strength is wasting away, turning to flab. When they come to look in on me, they turn me over and rub oil into my flesh where it meets the mattress. Straining my neck towards their hands, I can see that my skin, once red, is now wearing thick and grey like animal hide. I am glad there are no mirrors.

When I say they, I mean the two nurses. Apart from Spotty, the greasy-haired young female nurse, who seems about thirty, thirty-four, there is a male nurse. He's the kind of man I used to find attractive. It's irritating and amusing that, of all things, I remember my sexual preferences. Tall, dark and foreign, he has a large hooked nose and hair that curls into very deep brown eyes. His voice – not that he ever says much to me – is rich and melodic. When I first heard it I was happy because it triggered a memory: from the folds of his throat came the dark voice of Count Dracula.

Though he is tall, he is very thin. His chest falls away from his shoulders giving him the pinched look of a Romantic poet about to catch TB. When he smiles, which is normally only in scorn, there are gaps at the back, teeth missing. And he's got a big cock.

I only know because the bastard pulled it out on me one day. He was changing my colostomy bag and draining my catheter. They don't change the bags all the time. Mostly they empty them. Changing them takes longer. They are meant to clean the little bit of bowel they've pulled through the stomach muscle. It's called a stoma, apparently – Spotty explained it once – but it looks like a misplaced anus. Sometimes, when they change the colostomy bag, the stoma bleeds.

That day was a changing day. They normally empty the old bag first, clean the area and cut the attachments to size, before they fix on the new bag. He took the bag out without emptying it. Little bits of shit dribbled over my belly. He looked me in the eye, waiting until he could see he had my attention. Then he picked up the full bag and waved it in my face.

'You sure shit lot for old lady.' He hardly ever uses articles, leaving his words to float free of the precision grammar could offer.

He held the bag right under my nose. I thought he was going to pour it all over me. He held it there, grinning down at me. I tried to scream, but no noise would come out and it hurts yelling through plastic. I shut my eyes. Anything not to see his face.

I heard the bag smack onto his trolley. My stoma and the surrounding area was stinging, sharp pain searing into the broken flesh. He hadn't bothered to clean me yet. Then I felt his hands close around my catheter.

'Look at me, lady,' he said. His fingers, cold and slick with lubricant, traced over the catheter, nudging the lips of my vagina. 'Look at me, just taking piss.' He removed the draining tube. The catheter began to empty, lukewarm piss on metal bedpan. 'Taking piss, get it?' He let the urine splash onto the bed sheets. He held it like a hose, playing with the stream until the bag was empty. Then he got his penis out and started waving that around.

'Just taking piss,' he said, laughing. I could see gold fillings in his molars.

Steve – I

They say time is a healer. They sit you down at your own kitchen table and turn their backs on you to make tea. All you can do is stare at the Formica. There is a patch of dried-on dirt, the remains of Fran's last attempt at a sponge. You've been avoiding wiping it off.

When the tea is made, they place the mug in front of you, sometimes with a hand on your shoulder, lightly, briefly. Sometimes they save the touch for when they are sat down opposite, and reach their hand across to finger your sleeve. 'Time's a healer, Steve,' they say, but they never bloody look you in the eye.

It's been nearly a year and a half since then, sixteen months since Fran died and I know now it was their shifting eyes that spoke the truth. All I can see is that time pulls you apart, leaves you broken open – an easy target. I knew back then that things would never be the same. How could they be with Fran dying? But I didn't ever imagine this. I've never been one for horror stories.

It all started when Fran saw the job in the local paper – caretaker and gardener for a nearby care home. I thought she was having me on at first. I mean, I'd retired, sold off the business. We didn't need the money. But Fran wanted me to keep busy. She didn't want me moping about fussing over her and it would be something else to think about when the time came, she said. She thought it would keep me fit, all that manual labour, plus I'd be my own boss and that. The hours were flexible and it was close enough to home so that I could pop back if she needed me.

I went for the interview and the rest is history. Three months after I started, Fran was dead. I've been here ever since.

It was the machines that clinched it for me. I like machines. In the good old days, when the business was still running well, we had ten working coaches. It's true that two were back-ups, kept inside the garage for emergencies, but all of them were state of the art, kept in tip-top nick by our fleet engineer. An industrial floor cleaner and a flash lawnmower aren't exactly Bedfords or Leylands, but the idea of being around that engine hum was enough to tip the balance in Fran's favour. Plus I didn't have to go near the clients – wasn't to even go in their rooms – and the morgue and the waste incinerator were looked after by a specialist. It sounded ideal.

With the hours being flexible and that, I started out working odd hours to fit in with caring for Fran. The care home was good about it. I could work over the weekend if I needed to and as long as the place was clean and tidy, they were happy. Looking back, I see they were playing me a fool's game, but a man can't think straight at a time like that. We'd been married forty-seven years, sweethearts longer.

Seeing as it was Fran's idea, I had no cause to argue. I wanted to be there with her all the time, but as soon as she forced me out it made sense. Even with the nurse doing nights, I hadn't really had a break. Somehow it gave me more energy, pottering around the care home. March can be a funny month and most of the spring flowers had already come and gone – it was one of those years when spring was early – but there was still lots to do in the garden, repairing the lawns, weeding, mulching soil, and general tidying up of climbers and shrubs. And inside the corridors were in desperate need of cleaning. It gave my mind a break, got my limbs going with all that bending and moving about and all that fresh air. I hadn't done any exercise for months, just trapped indoors minding Fran.

I'm not complaining. Don't get me wrong. Fran was my backbone. It's just we both knew she was dying and this was, well … 'If there's a heaven,' she said, forcing herself higher up the pillows, 'I want to know where to watch over you.' Her eyes sparkled at me, playing with me like they always did. 'If there's nothing but a kind of blackness, at least I can picture you getting on with something, not just mooning about the house.' I could see her finger lifting, attempting a wag, and I realised the job was for Fran too. She was always a nosy bugger and she wanted new things to think about.

It's stayed with me, that. At the time I could see her logic, but I can't bear to think of it now. I wouldn't want her to see me here. Still, back then I would come home and distract her, tell her everything. She had opinions about it all – well, at first. The last month she was struggling to remember, falling in and out of consciousness. I just sat with her for hours, holding her hand. Got special leave to be with her the last couple of weeks. You just don't know when it's going to happen and you don't want to not be there. You have to be there.

The day of the interview, she had Mrs Tace down to a tee. 'Mutton dressed as lamb, I'll bet,' she said. 'Trying to attract a younger man.' All I'd said was that she wore high heels and Fran kind of picked up everything else, like osmosis or something. But she was good like that, could always read me. 'Good rack?' she asked. I hadn't wanted to say. It annoyed Fran that I didn't like to talk about boobs. 'Don't mind me,' she used to say. 'Look all you like, I shan't stop you.' She laughed at me and all but, really, I didn't think it was so funny. She was always the one that used to make light of things; through everything she was the one who kept her humour up.

I told her about Mrs Tace's heels because I could see they were going to cause me trouble. Heels on those floor tiles were bad news. I saw all the marks when I went in. They'd been looking for a caretaker for over a month – the floors were terrible, pock-marked with little black circles. I tried to tell Mrs Tace, but she wouldn't listen. Image is everything, apparently. And she can wear the heels if the caretaker properly cleans the floors. She's a right ray of sunshine I can tell you. But then, she won me over. Even at seventy-one she could see I was a lady's man. I could hardly concentrate on what she was telling me, she had her cleavage shoved so close to my face. I caught the gist of it: clients' rooms, morgue, incinerator, her office, all out of my jurisdiction; hours flexible – especially considering my age, my wife's health and that. It was the strangest interview. The moment I mentioned Fran the job was mine, like having me preoccupied was just what she wanted. Trust Fran to know I spent most of the interview gawping at Tace's tits. 'Tasty Tace' she called her. And she is, just my type, nothing like these skinny modern girls, but a real woman, fleshy and proud.

Funny thing is, Fran was right about Tasty Tace. After the twenty minutes or so of the interview, she took me round to meet the other staff. The moment she saw the live-in nurse, Milo, you could tell she fancied him. He's one of those young, tall lads from Eastern Europe. Women always seem to like them foreign, and she was all over him. 'Steve, this is Milos' – she said his name so quickly, burying the non-English sounds with a breathy whisper, that it was hard to make sense of it – 'our resident nurse. We don't know what we'd do without him.' She knew what she'd do with him, though, that much was obvious. She adjusted her skirt as she walked towards him, smoothing her hands over her hips like she was pointing out her curves. And then she kept pushing her hair off her face all the time. Milo didn't look the least bit interested. He shook my hand and told me to call him Milo because it's easier to say. Seemed a decent sort of bloke. I think we're too soft on immigrants in general, but that doesn't stop me treating everyone like an individual. It's only fair. And Milo seemed all right. God knows, I thought it would be good to have another bloke about.

Then she introduced me to the other nurse, Sarah. She's a funny one. She shook my hand and all, but she's got shifty eyes, darting about behind her fringe. No, I didn't like Sarah from the start. Even then she was twitchy, sizing me up. She offered me another old classic. 'Sorry to hear about your wife, Steve. I'll pray for you.' Pray for me. What a lot of cobblers. God's like Santa Claus for grown-ups and it looked like she knew it too, feeding me a lie. Fran told me not to be too hasty to judge. Always tried to see the best in people, did Fran. My Fran. How could she have known that Sarah's beady eyes would haunt me like this? I christened her 'Sour-grapes Sarah' – it's the sort of name Fran would have given her if she'd lived to hear more about her.

I didn't meet anyone else that day. I would start the next week, once arrangements were made for Fran – I had to get a mobile phone, Fran's friend Jean from over the road offered to pop by when I was out, and James, our son, promised to come over for a couple of weeks. Sour-grapes Sarah and Milo went off in different directions and Tasty Tace showed me to the door. I couldn't quite believe I was about to go back to work at my age. But nothing was real back then. I was sleepwalking through the days, thinking about every breath, every passing moment, hoping to keep time on hold. Somehow I lost sight of the big picture. I didn't want to look the future in the face. It was too bloody much. Fran was always much better at taking the bull by the horns. She wouldn't be stuck where I am now. I just didn't have the balls. Never thought I bowed to authority till now.

My first day at work, things were looking up. Fran was having a good day. She wasn't in much pain. I'd left her sleeping after lunch and Jean was dropping by a bit later to check up on her. I could get in two hours' solid cleaning the corridors before heading back home to make Fran's supper and chat a bit before the nurse arrived. I was feeling bright, you know. A bit nervous, it being the first time I'd left her. But Fran was so pleased I was getting out, not going would be letting her down. I couldn't do that.

The care home is only a few streets away. I could walk it, but mostly I took the bus, like I did that day. I popped into Mr Raja's for a copy of the *Sun* and waited in the spring sunshine until the bus came. Five minutes later, I was strolling into the home.

My first task of the day was to collect my keys from Tasty Tace. I walked up the driveway to the entrance and pressed the buzzer. Peering through the glass, I could see that there was no one behind the front desk. I thought it was a bit odd not having someone there, but then after only a minute or so, Sarah arrived to let me in. She glanced over me, like I was a delivery rather than a person, and pushed the button to release the door. Then she picked up the phone with one hand and held the other out flat, stopping me in my tracks.

'One minute, I'll let Alexa know you're here,' she said. Then she spoke into the receiver, 'Alexa, it's Sarah. Mr Green has arrived.' There was a brief pause. 'Of course.' Sarah put down the receiver. 'I'll show you to her office.'

'No need, Sarah. I remember the way.'

But Sarah wouldn't listen. She walked slightly ahead of me, answering my attempts at conversation with single words and grunts. I gave up and walked in silence two paces behind her. She even knocked on Tasty's door for me. It was like she thought I was senile, occasionally looking over her shoulder to check up on me. Thankfully, Tasty's office is less than a minute's walk from the front desk. A straight walk down one corridor hardly needed an escort, but as soon as Tasty called me in Sarah walked away, her smile fading to a sneer as she turned to face the corridor.

I pushed open the door to reveal Mrs Tace behind her desk.

'Welcome,' she said. 'Do take a seat.' She swivelled in her chair. I used to have one of those chairs myself, not because it was comfy, but because it felt business-like. It was like playing office and there was something of this in the way she made it spin around. It felt calculated. I should have thought more of it.

Having turned the chair in my direction, she placed one manicured hand firmly on the table.

'How is your wife today?'

A stupid question.

'She's doing well, thanks,' I said. There was no other answer. It wasn't as if she wanted to hear the truth. 'Still dying' isn't exactly small talk.

'Good. We want to try and help make your time with us as easy as possible. Please do come to me if you have any difficulties or you need extra time with your wife. As a care home we understand the importance of the carer and their needs and we like to look after our staff. We are interested in the whole person, not just their function.'

Even at the time, it felt like she'd prepared the speech. It was like something you would save up for a newspaper interview. It's something I'd enjoy quoting back at her – not that it would do me any good. Her use of the words 'function' and 'person' so close together worried me. I had to fiddle with the collar of my shirt, loosening it a bit, to relax again. I should have trusted my flight instinct.

'There are a few things you will need to know about, to help make us an efficient team. As I said in your interview, your jurisdiction is quite distinct. You won't need to interact with our clients or clean their rooms. Milo and Sarah take care of the clients. The basement machinery, morgue and waste incinerator are maintained by a specialist who will be introduced to you on his next scheduled visit. In your daily routine here, you will not normally need to visit the basement. Any biological waste from the communal areas should be incinerated, however. Stan, the specialist, will show you how on his next visit. In the meantime, please ask for Milo or Sarah's help should you clear up any hazardous waste.' She appeared to be reading from a list on her desk. Her head was bent down and she spoke without looking at me – her eyes, lifting now and again, in my general direction, peered over her reading glasses – but the papers in front of her looked more like bills to me.

'At present we have a small number of clients on our list.' She turned a piece of paper over, revealing a plan of the home, names dotted about in different rooms. 'Several are very sick. Do not be surprised, therefore, if the day room looks a little empty.

'You are welcome to use the kitchens, for boiling water etc. We only ask that you avoid disrupting any food preparation for clients.'

She whipped the paper onto its front, leaving its blank side glaring up at me and took off her glasses. Her recital of the rules had been almost breathless.

'Do you smoke?' she asked, fixing me direct in the eye.

I nodded uncomfortably.

'Smoking is strictly prohibited inside the building, but you are free to smoke in the grounds. In the event of a fire' – her eyes moved back to her desk again – 'we congregate at the front of the building. If you are inside at the time of the alarm, please check your immediate vicinity for any clients and follow instructions from Milo and Sarah. Under no circumstances should you attempt to rush into the building if you are outside, nor should you attempt any heroics. Milo will talk you through the process in greater detail. Right.' She started to gather her papers, dropping them against the table to align all the edges. 'Unless you have any questions, I'll show you to your storeroom.'

The storeroom is just outside Tasty's office, opposite Milo's rooms. Back then, it was a mess, brooms and cleaning products strewn randomly on shelves and covered in dust. Tasty held out a set of keys.

'These are yours. They let you into the building through the front entrance, the kitchen door and fire escape. This one opens the storeroom. Milo, Sarah and I all have keys to this room so that clients' rooms can be cleaned and any spillages dealt with in your absence.' From the state of the storeroom it didn't look like any of them had done much cleaning over the last month or so, but it made sense they had access to the place.

'This is not your private domain,' Tasty continued. 'Please do not treat it as such.' She peered at my newspaper. I think the stuck-up cow was trying to tell me not to hang up calendars of naked girls. At the time, I nodded, but now it makes me feel sick; the idea that she thought she was a good judge of what's decent is laughable.

'On the other hand,' she added, 'you can consider the garden shed your own. Milo does have access to it, but only as a precaution. I won't walk you across the lawn.' She smiled. Those shoes again, I supposed. 'Everything in order?'

I told her I planned to start indoors today, though I might take a quick look at the garden shed. I wanted to get started on the floors.

Once she'd gone off back to her office, I had a right lark. No one in the building knew how to work the floor polisher and with no supervision I could take as long as I liked. I found the manual hidden under a pile of old yellow dusters – it should all be in a box file now, ordered, protected with all the other manuals – and checked the descriptions against the real thing, matching part to part, and working through the mechanics of the machine. It's a lovely great thing, but it's heavy, which makes it tricky to handle. Once you've got the wheels spinning polish on the floor, you need to kind of hold the machine up. Keeping the wheels hovering slightly above the floor maximizes its cleaning power and this makes controlling the machine quite difficult. The spinning motion of the polishers pushes the thing all over the place. If you didn't hold on it could run into a wall, ruin the skirting board, or knock over an unsuspecting client. But I love a tool that needs to be mastered and I was like a boy in a sweet shop. All the time I spent working out the machine, test-driving it, was like a gift.

I'd only done the ground-floor entrance hall and corridor when I realised it was time to pack up and get back to Fran. And though I felt guilty – nearly one and a half hours not thinking of Fran – I also felt refreshed. It's another of those things no one wants to talk about or tell you: sometimes you need time off, time not to think of anything. It's not that the situation goes away, or that you don't feel it somewhere deep down, but it's like stepping into a warm bath – you feel immersed in something else.

You need it. You need to pretend things are normal sometimes even if the normal is that everyone dies, that we're all little parasites on the face of the earth.

There is nothing left to distract me now.

That afternoon, though, I felt bloody marvellous. Good solid work. It's old-fashioned, but it's honest. I was tired and had more of a sweat on than I'd had in weeks, but I felt strong, capable, like I did years ago when I'd first started to earn. Fran was a genius, a little marvel. She knew just what makes me tick.

Even though I hadn't had a look in the shed, I wasn't worried. I was happy to spread out the excitement. I needed to get back and prepare dinner before the nurse arrived. I needed a bit of alone time with Fran. If she was up to it, she'd want to hear everything I'd done. She was like that – interested in everything.

No one noticed me going. I didn't need to clock out or anything. Tasty had told me just to keep a log of my hours. They'd be able to see if I was doing my job. On my way out I looked at the gleaming floor. Though I couldn't get rid of a few dents from those heels, the black marks were mostly gone. It looked good. It looked bloody good.

You can't believe it when they tell you it's back. You've fought it once, the cancer, and it was odd the first time, looking at your healthy wife and wondering where they could see anything wrong. Day before the check-up she's doing her usual full day's work: after-hours secretarial, the office books, your tea. Then – her without so much as a pale face – you're told she's sick.

This time round, you sort of know what to expect, but you think you beat it once, why not twice?

Metastases, they tell you. Like you know what it means. You nod and watch your wife die from the inside out.

They start up with the treatments again – chemo, radiotherapy. It's meant to control the cancer, slow its growth. You watch as her hair falls out again, as the hormone shit they put her on bloats her slim figure and turns her into a bald man in drag. You pretend you can't see it. You pretend you see only the beautiful woman you married and loved all those years. You pretend you're the man who only ever sheds tears over happy things – your wedding day, your son's birth – and instead you go to work to cry.

When the coughing gets really bad, you get the nurse to call the doctor and you hold her hand while they drain her lungs. Pleural effusion it's called. You're careful not to hold too tight because her skin feels like rice paper and you don't want to wear it away. When they're done and she's breathing easier, you go downstairs, open a window, roll and light a fag, thick blue smoke twisting away against the night sky.

You put up an old photograph of your wife at work, one taken before the cancer. You go to work, the photograph in the background, watching over you, and you pretend your golden years together are still to come. You try hard not to think about how many more months until she's dead. You cannot imagine that emptiness.

The next day Fran wasn't doing so good. I got Jean to come round before I left for work. I'd had to up Fran's morphine during the night. It's scary stuff. Made Fran a bit distant. But it was an unfocused and uncertain Fran or a Fran in agony. It wasn't a hard choice. And sometimes it seemed to jog her memory, take her back to the good old days. One time, I woke in the night to hear her shouting, 'So many colours.' She swore she could see fireworks through the window. 'It's for the end of the war, you know. Mum says it never has to be dark again.' She could only have been six the night of the celebrations and somehow she'd got a glow of youth on her through the memory, cheeks all hot and rosy, pushing up against the pillows, the whites of her eyes flashing in the darkness. It took her a long time to fall asleep again. I sat next to her, carefully stroking her forehead.

On that second day of work, the morphine just eased her back to sleep. I left Jean sitting in the green armchair in Fran's room with a mug of coffee and the crossword; Jean telling me to get off before Fran found out I was a shirker. Pure salt of the earth is Jean. Don't know what we'd have done without her.

I was happy to leave Fran asleep as she might be brighter later and I preferred to sit with her when she was awake. And I thought I might have tales to tell once I'd had my first look at the shed.

I'd had high hopes of the garden shed. It's right at the back of the garden, in the far right-hand corner, set into the shade of the laburnum. I knew it would look pretty when the laburnum flowered, yellow petals fading into dangling seed pods. They're poisonous of course, but everyone's happy to put up with a bit of poison for a brief duration of sunlight dancing among the leaves. At least, that's how I saw it then. But it was too early in the season for laburnum flowers yet and the shed sat dank and dark, flush against the fence, tucked behind the tree trunk as far from the home as possible. It's much more like a den than a shed. I'd have loved it as a nipper; it's a perfect little hideout.

The padlock on the door was a bit rusty, but once I was inside the light fitting still worked, revealing a jumble of tools, a wheelbarrow, a lawnmower and various sacks of compost, plastic pots, gardening gloves and the like stacked against the walls and spilling from precarious shelves. Because of the tree and the fence, there wasn't much natural light. I stepped inside, took a deep breath, smelling a mix of chemicals and damp earth, and felt safe. It was as if I was a million miles away from anyone. I stood there a while just breathing. It smelt like my dad's old shed, only with more earth and less damp. Dad's shed always had a tinge of mould to it, with bits and pieces of old rope and rotten wood from repairs to the barges lying about, back when his business was freight, up and down the canals. Back when the docks were still big business. Even then Dad was a visionary, already scrimping and saving to get his first mechanised road vehicle. He never looked back. Said driving was easier on his leg. Shrapnel had torn through the muscles and ligaments around his right knee and when they healed they tightened so one leg dragged a bit behind the other. Saved him from a second call-up, though.

Thinking of Dad wasn't easy. He was proud of what I did with the firm, turning from freight to people, trucks to coaches. But he would have hated to see it sold off bit by bit, not even the name intact. There was nothing I could do, though. James didn't want in, Fran was ill for the first time and the cowboy drivers, operating illegally without coach safety checks or proper premises, were cashing in on low overheads, driving us off the roads. It was time to quit. At least he didn't live to see it. The site's gone residential now – a prime bit of real estate. The whole neighbourhood's changed. But right there, in the shed, it felt as if time had gone into rewind. I could smell the horses, the manure and straw mixing in with a stamping of hooves and the twitching of flanks as my Dad settled harnesses. There was gentle clinking of clean chains. Some of the barges, driven by coal-burning engines, were beginning to smoke; the air heavy with the dense fog that marked the sun's rise and fall with deep stripes of reds and pinks and yellows.

I breathed in and out, falling into the rhythm of those days gone by. I knew it was nostalgia. I knew back then they wouldn't have been able to treat Fran, but I was grateful for those memories. Once we had been young, the world too small to hold us.

I've no idea how long I stood there staring into the past. It was only when the wail of an ambulance went by that I shook myself back into the present. I'd decided that, since I hadn't seen any old people in the day room, the driveway and front of the home should be tidied first. The flowerbeds and lawn were badly in need of attention. It made the place look shabby and uncared for. The lawn desperately needed mowing and bits of the edges had crumbled into the beds and needed repairing. Then there was weeding, pruning and mulching to be done. I wasn't planning on planting anything just yet. I wanted to see what was there already, see the seasons pass over before I made any big changes.

It didn't strike me as odd that I hadn't seen any old people. I took Tasty's word for it when she said they didn't have many clients just then. I didn't know how these homes worked. Fran had cared for both our parents at home. That's what families did: cared for their own. At one time we had both mothers in the house. It wasn't hard at all, though I've started to question my experience of that; it was Fran who did the caring and she was never one to complain. Back then she said it filled the void James had left.

Deciding not to properly sort out the shed until the gardens were shipshape, I found the tools I needed and took them in the wheelbarrow, which could double up as a vessel to drop the weeds into – I would weed and prune, then mow the lawn, then mulch – and pushed off over the back garden and along the path around the edge of the home. There wasn't a path from the shed to the patio and though I looked for planks, I couldn't find any, so I just struck out across the lawn towards the concrete hoping I wouldn't do too much damage. As I wheeled past, I saw Milo sat at his computer. I raised my hand, but he didn't see and kept squinting at the screen. There didn't seem to be anyone else about. Tasty wasn't in her office and all the other windows were empty. No faces, old or young.

It was very restful to be working alone. After a few minutes down on my knees by the flowerbeds, I found myself whistling tunes Fran and I had heard on the hospital radio. I heard more of them than her because I couldn't be with her for the radiation treatment and had to wait outside. Fran said it was strange that something everyone else ran from could do you any good. Apparently they stand around aiming the machines at you, taking their time and then just as they press the button they run out, dashing for the safety of the corridor, leaving you half naked and fully exposed to the burning rays. She had scars from it.

I've always been a good whistler, but truly I hadn't found myself carrying a tune for some time. Yet again I sent a silent thank-you to Fran for knowing me so well. Who else could have sent me back to work knowing it would do me the world of good?

The flowerbeds were terrible: lots of weeds to pull up, summer-flowering herbaceous perennials to lift and split and shrubs and roses to prune; and that's not mentioning the climber on the north-west wall. It was satisfying but tiring work. I was out there about two hours with no sign of anyone, but I didn't think to be unnerved. My hearing wasn't as good as it used to be and I thought the clients could be watching telly in their rooms or just resting. It was a care home, after all, not a nursery. There was no reason for there to be lots of noise. I was used to Fran passing the time with crosswords and jigsaws, newspapers and daytime television. I just didn't think to notice the silence. It was bright for March with a lovely cool breeze gently blowing through the trees, perfect gardening weather. Beads of sweat were slowly falling into my eyebrows, but I brushed them off with my arm, lost in the rhythm of the work. I was making two piles in the wheelbarrow: one for composting, one for the bonfire.

But it was this contentment, this rhythm that made the sound of the telephone so shrill and alien. It was coming from Tasty's office. I was right under her window at the time but hadn't noticed her come in. The window was slightly ajar. I couldn't help overhearing.

'Home Comforts Care, can I help?

'Ah, Graham, thanks for calling back.' There was a pause as the person on the other end spoke.

'For heaven's sake, Graham, relax. He's in his

seventies and his wife's sick.' Another pause. They were talking about me.

'I know, but trust me, please.'

Then followed a long pause. Whoever Graham was – I know now he's the home's doctor – he had a lot to say and presumably it was still about me, even though I'd never met the man. It was an awkward few minutes – me hunched down on my knees under her window, trowel in hand, barely breathing, trying not to draw attention to myself. Then Tasty started in again.

'The jurisdictions are there for a reason. Stan will come over next week and show him the ropes, then that will be it. He won't need to go down there. Can we drop it now? I want to talk to you about the old woman.' At least they were moving on from me, but I still didn't dare move in case she realised I was under her windowsill. I stayed as still as I could, hearing Tasty's side of the conversation and waiting for the phone call to end.

'Yes. She's not responding as well as we'd like.'

'When you get a chance, please, Graham. There's plenty of time still, but we'll need to start planning ...'

'Yes. Okay. Friday, then.'

She clicked the receiver back down. I could picture her, chin on hands, lips pursed, eyebrows knitted in thought, elbows up on the table, pushing her cleavage together. I didn't know how long I'd have to wait, but I didn't want her knowing I was sat out there listening in. I could feel my heart knocking at an unwelcome pace and for the first time I wondered why they had hired me. I'd thought they couldn't find anyone else, but I began to wonder if there was more to it. I didn't think I came across as senile, but I was over retirement age and I had a sick wife. Most employers would run a mile.

Finally, some minutes later, Tasty left her room, flouncing out of the door with some energy. When I told Fran about the whole thing later, she said she thought I was being paranoid. Graham would have been questioning the wisdom of employing an old chap like me, and Tasty was just standing up for me, proving that some employers valued the loyalty and work ethic of older employees. I think, had it been any other time, I might not have been able to let it go. 'He won't need to go down there' was a statement that didn't seem to fit in with Fran's theory, and now, over a year and a half later, I hear it floating out of the past. I should have paid more attention. I know why they didn't want me down there. I know what they do.

It's always the little things that sadden you. The first time round, when Fran was in the ward after the operation, there were six of them in there, recovering from having different bits cut out. One lady must have been in her eighties. For the couple of days we were there, she didn't have one visitor. And there's no privacy, so now and again she would offer a few words, answer questions about the time, or the date, or the food, but mostly she would just have to watch everyone else's visits, listen in to conversations.

One lunchtime this lady had ordered yoghurt for her sweet. The nurses had come round and delivered all the meals, but with so many patients there was no time for the details. You got your meal. You ate it.

The lady had got herself sitting upright with the table pulled over the bed. She'd managed the soup, drinking it like tea, but the yoghurt was tricky. God knows what bits she'd had chopped out, it didn't matter, because this woman's hands shook and her knuckles were swollen, all purple and stiff. She picked things up as if the ends of her fingers didn't work any more, like the tips were no good.

Well, I wasn't really watching her. I'd been helping Fran. Just out of the op, Fran's right arm wasn't working properly and because they'd taken lots of lymph nodes, the swelling was terrible. She needed me to help cut up bits of food and open things for her. She had the yoghurt too and it was a bugger to open. The foil was really stuck down tight. While I struggled with it, Fran was watching the old lady. She couldn't open hers either. So Fran made me go over there to open the yoghurt pot for the old woman. 'That's so thoughtful,' she said. 'You're just left to get on with it, aren't you?'

I often think about that. You're just left to get on with it.

I don't know what happened to her after we left. She was still there, staring up at the ceiling, waiting to get well. Waiting, anyway. I've learnt how that feels.

The rest of that first week at work was uneventful. I restarted a compost heap out behind the shed, close to the back wall – you could tell there used to be one there because of the hedge, grown like a little border wall around a scrubby patch of ground. I mowed the lawn. I did both the front and the back on the Wednesday. I did a bit of work on the clematis on the Thursday and started to tidy the beds in the back garden. It was quite a job, but I didn't have time to complete it on Friday. Tasty had stipulated floor cleaning twice a week and I'd been neglecting the inside of the care home for the gardens. I could see that there was going to be quite enough work to keep me busy.

I could have gone in Saturday, but James was coming. I was going to pick him up from the airport. Fran was excited about it because he was bringing his girlfriend, Michie. Michie is Japanese-American. It would be her first time in England. We'd heard a lot about Michie – well, Fran had – but we hadn't met her. It was the first time in years that James had had a serious girlfriend and Fran was desperate for him to settle down. She'd been waiting for grandchildren for so long and Michie was her last hope. She wanted to see this woman before she died because she thought she'd be able to imagine what her grandchildren would look like even if she never got to see them. Poor Fran. Sometimes she could be really daft. Turned out Michie was a similar age to James. I know these days you can have children in your forties, but you have to really want to. It soon became clear that neither James nor Michie did. Fran's endless anecdotes about how lovely James was as a child fell on deaf ears. There would be no pitter-pattering of children's feet.

The idea of James coming over was to look after Fran while I was at work. We'd planned he would stay two weeks. Enough time for me to get to grips with the new job and to ease the burden on Jean. Fran didn't want to be a burden to anyone.

But the plan fell apart almost immediately. I spent more time at home the two weeks of their stay than I did in the following months of Fran's life. Michie didn't think about Fran and wanted James all to herself. She was polite enough, but I couldn't help thinking her a cold-hearted bitch. Fran was dying, for god's sake. James should never have brought her. He must have known what Michie would be like. Instead of looking after Fran, he spent two weeks sightseeing, going to Buckingham Palace and the London Eye. To be fair, he did make Fran the odd cup of tea and he did sit with her in the early mornings and, when I made a fuss, he went to one of her radiology appointments.

Fran never said a word against him. 'It's so good to see him, Steve. Our boy. So good of him to come.'

Nine weeks later she would never speak again.

I know he feels it now, James. I know he does. But we've never talked, not like he used to with his mum. He promised Fran he'd call me every week. And he did. He called every Sunday. But our conversations were full of what wasn't said. I didn't know how to get the words out. And despite his fancy education, he couldn't find the words either. It was a right cock-up. It's almost a relief, not talking now; the weight of everything I could have said makes my syllables blur into senile gibberish.

And I can't forgive Michie. That's a barrier.

One of the days they were staying, they planned to go off somewhere in the afternoon so they'd asked me to do a morning rather than an afternoon shift. I came back just before lunch. Must have been noon. I came in through the front door and nearly crashed straight into James, walking up and down the hallway talking on his phone. He looked at me, put his hand over the mouthpiece and mouthed the words, 'Work. Michie's with Mum.' So I went straight up. I mean, Michie was American really, so it wasn't that her English was bad or anything, she just didn't show interest. She treated Fran like a small child: ignoring her when she was quiet and then offering food or drink, or suggesting she needed the loo, every time she spoke up. 'Are you all right, Mrs Green? Would you like more water? Can I get you a sleeping tablet?'

I know I sound like a bastard because she was attentive in certain ways and that, but Fran wasn't a person to her.

When I walked in the room, Fran was awake lying flat on her back staring up at the ceiling. Michie was sat in a chair by the window, reading one of her fancy law journals. I'd told her Fran found it harder to breathe lying down.

'All right?' I asked them both.

'Steve,' Fran said, trying to sit up, 'how was your morning?'

Michie nodded. 'James had a work call, so I came to sit with Mrs Green.'

'Call me Fran, dear.'

'I'll let the two of you have some quality alone time,' Michie said, getting up. As she walked out of the room, Fran spoke to her back, 'Thank you, dear.'

Fran waited for her to start walking down the stairs and then looked up at me.

'Could you help me with my sweater?'

All morning Fran had been left half dressed, her jumper wrapped up under her arms, a misshapen bundle against her back. She'd have been uncomfortable for hours, lying on that clump of material. It would have added to the pressure of breathing on her back. I eased the jumper over Fran's chest and down her spine, plumped up the extra cushions and pillows and helped her to sit up. Her breaths were coming quick and hard, making that sickening rattling sound.

'Oxygen?' I asked and she nodded. I pulled the

mask from the bedside table and gently laid it over her nose and mouth, settling the elastic above her ears and over the remaining strands of her hair. James, it turned out, had been on the phone with work colleagues for over an hour and before that he and Michie had been discussing some law case. They'd talked shop all morning at the bottom of Fran's bed.

'They arranged the meeting to fit in with James,' Fran said, her words broken by oxygen hissing into the mask. 'Got up specially early to get his opinion.'

I thought it was a load of cobblers. James would be free all afternoon, sightseeing with Michie. I've never asked him, but I suspect he said he was busy that afternoon. Maybe I'm wrong. Maybe they were going to court early over in America and wanted to talk to James first, I don't know. It pains me to think about it, James leaving his mother on her back all morning, her jumper up under her armpits. It makes my fingers curl and itch into fists.

It was during the first week of their stay that Stan came to show me the basement machines. I was trying to be professional and that, trying my best to take everything in, but, looking back, with all that was going on, I couldn't have been playing with a full deck.

Stan's a nice enough bloke. Similar age to James but one of those wiry chaps who can't keep still. When he's not eating or drinking, he's smoking or sucking on cough sweets. It's a strange habit. Makes him smell a bit funny, like he's covering something up. Fran reckoned he might be an alcoholic or maybe he was getting a high off them. On the packaging it says consume no more than one pack a day. Stan sucks his way through a lot more than one pack in a day. And they're full of paracetamol. Must do terrible things to his liver. But it wasn't my place to say. I don't know him that well. We've had coffee together when he's been here. Shared a smoke on the fire escape if the weather's not been too bad. But it was just small talk. Nothing deep. He has said some interesting things though, now and again. But whether he really knows what goes on here, I can't say for sure. Still, even that first time, when I was out of it, he dropped a few choice morsels.

When he turned up, Milo came to find me in the garden and all three of us went down into the basement, along the corridor beside the morgue and into the outhouse. You can only get to it through the basement. There aren't doors on the outhouse itself. Something about the incinerator needing to be properly contained. Seems odd to me to keep a morgue and a furnace close together, but Milo said it was useful seeing as half the waste needs to be kept cold until they fire up the incinerator. And they've placed the incinerator well. It's kept away from the morgue's adjacent wall, but close enough to the main building for the chimney to sit flush against its outer walls. It keeps the outline of the care home more streamlined. Though whether it was built with this in mind seems unlikely. The whole thing seemed alien to me. I was used to workshop waste, oil, scrap metal, nothing like this.

Milo was meant to have shown me the basics, but I'd had no need to clean up anything clinical or anatomical, no human waste or anything, so the both of us just waited for Stan's visit. The only rubbish I'd had so far was from the garden and most of that went on the compost. Though I was keen to see the incinerator and find out how it worked, I wasn't so keen on going by the morgue. They give me the creeps. Fran said she thought it was weird the home had a morgue at all, but Milo said one had been installed when there'd been a pile-up at the local crematorium. Funeral parlours had filled up and there were fears about the spread of disease. It's not a huge morgue, but it means they can store bodies here and send them direct to crematoriums. One of the local funeral parlour directors comes and deals with the care home's dead on the premises. I don't like to think about being above a load of preserved dead bodies. I used to tell myself to just get on with it, it's the way life is. But not any more. I've got nothing to get on with. I feel the chill of the morgue penetrating the floors, seeking me out. I don't believe in the crematorium pile-up story any more.

But that day we weren't talking about the morgue, we were talking about the incinerator. Stan, apologising to Milo for the repetition of information, gave us the whole spiel. The incinerator was a fairly heavy-duty model, unnecessarily large for the care home. Stan offered the information between regular clicking pauses when his tongue flicked the current cough sweet from one cheek to the other, knocking it against his teeth and leaving trails of saliva to collect in the corners of his mouth, which he slurped away by sucking in his lips like an old man with false teeth. It makes long work of anything Stan has to say. This fact about the size of the incinerator was of passing interest at the time. The money had been spent after all and since they had the machine it made sense to use it, even if they did so at less frequent intervals than it was built to withstand. It is a particularly effective model, meeting strict air emission regulations and with preheat and secondary chamber temperatures reaching up to 2000 degrees Fahrenheit even human bones can be reduced to a sterile white ash.

Stan took us through procedure, right from bagging and labelling of waste at source, through waste storage, to incinerator operation. As the machine has digital controls and recording systems, Stan comes and takes the reports so there's no need to write anything down. You have to get dressed up in fireproof safety gear, leather aprons, arm guards, gloves and a high-temperature safety visor. You end up looking like something from a science-fiction film.

The operational procedure is very simple. You de-ash in the morning or when the unit is cool. We could run the machine for ten hours every day, but due to its capacity, we run it twice a week. It doesn't do sharps or anything, so those get sent off elsewhere – Milo sorts that out.

Once the controls show the right temperatures and times, you put the waste on the hopper or automatic loader, close the lid and press the load switch to begin the cycle. The door on the primary chamber opens and the ram pushes the waste into the chamber. When the ram withdraws the chamber door automatically closes and the treatment process begins. It's a fantastic machine. Even with the added pressure of James and Michie's visit, I was sharp enough to realise the machine was far in excess of the home's requirements.

Back upstairs, away from the noise and heat, Stan, Milo and I sat and had a coffee in the kitchen. It was my first cup of Milo coffee. He makes it really thick and grainy. It's Turkish coffee apparently. I quite like it, especially when it's had a good few sugars added, but I still prefer an instant if it's going. Milo's coffee's a bit rich for me, but I drank it to be social. If he went to the effort of making it, it only seemed right to drink a cup with him.

We were sitting in the kitchen and Stan asked if I had any more questions. Well, I'd already asked quite a few, being interested in machinery and that, but there was really only one left that was niggling at me.

'Why doesn't the home treat transferred waste from other sites?'

'No idea, mate,' Stan said crunching the last of his cough sweet. He was stirring sugar and milk into his cup. He swallowed the sweet, lifted the cup and blew over the surface of the coffee. 'I keep telling them they could make a fortune.' He took a tentative sip. 'Thanks, Milo, great coffee.'

'Licence issues, Alexa told me,' Milo said, leaning back in his chair, offering the statement to the ceiling. Alexa is Tasty's real name – Alexa Tace.

I nodded at Milo's answer and left it at that. There was so much to be getting on with that I didn't have time to think more about it. It seemed reasonable enough at the time. Other things clouded out the home in those days. Fran was so much more important and I didn't want her left too long with Michie around. Didn't like the idea that she was lying flat on her back, her clothes twisted under her, taking shallow, painful breaths while James and Michie talked law.

Now, of course, I know different. There aren't any good reasons for refusing to make money out of machinery like that.

It was during those weeks of James and Michie's stay that Fran's 'save it for later' habit really took hold. It was another reason not to think too hard at work.

It started years ago, back when Fran and I were recently married. We'd both grown up through the war and then when we were starting out together there was still rationing so neither of us liked throwing things out. There might be some other use you could make of a broken chair, Fran would darn the holes in our socks, her stockings even, and we'd always keep leftover food. If you couldn't do anything else, you could do a soup. Didn't matter if it was a thin soup, there'd always be rings of fat floating on top from the gristle of yesterday's meat or the cooking oil. So the idea of saving things for later was ingrained and that. It was what you did.

When we started trying for babies and found it wasn't as easy as we thought, Fran was already building up a trunk full of clothes and bibs and useful things that other people had saved for later and passed on. After a year or so she fell pregnant and we were happy. Like Dad, I'd seen a gap in the market. His haulage business was running but not turning as good a profit as it had done in the past, so he'd let me buy a couple of coaches to take people on holidays or do school trips, and I was turning the business round. Things were looking up. We were working like donkeys but we had a baby on the way and the business was going well just as I was about to inherit the lot of it.

Then Fran had the miscarriage.

There aren't words for it, the sorrow and that. She was six months gone. Our child looked like a real baby when it came out. I was there with her in the hospital and saw little Maggie being born. But Fran didn't want to look. Maybe that was what did it. After that everything had to be saved for later.

Everything had a purpose, was useful for something. The loft, which I normally filled with spare tools, Christmas decorations and that, became a treasure trove of old furniture, kitchenware, light bulbs, you name it we had it. Anytime anything was replaced in the house, we didn't chuck out the old versions, we put them in the loft. Just in case we needed them later, was always Fran's excuse. It started with the trunk of Maggie's clothes. They were put up in the loft and they never did come down. When we finally had James, several years later, Fran had built up a new trunk. Both were up there when we moved. We had to get rid of a lot of stuff when we sold the business. There just wasn't the room for it. It was weird moving in somewhere with no room full of spares. Like a clean slate.

Then, with James and Michie over, it started again. James brought Fran the latest electric blanket. We had to switch the plugs and that, but it worked like a dream and she could reach the controls easily herself. Instead of throwing out the old one or giving it to charity, Fran said we should 'save it for later, just in case'. Maybe someone else would need one, or the new one might break.

I didn't really think about it. I put it up in the mostly empty loft.

Then she started saving other things for later. She didn't seem capable of eating a whole meal. Even breakfast, the cereal all soggy, milk curdling in the bowl, would be left beside her bed. 'I'll save it for later,' she kept saying. I found myself throwing so much food away. It would go off on the bedside table or the plate would go in the fridge and never come out again. Later wasn't ever going to come. The late Frances Green would come first. So one more mouthful now was what I tried to stick to. Getting her to eat a little more, keep her strength up. But I knew I was fighting a losing battle. Katrina, our Marie Curie nurse, was ever so good, letting me talk to her about it, telling me she tried to encourage Fran to eat a few of those saved meals during the night when she was wide awake and unable to sleep. Telling me to stay positive, even if it was only for Fran.

So I bought Tupperware for saved food and reordered the loft, pushing the few things we'd saved from the old place to the back, making room for all the new bits and pieces Fran wanted saving, and I tried to tell myself later was a positive thing. If Fran could imagine wanting things later, she still believed in later.

James and Michie thought we were both mad.

'Why do you need to keep this, Dad?' James would ask.

'Your mum wants me to save it.'

'But she'd never know. It's not like she can climb up into the loft.'

'It's what she wants.'

James didn't see the sense in me going along with her. He didn't see that, just like Fran, I needed to believe in later too.

I came back from work one day and found James on a ladder up to the loft. There were boxes of things in the front room. Michie was sorting through them.

'A pile to keep, a pile to throw out,' she said, not looking up at me.

'You have to face up to it, Dad,' James said. 'It's better to sort through it all now.'

I knew what he meant. It wasn't just Fran's death he wanted me to face up to, it was mine. As Michie inspected the family china, packed for safekeeping, they were sending us both off.

'It's good to know what's what,' Michie said. 'Have you done an inventory?'

'What for?' I asked.

'For your will,' she replied, making the statement sound like a question, raising the pitch of her voice for her partner's silly, senile father.

I was bloody annoyed, I can tell you. I got them to put it all back, Michie shaking her head and tutting under her breath. But I suspect they looked through it all when I went out again. They might even have taken some things. I don't remember everything that was up there.

It was the same when Fran died. Michie didn't come back, thank Christ – I don't think there's any love lost there – but James managed to make it back in time for the funeral and then spent most of his time trying to force me to go through Fran's things. I kept saying, quietly, that I wouldn't do it. There was no Michie to egg him on, so he gave up in the end. Perhaps, after all, he didn't have the heart. And Michie did well out of it anyway. Fran wanted her to have some of her jewellery. 'For the daughter I couldn't have.' That was what it said in her will. Only I knew that Fran meant Maggie as well as a daughter-in-law. Michie probably thought it was junk, but luckily I didn't have to see her face when she got it. I wouldn't have left her anything. They're not married, they don't plan to have kids and Michie treated Fran like a sick cat that it would be kinder to put down.

Fran was exhausted when they left. Worn out with the effort of being nice and putting a positive slant on everything. She had decided Michie was all right because Michie loved James. She kept saying she was doing all right and didn't need too much help because she wanted to spare James's feelings. She spent the week after their stay on a high dose of morphine and pretty much constant oxygen. Fucking knackered, she was. It wasn't easy seeing her like that and keeping going to work, but Fran wanted me to go. She wanted me to keep busy, to get some exercise. So I went through the motions: set to cleaning out the shed, made lists of things to replace and order, threw things out; made myself a cleaning and gardening schedule to help me keep track of tasks; kept my head down, myself to myself, my mind nearly always a few streets down with Fran and Jean. I didn't think about the clients in the home. I didn't think to question the size of the laundry bundles – always tiny for a home with so many beds – or the silence that hung about the place. I just got up, saw off Katrina, helped Fran to breakfast, saw in Jean, went to work, came home, helped Fran to her hospital appointments or talked to her, or just sat with her, made supper, had a little chat with Katrina when she came, and went to bed. I was too tired to think clearly about things. I got flashbacks to the past, but couldn't see the present, it was just something to be lived through, like I was walking in a strong headwind.

Midway through June, the hospital told us Fran had only a couple of weeks. I told the home and they let me take time off so I could spend those last days with Fran. With Katrina's help, we could keep Fran at home. James didn't fly over. It was just me, Fran and Katrina. Jean was a right little gem as well. She dropped round and helped me cook some meals, sometimes sat with Fran while I nipped out to the shops and then as Fran got worse, brought food in for us. I don't know what we'd have done without her and Katrina. They were fantastic, the pair of them.

Fran couldn't really talk near the end. She spent more and more time sleeping. I'd be there with her, holding her hand. Even in the night, I found it hard to rest. I'd sit up with Katrina until she forced me to go to bed. She said Fran would want me to sleep. She said I wouldn't be much use to Fran if I couldn't get some shuteye. So I would go down the hall and toss and turn, waking at the slightest noise – a car horn, a plane passing overhead. If I heard her cough, I'd be back up, in my dressing gown, my head around her door. 'She's fine, Steve,' Katrina would say. 'You okay?'

Sometimes Katrina and I had a hot chocolate together, sipping quietly at the foot of Fran's bed. When I was done, Katrina would send me back to bed again. 'I'll wake you, Steve, I promise,' she said.

She didn't need to wake me. Fran died in the daytime. It was just Fran and me. I didn't even see it happening. She seemed to be sleeping. I was holding her hand, stroking it gently, and it was only when I leant over her to brush a couple of wisps of remaining hair off her face that I realised she felt cold. It was that peaceful. I kept sitting there, didn't move anything, kept talking at her, until the doorbell rang and Katrina helped me go through all the form-filling and the notifying. She knew the moment I opened the door. I stood there, in the doorway – maybe I was a bit slow – and she looked at me and said, 'I'm so sorry, Steve.' And she meant it. 'It's what she would have wanted, the two of you alone together.'

I stayed off work another week. We got the funeral arranged quickly, and like I said, James flew back for it. I wasn't sure that I'd go back to work, but I knew it was what Fran wanted, what she'd imagined and I wanted to stay true to that. So I went back. It was searing hot by then and the whole place smelt of dust and decay. It was so depressing. So I did my best to keep out in the garden, coming back in those lonely evenings to water the lawn. I had to wait till dark because of the hose ban. It gave me something to do, I'll say that for it. I didn't mind doing longer hours.

Milos – I

This morning I wake up excited. I am filled with positive feelings about my work. Smiling, I walk to my desk before going to the toilet. It's a detour, but I want to see the photographs as they are, ugly and beautiful all at once, laid out in a jumble. There are lots of Steve, the caretaker, sitting on the fire escape, mowing the patchy lawn, then a whole series of shots in the kitchen – its industrial size and metal surfaces make any shots in there perfect contrast pieces to photographs taken in the morgue, especially any that include the autopsy table. And smiling over them all, from her position on the upper left-hand side of my computer, a wedge of Blu-Tack distorting her chest, is my daughter, Jelena, healthy and unnervingly self-possessed. It is pleasing to have her looking down on these, my other, darker children.

I lean over the photographs, briefly nudging them with my fingertips, testing new arrangements, then walk back to the loo. I shouldn't take these photographs, but I'm an artist building a collection for exhibition. No one needs to know where I shot the pictures. I take them secretly, often shooting from my waist. I like to capture the edges of people. There's a good one of Steve's back, a rolled cigarette dangling from his silhouette, as he stares out at a half-cleaned window, soap slipping in thick legs down the glass. Inside, just visible through the blurred window, is someone in a wheelchair. The exhibition will be called 'Fractured'. I hope it will show that even in England, life can be lived in the shadow of a hollowed-out sense of humanity.

I am naked but the heating on the lower-ground floor is on and I am not cold. It's good to walk about like this. With my right foot, I kick one of Jelena's plastic balls sideways towards the patio and it bounces off the wooden ridge of the door, knocking against a leg of the coffee table. I count this as a goal.

In the toilet, my pee casts a long and refreshing yellow arc that splashes off the back of the bowl. Flicking the last bits out of my dick, I turn on the taps for a shower. I close the lid of the loo – no need yet to flush – and wet my hands in the shower. I reach for my toothbrush, squeeze on some paste, and get under the water, washing everything at once.

When I am dressed, I make my way out into the home, through the corridor to the kitchen for fresh coffee, bread and cheese. We only use the kitchen to impress visitors – clients are fed nil by mouth because it's easier – so I treat the kitchen as my own. I meet Sarah in the corridor.

'You're late,' she says.

Sarah is an unlucky woman. She has all the worst characteristics of English women: greasy hair, broken skin, her small features squashed into the middle of a face shaped like an upside-down pear; her skin is sallow and her cheeks are laced with tiny red veins, angry spots and pockmarks; her figure is solid, unremarkable. We flirt a little bit, now and again. She takes it well. It's nothing serious.

I look at my watch.

'Is normal time,' I say.

'Don't you remember? Didn't you wake up last night?'

Blankly I look back at her.

She rolls her eyes. 'Oh, god, Milo, it's like you're living in a dream world.'

I shrug. 'Good rest is half of work,' I say.

Sarah is already in her uniform, clipboard in one hand. She flicks through its pages officiously.

'We've got a new one in. Woman. In good condition. Sixty-five. Katherine Drasen. Arrived last night with the doctor. She is still flat out. She broke her nose in the fall and we are saying it was a stroke.' She looks up through several strands of loose greasy fringe, her eyebrows raised. I nod. Then after the briefest moment's pause, I hazard a wink. Women usually like to be challenged, but Sarah rolls her eyes again.

'Milo?' This is commanding and I nod properly now. 'She's been fitted out with all the usual for now: catheter, colostomy bag, drip. She's on a very heavy dose of morphine so we don't expect her to wake up for some time. You'll need to move her.'

'Right,' I say looking at my watch again.

'Milo, I mean it,' Sarah says pointing a finger at me.

'I know, I know, but can't I have breakfast first?' I smile weakly; sometimes it works.

'You've got half an hour to start your round. We've got a busy day today and I want you to be on time. You know what Alexa's like. No excuses.' She hands me a piece of paper from the top of her clipboard. To take it I have to balance dirty coffee cups across one arm like a waiter. Sarah watches me, suppressing a smile. She is getting me back for the wink. 'This is your schedule today. Usual procedure. Don't be late.' And with that she walks on past me down to the back stairs, teeth breaking through her grinning lips as she goes.

I read through the schedule as I go into the kitchen, pushing the door open with the same hand that holds the outline for the day. It's a good test of balance, cups on my left arm, schedule in my right hand.

I won't move the new lady every hour. We gave up on that long ago. Every two hours maybe is enough, sometimes less. I've even left it for a whole day a few times. I prefer to do it when they sleep anyway. It does mean that they get bedsores, but we want the muscles weak so I see it as doing a better not a worse job. Also, it means I can do everything at once: change their colostomy bags, do their bed wash, all that. Mostly Sarah and the doctor deal with the drugs, so I don't have to be concerned with them.

If a new woman came in last night, it means the other one will be processed today. I like seeing clients at this stage. I like to compare them. See how alike they are. If the old one isn't due in theatre until one o'clock this afternoon, it's perfect. Plenty of time. Sarah is such a worrier. I really ought to stop flirting with her. I like to tease women, but quite apart from her looks, Sarah doesn't have the right temperament.

Despite the huge barrel-like tins of instant coffee in the corner of the kitchen, meant for staff and visitor use, I make Turkish coffee. I like listening to the water bubbling slowly through the fine coffee grains, the steam and smell suffusing the kitchen, claiming the space. There is a sense of belonging in Turkish coffee.

I fill up the coffee maker, set it on the hob and get a cup out ready. While I cut bread and cheese, thickly buttering the wholegrain slices, I think about my usual chat-up line. It involves a photograph. I've never dared try it on Sarah.

I carry a photograph of a grey-haired man, cut from a newspaper, in my wallet. When I really want to get a girl into bed, I take out my wallet and point to the man's picture. His face is bland, stolid, his hair like a wig placed right at the top of his forehead. Sometimes they recognise Slobodan Milošević, sometimes they pretend to. If they look blank, I say 'war criminal' calmly, pausing, feeling for a reaction, and then 'national hero'. This shocks and thrills them. They love it. It's not quite the same now he's dead, but it still works. They like the distant mystery of my war-torn past. They don't ask me about it, which is useful. It means I don't have to embellish. Instead, it's left to their imaginations and this makes it much easier to fuck them. It was how I got Alexa's daughter, Lily, into bed.

The coffee whistles on the hob and soon I am sat out in the canteen munching and rereading the schedule.

It's now 8:30. The ward round for both the old woman and the new one need to be done this morning. Best to save the old one till last as she needs a proper wash before theatre at 1:00. I also have to fit in the old man before then. There are no visitors today, except for Mr Brown, which is good. It's more complicated when a crossover happens during visiting hours. Then everything goes on hold. Today packages can be cut and couriered during theatre. I will do the drop-offs. There is no exchange. Sarah says all packages must be quality checked before money changes hands. Then back for a final check of the new woman, and the old man. Mr Brown will be told his mother died in her sleep. A body will be ready and waiting on the bed in her room, and Mr Brown will come, probably without his wife who hated her mother-in-law, to pay his final respects. He will be feeling relieved because there wasn't much money left to pay for her care. Of course, that's why they picked him to be the grieving relative. His river is dry.

With any luck Mr Brown will opt for the home's funeral arrangements and the body will be cremated by the care home's associated funeral parlour. They usually take that option: it's easier. Unless, at the last minute, remorse catches up with them and they suddenly want a grand funeral to pay off their guilt. Then it is all much harder to organise.

After the funeral, we won't see Mr Brown again.

The whole schedule thing is stupid, though. I'm meant to read it, fold it tight in my inside breast pocket and then shred it at the end of the day. I keep telling Sarah to just tell me what to do. But she says the schedule is created so that there can be no excuse for not knowing the plan. We tried using a white board for a while, but because we had to make the board look real, the actual schedule got lost under lies. Now we use the board only for visitors. It looks more professional, more medical. But no visitors today is a good thing. It means I don't need to hurry over my breakfast and I will have plenty of time to take photographs. I shouldn't really leave last night's photos out on my desk either, just in case anyone sees them. I'll have to put them away in a drawer.

I fold the schedule and place it in my top pocket. My coffee is now pleasantly cool and I swing one leg up onto the plastic chair next to mine.

I told one woman, once, about what it was like building up to the war. My ex-wife Claire. She got me into this country. Married me even though she knew I was no longer in love with her. She was clever, and like all clever ones my teasing made her want to fight me first with words and then with flesh. She wasn't my first foreigner. They weren't hard to find along our beautiful stretch of coastline, mountains lending a romantic horizon to the beaches. But she was a little different. She kept coming back, waiting for me to finish my shift at the bar, waiting for us to be alone.

I made her wait three nights and the sex was so good I let my guard down. She left her questions hanging silently like a void between us that I couldn't help but fill. So I told her about my family, the army, university. I told her about wearing uniform and digging trenches in winter, muddy water freezing around my feet. I said the earth was hard and the skies high. I told her about how we were made to sleep outside to prepare for harsh conditions, how we learnt to kill straw bags with bayonets. That smoking kept us warm.

It was so cold, I told her, that I did not notice the hole in my chest. The whistling iciness, like wind blowing straight at my heart, was pneumonia. One day out digging I collapsed, a cigarette hanging from my lips. I passed out and came to in hospital. I didn't want to stay so I got up and walked unaided, with no proper papers, all the way home. It was over a hundred miles.

She understood my home was no place for an artist, not with censorship and the murmurings of discontent, so she married me and we flew here with my mother's *sarma* on our knees. The taste of sour cabbage and juicy beef was my first taste of freedom.

It didn't work, of course. We tried. But everything is different now. I met Ana and Jelena was born.

I lift my legs down off the chair, rubbing my ankles and calves; the veins there are dilated, twisted in raised knots. It's an old person's ailment. I drain the dregs of the coffee.

Jelena will call tonight. She will not be able to do much more than giggle a few unconnected words down the phone, but it will be so good to hear her. I close my eyes, sunlight sneaking in through the day room, damp and deep green, tinged by carpet and plush upholstered chairs, and feel my little girl in my arms. Her skin so plump and soft; the grip of her fingers tight.

When I finally get to the new woman, after breakfast and putting the photographs away, my trolley filled with a clean sponge and hot water, I am running a little bit late. Luckily, Sarah isn't around and the corridors are empty, as is so often the case, so it doesn't matter too much. I have my camera with me. It's not the best camera, but it's small enough and good enough for the kind of pictures I want to take. When I'm alone I can close the door, bring it out and get proper work done, but if anyone else is around, it fits on my belt like a large pager. I can still take photographs with it, but only without the flash.

The new woman's name is Katherine Drasen. It's such a familiar name, like Katarina Drazenovic.

She is sleeping. Out cold, her body hooked in place by plastic tubing, like something from a science-fiction novel. None of the clients ever seems quite real.

Pushing the trolley to one side of the bed, I make sure the door is firmly shut, then before beginning work I look at her through the camera.

She has a small body. They are often like that, as if age has had a shrinking effect, has weighed them down. Huge bruises cover her face, and she is bleeding from her nose. The colours of her face are vivid: blacks, greens, yellows, purples, reds, blues, like a rainbow.

So far there is just a simple bandage holding the bridge of her nose in place, but soon most of her face will be wrapped in bandages. It's important to obscure the face. In this case, it's a shame because for an old woman she's good-looking. Through the swelling I can see high cheekbones, a strong forehead and jawline. She looks like a woman who stood her ground. She seems young, even. That, too, will fade. The tiny likeness to the woman she once was will dwindle. Even now it would be hard to say what she would look like without the swollen mass of broken skin. A new, bland, virgin face is forming beneath. It's like a poor man's facelift. A bone snapped here, skin stretched there, the etchings of history cut away.

I see they have not washed her properly. There is a smudge of mascara under her right eye that must have fallen with tears, down towards her ear. With her eyes shut and a look of peace on her face, the mascara reveals the real sadness she has been brought to. It would make a perfect photograph for my collection and the room is light, so I shoot without a flash, dapples of sun playing among light-brown eyelashes, the blackness having smudged down her cheek. It's amazing that the smudge can be seen at all among the mess of bruises on her face, her eyes puffy, their colour deepening with every moment I stand watching them. I'll be able to use this photograph later if I need to touch up the colours of her face. False bruises make useful masks if the bandages have to come off.

I travel down past her neck and shoulders. The back of her left hand is punctured with a drip needle and wire, but apart from that her hands are strangely immaculate. They are clean, no scratches, no bruising even around the cannula, nothing. I capture the perfect fingernails of her right hand, palm up so that you can see the lack of dirt. Then I check her knees and legs, pulling back the covers. There are no bruises there either. It seems she only fell on her face.

Working quickly now, I take everything off her. I'm not meant to get her this cold, but it will make a good photograph because the shot mirrors ones I take later in the morgue. She is in a proper nightdress that can be unbuttoned from the sides. I have to watch as I turn her so that the drips and bags all stay in place. Her breasts surprise me. They are almost pert, like those on the body of a virgin girl.

I finish the pictures and begin to wash her. The water is still warm enough (I made it extra hot). Her skin smells fresh and despite the looser flesh, her frame is good, her shape still womanly rather than heavy and round. She must have taken care of herself. It makes me wonder about her, Katherine, Katarina. Did she know the origins of her name? A year here, a letter there, claiming foreign sounds, taming them, until the past is almost wiped clean, like I wipe her now. There is no chart hanging at the bottom of the bed, no nametag. Soon no one but certain staff will know her name, and no one will use it. She is no one. Like a cipher in a play, or a dummy in a shop window, she stands for every woman but is no longer one herself.

I take the sponge and wipe her labia, avoiding the catheter. I rinse the sponge in the basin, wipe her again, and then check her pussy with an ungloved hand, bringing my finger to my nose. I sniff. Just a hint of vinegar. As clean as it can get.

Her arse is now a useless hole, as the stoma on her belly has taken pride of place, and is clean. I wipe it and then pass the sponge over and around her legs, under her breasts, beneath her armpits, moving up, down and around like a child painting with a potato, blurring a neatly cut-out shape into a swipe of paint.

She is clean enough. I button back her nightdress and refold the sheets beneath her arms. She feels cold. There is a beige cardigan on the solitary chair. I take it and rest it gently across her shoulders so it covers her upper arms.

'Katarina,' I whisper, 'you should have stayed in east. They would not have forgotten you there. Here you are straw among whirlwinds.'

I won't speak to her like this again. These are my final words to a dying woman. However she came here, she will not leave. She is here because no one cares. If no one cares, you are already dead.

Everything is now on the trolley apart from the camera at my belt. I stand by the trolley and look at her for a moment, breathing slowly, thinking. And then my thoughts are not with her, my eyes no longer looking at her but through the sheets, the body, the bed, and out to something unfocused, images not of this time or place. Tonight I will talk to little Jelena. Tonight she will make me feel that only good can exist; all of this will feel worth it for one note of her laughter.

I wipe the back of my hand across my forehead, waking myself from the forgotten sounds of sea breezes, the sense of warmth from the sun and the cool mountains at my back. I turn and place a hand on the cold metal of the trolley. I have to get on with my round.

It is now 10:30. I can fit in the old man first. I open the door, push the trolley through and let the door click back on its hinges. The light in the corridor is brilliant, bursting through the large windows like a promise. Downstairs I hear Steve whistling. It's his favourite, something about angels. Unadulterated pop music. Meaningless, harmless, tuneless. But the opera of its day perhaps? No. It's nothing like opera. I let some thoughts run frighteningly close to stupidity. It's my way of keeping sane, holding conversations in my head, thinking through projects, plans, ugly hopes.

The old man is a floor down. I have to make my way to the lift, push the trolley through the doors and press the button. I am going right down to the ground floor first to refresh the washing water. I don't feel like it, but it could possibly be the best part of the job, boiling water. I push the trolley like a pram with nothing but shopping inside. I am careless. I like to hear the rattle of pans on metal, water sloshing. Why shouldn't I take what fun I can?

I do go all the way down to pour the dirty water in the kitchen sink and refill my bowl with urn water, scalding hot. Using boiling water saves on cleaning the bowl out and it means that by the time I am in the old man's room and have taken a few pictures, the water temperature will be perfect for his bath.

I come out of the kitchen, trolley still rattling, and get back in the lift. Steve is on the first floor. The whistling stops.

'All right, Milo?' he says, nodding at the sound of my name. He doesn't fully look up at me.

'Steve,' I say, halting the trolley for a moment. 'How you doing?'

'Oh, same old, same old. Beautiful morning, isn't it?'

The English and the weather, God. I nod back at him and watch as he pauses, takes the hip flask from the inner pocket of his overalls, sips, smacking his lips, and then holds it out towards me.

'Fancy a nip?'

I take it. I don't really fancy a nip, but I like the gesture. Steve is a good man. I like him. I drink deep and enjoy the burn that spreads from my throat through my chest. It makes me cough a little, and I splutter out thanks.

'That's the stuff, eh?' he says. 'On your rounds?'

I nod, my face hot, words lost. I don't normally find it hard to drink his whiskey, but the coughing has sent some of it down my windpipe and up the back of my nose, making my eyes water. Steve nods back and resumes whistling. I push the trolley further down the corridor. I keep meaning to ask Steve to share a *rakija* with me, but I always seem to forget. One day I will ask him. I think he will like the taste of it. The national favourite, it's so strong it partially evaporates on your tongue, so that you breathe it and drink it at same time. I must remember to ask him.

The old man's room faces towards the garden, which catches the sun in the morning, light slanting in at an angle. There's not much light left now as it's getting on for midday. He is awake, sitting up with his back against the bedstead, his short legs stuck out underneath him. His legs are useless lumps, the muscles too wasted to carry him. As I open the door he eyes me suspiciously.

'*Deda*,' I say, 'time for your bath.'

I'm not worried about him talking as he only has a hoarse whisper left, and even that is unintelligible. Still, he speaks with eyes that narrow, his lips pressing tight together. Without glasses, his face holds some sense of individuality. A scratchy grey beard grows across his chin, cheeks and upper lip. He has a nasal feeding tube taped across his face and, mistrustful of my movements, I cause him to wince.

I talk to him in Serbian. It's nice to speak freely, to be heard and not understood. I pull back the sheets and photograph his feet, the thick yellow nails like hard cheese. I will have to cut them. I pull his pyjamas down and photograph his penis like it's a sausage waiting to be sliced and eaten with a thick hunk of bread. I have to bend in quite close to capture it. It looks best pushed up onto the slack blubber of his belly. The catheter wire looks like a twist of intestine fixing the sausage to its string. As I try out different angles, the old man coughs and hacks, then spits at me. His phlegm lands in my hair. I smile. This makes my job easier. I look straight at him and turn the screen of the camera his way.

'Look,' I say, 'your manhood.' And there is the picture for him to see. 'Is small, eh?' I smile again, not looking at him. The smile is at him not with him. 'Winter either bites with its teeth or lashes with its tail,' I say, softening. Old age is the winter of life, even more cruel than we imagine.

I take the camera back, unbutton his pyjama top fully and photograph his weak chest, its sparse hairs white and grey like seasoning on thin soup. Finally I train the lens over his face and take a series of photographs, the blood-red skin fading as his anger is worn to despair. Then I cover the beginnings of his beard in lather, photograph him again and uncurl the long barber's knife. It occurs to me that I might seem threatening, wielding this sharp razor so close to his jugular. I swipe, shoot and wipe until his pallid face is clean and empty.

The water is perfect now, if a little cold, so I soap his body, washing carefully around his stoma so infection doesn't take hold again. The soap makes him suck in air. It must hurt. I pay little attention. I see time is moving fast and I should be seeing to the old lady. I'll have to be quick. I push back his foreskin and clean around the shaft of his penis, then around the slack skin of his scrotum. My touch makes his penis stiffen and when I look up his eyes are fixed to the ceiling. It's shameful for him, but I feel no pity, not after he spat in my hair. I change his shit bag. It's too old to empty again. I will have to leave his toenails. There isn't time. There is never enough time.

'Just been cleaning old lady,' I say in English as I work. 'Nice tits, you know. Maybe like your wife?'

I know it's cruel, but I have to keep my own dignity. I want to get back at him for hacking at me. He doesn't respond. He has no more fight in him today.

Before I leave, I place the big holed glasses over his eyes. He has two pairs: one black, one white, the lenses like giant sieves. They cover most of his face. He looks like a bee, or a wasp, or a fly. He does not need them but we like him to wear them. It helps secure his anonymity.

'Got to buzz.' I chuckle, clanging things onto the tray and walking out. I never tire of this joke.

In the corridor my stomach rumbles. I'm hungry,

but I don't have a lot of time to sort out the old woman before theatre. I'd like another coffee, perhaps a cigarette, but it will have to wait. I slam the colostomy bag in the biological waste bin and go back down to the ground floor. I need to prepare the trolley with fresh hot water, new supplies, proper surgical soap, clippers and a clean razor. I'll be doing a thorough job on the old woman and given that it's eleven thirty, I only have an hour and a half to complete her. It pisses them off if I miss deadlines too often. I'll just have to push my cravings aside. I cheer myself up by thinking of the photographs I can take. Images from these last rites washes are good. They show people as packages of tissue, revealing the very heart of the home's business.

The old woman is unconscious. Her drip and feeding tube have been removed in preparation for theatre, so she sleeps unaided. Over her time here she has grown heavy on the food we force into her. She twitches like a fish dragged out of the sea, her belly pregnant with unsaid, unspeakable events. Her skin has a sallow, grey tinge like dirty bath water. I take her clothes off and already it feels like I'm touching a corpse. The new lady will have to put on weight or the resemblance will be strained.

I roll her onto a plastic sheet. It's not easy, requiring lots of pushing one way and then another, manipulating limbs, pushing the plastic beneath heavy flesh. When she's safely on the plastic, I cover her torso with the nylon sheets again and take up the clippers. It's important I shave everything but her eyebrows. Hair gets in the way, makes incisions harder. I am not sure if they will want to cut into her head, but it's best to shave it anyway. We can always put her in a wig. Also, shaving heads is fun.

I make sure her head is properly on the plastic to keep the hair from falling to the floor and take the scissors to the longer bits of her limp hair. I stuff most of the hair into a bin liner. I have to cut the long strands because the clippers catch on longer hair, ripping it from the scalp. As I cut, the woman looks less and less like a person and more like a collection of features and limbs; a series of parts. She becomes a drag queen without drag. Something in her appearance makes me think of a famous singer from back home. I begin to sing one of his tunes to the whine of the clippers, imagining an accordion backing and lilting vocals. I stop to take a few photographs. Maybe I could post them on a website, put them next to press photos of the singer. They would be round the internet in no time.

I read somewhere, once, that he said something about his brains not being needed abroad, only his muscles. It's what I felt when I first came here. It's still true, I think. But men must act as men. If I can only get these photographs right – divorce them from the care-home setting, maybe claim they are from a different time or are digitally enhanced – I will be on my way to becoming a famous photographer. I will win grants and prizes and maybe then it will be easier to go home. I'll still travel, but Eastern Europe will be my base. There is no real life here without Jelena. But old habits, beliefs won't fade. I left too long ago. My home remains frozen in time as the land of misopportunity.

Humming, I break off the final grade and take the blades of the clippers straight to the skull, cutting close. Her head is like a naked baby in my hands: the skin is soft, unmarked.

I dust off the hair from the plastic sheet into a bin liner and pull the covers down so that I can shave her armpits. I've been lazy with the old woman in the past, but I couldn't believe anyone would take a look at the state of her underarms. Despite the neglect, there is only a smattering of straggly, wispy hair. Easy to remove. Next, I move on to her pubic hair. I have to keep her warm today so I'm extra careful with the blankets, making sure I leave as little skin exposed as possible.

I spread her legs. How did I get this job? How did I come to be here shaving old woman pussy? It disgusts me, so I put the lens of the camera in between us. I let the camera see what I don't want to.

It reminds me of stories from the war. Women on both sides were taken and raped, their bodies ravaged like the land, shamed, looted. If my family had been in a different place their lives would have been taken over by it, but being so close to the beaches, we hid our heads in the sand. It was not happening to us. It was not our friends, our colleagues who supported it, whose ideas, bodies, money went to uphold the land of our people. You only do what you can in war. If it does not taint you, why question fate? You are lucky. You just have enough food to eat. You are good at fishing. You stick together. You make do.

I was here, safe, or so I thought. But safety is no longer something tangible.

Here prejudice is covert; economics war. I look down at the old woman and her eyes suddenly snap open. She is not looking at me – her eyes still seem cloudy, blurred by drugs – but the atmosphere of the room changes. I have made a real woman bald. I have spread her legs on a narrow hospital bed, and now she lies exposed there, strips of light from between drawn curtains slashing at her body. I feel overwhelmed by an emotion I don't want to acknowledge, so I take a photograph. Once that's done I reach up to her face, running the fingers of one hand over her eyelids to shut her up. I still have work to do.

I shave her pubis and legs with a normal razor. I don't really need to do her legs so I don't bother about getting it perfect. I treat it more like an extra wash. It gives her legs a better sheen. Once all the hair is off, all the bits of left-over cream wiped off, I prepare the sponge bath with heavy-duty soap. I'm working at a good pace and the wash is well timed. Even though she'll have iodine splashed around her incision areas in theatre, it still helps if the client is cleaned not long before the operation. It stops too much dirt from building up again.

When I'm finished, I do not stand over her as normal. I am tired. I've pulled the blankets up tight beneath her arms and I do not want to look any more. She is small, her bald head round and shiny. It's like time has turned the clock back on her and instead of a grown woman, a child lies in front of me.

On the way out, I walk into Steve again. I hadn't heard his whistling. He looks up as I come through the doorway. I'm sure he looked into the room, towards the old woman. Steve is not allowed in clients' rooms. It would make me want to look.

I look hard at him and seeming to feel it, he looks back. After a moment's pause, he nods.

'Smoke?' I ask.

He nods again.

'Just need to get rid of trolley. Back garden?

Five minutes?'

'Okay, Milo,' he says, his head bent down, touching a finger to his cap in a mock salute.

Woman – II

Some time seemed to pass after the family came to visit. After they'd secured the feeding tube, it felt like I hadn't seen anyone for days. Perhaps they came when I slept. When I was awake there was nothing but the bland sameness of light and shadow on the wall, on the bed. If I was lucky, now and again I could make out a faint whistling echoing down the corridors. Though eerie, the sound was strangely comforting.

Then one day, without warning, Spotty brought more visitors.

'She's just through here' – I could hear her in the corridor – 'there we go,' she said, using that loud, demeaning tone. 'Visitors, Mrs Smith.' She directed this comment at me. I wondered if I had heard her correctly.

She held the door open and two people came in. One was in a wheelchair. She didn't look old. She had those really thin legs, all knee joint and bone. She was being pushed by another woman with glasses. This other woman was very tall and plump. Next to

Spotty she looked like a giant.

When they were in the room and the door was shut behind them, they stood still for a little while, looking at me. The one in the wheelchair put her head on one side.

'Mum?' she said, and moved herself closer to my bed, pushing the wheels with her hands.

I looked back at her.

'Mum, it's me, Ann. Claire and I have come to visit you.'

Did she really think I was her mother? The fat woman's mouth twitched at the corners, a grimace rather than a smile. Ann took my hand. Her head was just above the height of the bed. A better height for looking at. She stroked my hand.

The other woman had moved to the end of the bed and was fiddling with the blanket at my feet. She was very awkward. Ann was much more refined. Her little head jerked about on her neck like a bird on a perch looking out for worms. Even though she was in a wheelchair, she looked like she might fly away. Her fingers were quick and hard, calluses rubbing softly over the back of my hand. She looked into my eyes and raised her eyebrows, smiling in a hopeful but defeated kind of way.

'It's good to see you.'

I looked from Ann to Claire and back to the nurse, who was standing by my drip, arms folded.

'How has she been?' Ann asked her.

Claire didn't seem to want to talk. Her fingers worked through the blanket tassels in a defiant sort of way. Orchestrated disinterest, I thought.

'She's doing all right,' the nurse replied, 'aren't you? Her weight is up and hopefully her strength. If she keeps going like this we'll put her back on solids in a few weeks. We don't want to hurry you, do we?'

'And the bruising,' Ann said, her fingers still for a moment, 'when will it go down? It still looks so painful. Is she in a lot of pain?'

'Her nose is healing more slowly than we'd hoped, but she's in no pain.' She jerked her head towards the drip. 'She gets regular morphine.'

Ann nodded, her eyebrows tilting upwards at the centre in a commiserating, worried sort of smile. She gave my hand a tight squeeze and then started to rub it again.

'Has she said anything yet?'

It was Claire this time. She was still refusing to look at me. Her question had a tone of bitterness to it.

'Not yet, but give it time. We hope she will relearn to speak. We can't promise anything, but we'll do our best, won't we?' The nurse smiled at me, uncrossing her arms to pick up my left wrist. She checked the tubes and then took my pulse, two greasy fingers on my neck. She couldn't check it on my wrist, not with all the intravenous connections. I turned my head towards Ann.

'She seems to remember you,' the nurse said, 'that's a definite improvement.'

Ann was pleased with this. She squeezed my hand a bit too hard, but I couldn't tell her, and anyway, it was nice to have someone holding my hand. I didn't want her to stop. I felt tears coming again. It didn't matter that I couldn't place her or even remember her visiting before. This was kindness, affection.

'Look,' Claire said, 'I think the old bitch is crying.'

Ann shot Claire a warning look, 'Claire,' and turned right back, her forehead creased with worry.

'I'll leave you to it for a bit then, shall I?' Spotty said. She made it seem like she felt she was intruding.

She didn't fool me. 'I'll come and get you in ten minutes or so. Will that be enough?'

Ann nodded. Spotty left the room, making a wide berth around Claire as if she were a lot larger than she actually was. When she was gone, Claire walked over to the window.

'Well really, how you can hold her hand like that?'

She stared out of the window and then, as if suddenly reminded of something, reached into her handbag and pulled out a bag of toffees. She didn't offer one to Ann. She sucked the toffee out of its wrapper, pulling the plastic free with her fingers. The wrapper came away flat and sticky. Without looking at it, she dropped the wrapper in with the toffees and closed her handbag. Then she began to chew, moving the toffee around her mouth so that alternate cheeks bulged. The sound of it filled the silence.

Ann was still rubbing my hand, but she was no longer looking at me. She was looking absentmindedly at Claire. After a while she said, 'I thought you were on a diet?'

'I am,' Claire replied without turning. 'They're low calorie.'

There was a pause.

'Do you think she can hear us?' Ann asked.

'I don't know. If looks are anything to go by, she's fucked.'

Ann shook her head, in reaction, it seemed, to the swear word. It was as if, though she had heard it numerous times, she couldn't yet resign herself to it, hoping Claire would one day grow out of it.

'I really thought her nose would have healed by now. It looks all crooked, even under the plaster. And the bruising is still terrible. Do you think they're looking after her properly?'

'Don't pity her, Ann. She's on morphine, for heaven's sake.' Claire slurped through the sibilants, the toffee clicking against her back teeth.

Ann looked back into my eyes again.

'She can move her head. Maybe she can show us if she can hear.'

Claire grunted, her gaze resolutely fixed on the window.

'Mum,' Ann said, her head on one side, 'if you can hear us, shut your eyes.'

I shut my eyes. I was sure I wasn't her mother, but I wanted to talk to someone or at least have them talk to me. Ann seemed so sympathetic, sensible and caring. I hoped she might take me seriously.

'Claire, she shut her eyes.'

'You're sure she didn't blink?'

'Positive. Look.'

Claire turned to watch.

'Mum, if you can hear me, do it again.'

I shut my eyes again.

'See?' Ann said.

Claire frowned. She moved closer to the bed, peering at me through her glasses. Honestly, if I could have spoken I would have told her to make an optician's appointment. Those glasses were terrible. No one wears milk-bottle bottoms any more. Even I know that. It made her eyes tiny dots in the sea of flesh that was her sucking toffee face. She was grotesque, like a large burlesque monster, nostrils flared.

'Mother,' she said, 'can you really hear us?'

I shut my eyes again.

'Bloody hell,' Claire said.

'Oh, Mum,' Ann said holding my hand to her face, her eyes moist.

Claire leant over the bed. I could smell her breath, sickly sweet. She stared hard.

'I should have known,' she said.

'What do you mean, Claire?' Ann said, looking up at her.

'She couldn't ever bow out gracefully, could she? Could you?'

'Claire,' Ann said more forcefully. 'Claire, for heaven's sake, she's ill.'

'Well she should do us all a favour and bloody die.'

A fleck of her toffee spit landed on my upper lip, a tiny bubble that burst in the quiet, seeping into my skin. There was a knock on the door. Claire stood up straight.

'Time's up, ladies.' The nurse opened the door. 'Don't want to tire her out now, do we?'

Ann put my hand back on the bed and smoothed it down like a blanket. She looked at my arm and my hand, but avoided my face. Claire marched round the bed and took the handles of Ann's wheelchair.

'Bye, Mum,' Ann said as Claire turned her away from me.

The nurse held the door again. Claire didn't look back. The door closed and they were gone.

I stared after them for a while, my eyes fixed on the closed door. They had seemed so different. Like chalk and cheese. And yet, they were both certain of me. Could I be wrong? Could I be their mother?

Every day I wake up confused. It makes the terror of displacement commonplace. As I can't remember who I was, what I did, who I'm related to, my life is defined by what other people make of it. I'm out of touch, literally. I can communicate through blinking, but this requires great effort on other people's behalf. I can't question or complain. I am at a distance from them and from myself. I have to work it all out by piecing together snatches of conversation, trying to place trust in flashes of what seem like lucid memory. If I am a mother, I am a miserable one: either I have a son who won't visit me, or a daughter who hates me. Perhaps I want to forget.

I watch the patterns of shadow and light on the ceiling and I listen to traffic. It's like playing a waiting game, or a long session of hide and seek.

'Don't be shocked,' Spotty says to my visitors, just outside the door, 'if she doesn't look her usual self. She's sustained quite serious bruising and her nose hasn't totally healed yet. We've had to keep the plaster on.'

The nurses can't be trusted. Spotty said something about speech therapy, physiotherapy, but I don't remember receiving any therapy at all. Meals down a tube, drugs in a drip, shit in a bag and bedsores. Maybe this is how it always happens. Old age. Faulty memory. It all makes me very tired. If I can forget who I am, it follows that I can forget other things as well. I can't trust myself.

After the family, then Ann and Claire, there was one other set of visitors. They have only come once. Their visit left me with a lot to think about.

Early in the afternoon the nurses appeared and lifted me into a wheelchair. I hadn't been out of bed for as long as I could remember. It was exhilarating. Sitting up was such a novelty that it made my head dizzy, all the blood rushing through my chest. I could see much more sat up in the chair. The room looked so different. I could see cars out of the window, people on the street. I wanted to stay there, looking out, but with one of them pushing me, and the other pushing my various drips, they took me out into the corridor.

I knew I must have been taken through the corridor into the room when I first arrived here, but I have no memory of it. The corridor was long and bright with windows at both ends, and after an age of being in one room, it was like entering a church, the only movement dust sparkling in shafts of light. It was really quite a surprise. I expected something more akin to the rotted smell that seeps through the polish.

As they wheeled me to the lift, the nurses talked. It was, and is, like I am an object, a package they have to deal with and deliver to the right place. They think my silence makes me stupid and because of this they've grown complacent. It leaves me much to contemplate.

'When do they get here?' the man said, pushing all my wires out of the way of the lift doors.

'Two thirty.'

'Is really necessary I am there?'

'Of course you have to bloody well be there,' she pushed a weight of slick fringe out of her eyes and behind her ear. 'Just sit at the back of the room. You don't have to do anything, for God's sake.'

The lift started to go down.

'Who's coming again?'

'Ron James, you idiot.'

'Yes. Yes, I knew that. Her wife doesn't know, that's it, isn't it?'

'His wife, yes,' Spotty corrected him wearily. She must do it a lot. 'Don't say anything in front of the wife.'

The lift came to a halt and the doors opened to another corridor. There weren't so many doors down here and the light didn't run all the way through.

'Can't believe all are so bloody gullible,' the man said, struggling again with my drip and the lift doors. He had to push his whole weight against the open doors to keep them from shutting as he twisted round the drip stand. He did it with the kind of nubile energy a soldier uses to approach an assault course. There was an arrogance to his movements.

'They have not met before?'

'They didn't get on.'

They pushed me on into a large room with comfy sofa chairs and a view of the back garden. It wasn't much to speak of, a bit of dry yellow grass with a few trees, but I was pleased to see it.

'Then wife should be pleased to make a bit of money on her.'

They turned me away from the window and settled me in the middle of the room facing a huge television. I hadn't seen television for an age. I was rather excited, but they didn't switch it on.

'He uses it to gamble,' Spotty said. 'Right. Let's get the other one.'

They left me staring at a blank screen. I couldn't turn around to see the garden so I just waited and thought about gambling. It was a relief to be in a different room for a change. I was looking forward to meeting Ron James and his wife. How could he be making money on me? I wasn't sure what the nurses meant.

After some time, they were back with another wheelchair. I suppose I knew there must be other people in this place, but it was still a bit of a shock. I hadn't seen anyone else in here, apart from the nurses and visitors, and here was an old man, trussed up in much the same way I was, wires and tubes and weak limbs. They put him by the window, facing the garden. I couldn't get a proper look at him as he was behind me, but he was balding with those big old-man ears and a sack of a belly around which his arms were folded. They'd put him in a light-brown cardigan. As they pushed him past me, I saw he was wearing huge bee-like glasses. They were black all over with tiny holes and they covered half his face. I'd seen them before. Someone I knew had had to wear them after they had a fall. They kept seeing double. Or was it a cataract operation? Anyway, I knew he could probably see something, but he hadn't bothered to turn his head. He just stared straight ahead, looking like his thoughts were elsewhere. Perhaps he didn't have any thoughts. Maybe that's why they put him by the window.

'I'll be in reception if you need me,' Spotty said. 'Just sit at the back of the room and let me do the talking.'

She left the room and the male nurse walked towards the TV and switched it on. He flicked through the channels looking for something that interested him and picked a chat show. He sat on one of the comfy chairs, one leg hanging over its padded arm. The chat show wasn't very interesting, but it was a damn sight more interesting than anything I normally did all day and I was fascinated. The female presenter – there were two, one male and one female – was wearing a deep-green dress cut in the 1950s style, with a thin shiny belt tight around her waist. It was beautiful. I was so pleased that I could define the style of dress and felt sure that I'd had one like it once. I started thinking about what my dress would now be worth and whether I would still get in to it. Foolish, happy thoughts.

Then the cookery slot started. A simple dish for one: Spanish omelette and green beans fried in garlic. An awful lot of fat, I thought, but it was fun to watch them chopping and boiling and frying. It made me realise how warm the room was, much warmer than my room upstairs.

The chef offered the dish to the presenters and they took delicate bites, licking their lips and pushing spare millimetres of bean into their mouths with their fingers. It made my mouth water. Real solid food. I could feel the textures. They made all those 'mmm' noises, their eyes widening with pleasure. Then they said what was after the break and tucked in as the screen flickered to adverts.

I closed my eyes, imagining that omelette, its smell, and then I drifted off. I didn't mean to. I wanted to watch more television. I could sleep anytime. But the room was so warm and the imagined taste of real food in my mouth gave me a sense of ease I hadn't felt in a long time. I woke with the sound of the door opening and Spotty's voice guiding the visitors into the 'day room'. It made me smile because it was the first day I'd been in that room. 'Occasional room' might have been more appropriate.

The television had been switched on to a nature programme and the male nurse was no longer in sight. I imagined he was sitting at the back of the room somewhere, reading a magazine no doubt.

'Mr and Mrs James, if you'll just follow me, ah, there she is.' Spotty started to walk in my direction. I hadn't seen any other women in here so I don't know why she'd had to look around for me. She was such a bad actress.

The couple in her wake were cowed somehow, their shoulders hunched. They didn't look directly for me, but around at the room, rather greedily I thought.

'Watching television, eh?' Spotty said. 'Look who I've brought to see you.'

I looked. Presumably, this was the infamous gambling Ron. He was wearing one of those fake suede jackets that does up with a zip. He didn't look a great deal younger than me, his hair white with a yellowish tinge, like his fingers. His wife wasn't much better. She had squeezed herself into a pair of wedge-heeled ankle boots and a light-blue pair of jeans. A black overcoat hid her upper half, but she still managed to look like a pear. Her hair was cut very short and coloured a deep purple. The burgundy of her lipstick ran up her face in fine wrinkled threads. She looked like she'd eaten a spider. To top it off, her eyes were hidden behind round gold-rimmed glasses. The gold rim caught the light every time she moved, even slightly, so that it was hard to focus on her face and her expressions were lost somehow behind the movement. The pair of them were decidedly shifty. I could see why his mother and Mrs James wouldn't have got on. She looked trashy.

'She likes nature programmes. Watches them all, don't you, Ruby?' Spotty said.

Ruby? Well, it was a new one at least. I rather liked it.

'She always did like the telly, didn't you, Mum?' Standing behind his wife, Ron almost shouted the words, getting louder as he addressed me.

The nurse put a hand on his arm. 'Remember what I told you. She still can't articulate yet. Don't expect too much from her. It's not easy, is it, Ruby? But we're doing our best, aren't we?' She bent over me, smiling at me. I wondered who Spotty was doing this act for.

'Nice and warm in here, isn't it?' Ron's wife spoke up. 'Is it all right if I take off my coat?'

'Of course. You make yourselves comfortable. We'll bring the tea trolley round in a few minutes. All right?'

They nodded at her and she walked away.

'Would be all right, wouldn't it, this? Comfy chairs, bit of a view, no need to cook or clean. Look at the size of the telly.'

'Okay, love. I see your point, but isn't it what we all deserve?'

'Bloody well should be the price we're paying. Who's going to do it for us, eh?'

Ron smiled weakly at his wife, sighed and turned towards the screen. Neither of them was making any attempt to engage with me.

'I mean, it's not like your Tom is going to bother, is he? My savings. That's all we've got.' It was her turn to sigh.

Before she could start up again, Ron changed the subject.

'Think you can smoke in here?'

'You should know. You've been here before.'

Ron looked up at the ceiling, pausing for a moment before he spoke. If he'd been here before it wasn't to see me. He could have come to check it out before I got here, but I didn't remember ever seeing him before.

'Not to this room,' he said. 'Only been in her room before.'

'Oh, well, I doubt it. It's a health place, isn't it?' She turned her head, studying the room, her eyes narrowed.

Ron looked around, rather desperate.

'Hey, mate,' he said, calling out to the male nurse. 'It all right if I smoke?'

'Not meant to, but be my guest. You're paying, eh.' He gave a little verbal wink.

Ron smiled.

'Too bloody right I'm paying,' he said to his wife and pulled a pack of cigarettes from his pocket, tapping one out with expert fingers.

'Give us one then,' his wife said.

They both lit up, inhaling deeply.

'Bet you miss these, eh, Mum?' Ron smiled, his eyes focused below mine, somewhere around my cheek. I wondered if I had something there, some smudge or fallen eyelash. Perhaps the bruising had got worse again.

'Sorry we haven't come together before. It's not been easy.'

'We're very busy,' the woman said between sucks, blowing out smoke with her words and lengthening the legs of her spider mouth when she paused to inhale. 'Business is booming. My new ideas have done wonders. Ron says they can't spare me.' She took another drag. 'You always did prefer Ron on his own, anyway, didn't you?'

Ron broke across her, cutting off her line of thought.

'Where's this tea then, eh? I'm parched.'

'Yes,' his wife said, turning her attention away from me. 'They always this slow?'

The credits were running for the nature show and the music disrupted the conversation.

'Mind if I put the racing on, Mum?' Ron asked, getting up out of his seat before I could nod, blink, or make any response. 'I want to see the three ten.'

He changed the channel. Horses blurred across the screen, the voice of the commentator loudly cheering along the race. The noise was unbearable. Mr and Mrs James watched it avidly though. I looked at them, trying to remember. The smell of their cigarettes was making me sick. I looked down at my hands, trying to trace the remnants of any discoloration. There were none of the tar stains I could see on Ron's fingers. My hands were their same, tight, pale selves. They looked like white cabbages with extra-large green veins, all the leaves curling inwards. As I stared at my hands, thinking of cabbage leaves, the memory of a sweeter, rounder tobacco smell took root. Suddenly, I could see my father sitting in an old upholstered armchair with thick clouds of smoke billowing around his head, one hand clasped around the end of his wooden pipe. I could hear the clack of his teeth gripping the pipe as he smoked, taking it in and out of his mouth, repositioning the mouthpiece to allow for speech. The promise of words was there. I could see the glow of the tobacco and the warmth of the hearth reflecting off his glasses. He opened his mouth to speak, but the memory was broken by Spotty. She had come back with the trolley, bumping through the doors towards us, a huge steel urn and cups and saucers clattering on top. I couldn't recall anything else.

''Bout time,' Mrs James said, getting up to find a bin to crush away the last of her fag. Ron was already on his second, ash littered at his feet and one fag butt pressed down onto the television table, its filter jutting at an angle towards the wall.

'Better put it out, love.' She'd brought the bin back with her. He looked up at her, then the approaching nurse, took one long drag and pressed it hard against the bin liner. It singed a hole through the plastic, releasing a sudden smell of burnt hair.

Spotty was making a horrid racket with the tray. She looked at the pair of them, sniffed, and visibly shrugged.

'How are you getting on? Tea?'

'Milk and two sugars, please,' Ron said.

'Just the one sugar for me,' the wife added.

Spotty poured the tea into white coffee cups that sat a little awkwardly on their saucers.

'Biscuit?' she held out a plate of custard creams, bourbons and plain digestives. Ron took two digestives and his wife took one of each and balanced them on her saucer. Spotty's buzzer sounded. I knew what it was straight away, though I had never heard it before. It was clipped to her breast pocket. She read the message and shouted to the other nurse, 'Can you take over? The others are here.'

Old lazybones came and took the trolley from her and she left, muttering something about perfect timing.

I watched the Jameses sipping their tea and wondered how they would look if you stripped them of their skin. All those cigarettes would make their insides coarse and black with tar. Their faces were fixed to the screen, watching the racing. They looked tired and angry almost. Ron had his cup held halfway up his chest, waiting for the end of the race before he took that first sip, his mouth open slightly with anticipation. I tried to remember things about racing, but I was sure I wasn't the betting type. I had a vague memory of wearing a hat, and I knew you wore those at races, but you wore them at weddings too.

When Spotty came back in the room, she was

followed by two new visitors. They weren't there for me. They were there for the old man. Well, someone else with visitors. That was interesting.

Mrs James turned around to watch them come in and looked back at me.

'They could have done a better job with her face, Ronny. All that money and she's still black and blue.'

Ron mumbled his assent, his shoulders high and stiff as he watched the race.

As Spotty and the new visitors passed our group, they said hello.

'We've seen you before, haven't we, dear?' the woman said looking at me, and then turning to Mr James, 'You must be her brother.' Mr James froze, his eyes unfocused and wide, the teacup still inches from his lips. 'We met your daughters last time we were here.'

Mr James still couldn't quite spit out any words, so his wife did it for him.

'I think you must be mistaken.'

'Oh,' the woman said, 'oh, but I'm quite sure …'

'Yes, well this is Ronny's mother and we don't have any daughters. We've just got my son, Tom.'

All of the visitors, except for Ron who was still staring into space, his teacup now rattling on its saucer, looked at one another. You could see they were all certain that they were right. All of them but Ron, to whom no one was paying any attention except me. Ron looked scared.

Spotty laughed. 'Oh, dear,' she said, 'this does happen often. It is so easy to confuse people, isn't it? This is Ruby. I think you met Mrs Smith last time you were here. She was with her daughters, Claire and Ann.'

'Well,' the woman said, 'I'm sure' – she frowned,

staring at me – 'well …'

'Mrs Smith has a broken nose too,' Spotty said, smiling. 'Funny how sometimes people look alike.'

'I don't know,' the woman said. 'They look too alike.'

'Come on dear,' her husband said, putting an arm on her shoulder, 'we're here to see Father.'

'Yes, of course,' she said, allowing herself to be drawn away, but keeping her eyes fixed on me.

'I'm so sorry,' her husband said.

'Oh, it happens all the time,' Spotty added again.

'No offence,' Mr James said, springing to life, his tea abandoned on the floor. You could see he was trying to temper the indignation lighting his wife's face. He watched them walk off and once they were at some safe distance, he breathed out. Remembering his tea, he took it up and drank it down in one gulp.

'We'd best be going,' he said. He handed his wife her coat. She didn't look like she wanted to move. Her lips were pressed so tightly together they were almost invisible, all spider leg and no body. 'Love,' he said, 'come on.' He signalled to the nurses who must have been behind me with the old man. 'We've got to be off now,' he spoke loud enough for them to hear, but didn't shout. It was more like a very loud whisper, as if there was something he didn't want to disturb.

'You just let them insult her,' his wife said. 'Not that I'd normally mind, but she can't exactly defend herself.' She gestured towards me, her hand waving down over my face and body, hoping to exact some response. She looked like she wanted Ron to start a row.

'It's all right, Lynne. No harm meant,' Ron said, touching her arm.

His wife raised her eyebrows and pocketed the rest of her biscuits.

'Let's go, then, if we're going,' she said, reaching for her coat. She pulled it on as Ron marched towards the door. When she lifted her arms into the sleeves, a thick tyre of yellow-white flesh spilled out beneath her jumper, bulging over her trousers. Her jumper was far too short, despite the high-waisted jeans. She didn't seem to notice the exposure.

'Bye, Mum,' Ron called from the door.

Lynne didn't look back.

I looked across the day room, searching for something to cling on to. I had another new name. Ruby James. I'd been called Ruby James, Mrs Smith and Diane Eames. It did not make sense that I could be all three: which one was I? Could I be none of the three? And if I wasn't these women, then where were they? Why did the home need me to stand in for them? I felt the itch of my bandages, the skin healthy beneath. Money was being made from the blank mask of my face, that much was clear. Why else would they go to all this trouble? But how and who and where that left me, I could not fathom.

The TV was still showing racing and I watched one horse after another rush across the screen; clods of earth flying up and behind their pounding hooves, the integrity of the ground destroyed by their collective speed.

Steve – II

It was about three months after Fran died when I first started to wonder what went on in the home. It was September, I remember because I'd started to scarify the lawn, clearing off the thatch. That day, though, I was inside, working on the floors. Something just felt different, like there was a tension in the air. I kept seeing Milo rushing about with his trolley. I wasn't used to seeing him so active, which in itself I should have found strange. There's only him and Sour-grapes that provide the nursing care for the whole building and Sour-grapes was even less visible than Milo. Something about his face that day snagged at me, turned my attention outwards.

I bumped into Milo several times. In the early morning, I was polishing the first floor. I could hear Milo going up and down the lift with his trolley. He has a real particular way of walking, almost struts along as if he's always being watched. It's probably his height. He doesn't look gay or anything, just very continental. No one of my generation would walk like that. It's a youth thing.

I was surprised he went up to the second floor because I didn't think they had any clients up there. Not that I knew for certain, I mean, I kept to my patch and didn't go nosing around, but there was something about the air up there, plus it was always dusty, like no one was walking about, churning things up. I'd stopped bothering to clean up there as often and no one seemed to have noticed. There was no riot act read by Tasty or anything.

So I was cleaning the first-floor corridor, enjoying the feel of the machine humming away in my hands. I was whistling one of the hospital-radio tunes I liked. It made me think of Fran, my darling angel. And I was minding my own business, you know, letting the machine guide my thoughts, focused on the job and that.

Milo was on the second floor for ages, but not moving about. He seemed to be only in one room. Because his trolley makes such a racket, I can normally hear where he is. Well, he was up there and silent for quite some time. Then as I was working my way back along the corridor, I heard him go right down to the ground and then back up to the first floor, the lift doors opened and out came Milo, pushing his trolley ahead of him. I turned off the machine to say a few words.

I used to carry a little hip flask of whiskey. I'm not a heavy drinker or anything, but I found it helped to take a sip now again, kept me going when Fran's face hovered in front of my eyes for hours on end. I offered Milo a nip and we chatted for a few minutes. I gave him plenty of time to talk, asking about his rounds and that, but he didn't say anything about why he was extra busy, just nodded and got on with it. So I left him to it.

I don't know what it was, but just the whole atmosphere that day made me hang about. It wasn't long before I'd finished the corridor, but for the first time since I'd started working there, I wanted a little peek at a client. All over again, Milo was spending ages in one room. It wasn't that weird, I mean, giving Fran a bed bath took quite a while, but even thinking about Fran's care made me wonder what these clients were like. It wasn't a nursing home, it was a care home, so they shouldn't really be sick, but I hadn't ever seen anyone. It suddenly struck me. Why hadn't I seen any clients?

Tutting and shaking, I thought I'd better take myself downstairs. I didn't see any point in sticking my nose in when I'd been told right from the offset that the clients weren't my business. I wasn't being paid to make up stories. So I manoeuvred the machine into the lift and started work on the downstairs floor, which was much more extensive and would keep me busy.

Partway through the ground floor, I heard Milo's trolley and rather than bump into him again, I decided to have a quick coffee break out on the fire escape. It's good out there. You're out in the fresh air – well, fresh as it gets in the city – away from the warm smell of old people and you can look over the garden. It's not a bad view, even with the chimney and the outhouse blocking all but the home's driveway. You can't see the road, but you can see out over the railway line and off into the city. Most of the surrounding houses and flats are blocked by trees. It's quite a pleasant spot. I had a good instant from my flask, spiked with a nip of whiskey, and a fag and felt much better. I just needed to clear my head. It was crazy to go around snooping like some TV detective.

But as soon as I got back inside, I felt the itch to investigate creep back up along my arms, twitching at my eyelids. It was almost like I didn't have a choice. Fran had someone there nearly round the clock. The clients might not be sick, but what was their care like? Maybe they'd like to see a friendly face. So I took a bucket with some cloths and general polish that would do windows, metal doors or handles and started on the first floor, looking for cracks in doors, keyholes, any gaps where I could get a look at the clients' rooms beyond.

The first floor was a good place to start. It turned out that Milo was still up there. The door, whether by design or accident, was ever so slightly ajar. I could see inside the room to where Milo was leant over the bed. He was giving the client a bed bath. I could see the sponge and the client lying on the bed. The bed-ridden person was bald. It was a strange sight. I peered up and around Milo's back, trying to see better. It looked like he was measuring them with something, leaning back, down and to the side, checking them out from several angles. When I finally moved the right way and saw past him, I caught a glimpse of something I didn't expect: I saw a flattened breast.

The bald person Milo was washing on the bed was a woman.

I felt myself take a sharp intake of breath, quite loud. I had to step back, away from the door. It reminded me too much of Fran, her head beneath the wig she'd given up on. Did they have really sick people in the home? I'd had no idea.

My heart was going like the clappers. It was so loud I was sure Milo would walk out and want to know what the hell I was up to. But he didn't. After a minute or two I took another peek and saw he was tying up her nightie and tucking the bedclothes back under her arms. He was finishing up.

Thinking I'd better be doing something, I walked back to the lift doors and started to polish them. It was a good job too because Milo looked surprised to see me. I kept my eyes fixed on polishing, but I could feel him looking at me so I had to look round and nod.

'Smoke?' he asked and I nodded again. He suggested we meet outside the kitchen door. I gave him a mock salute as the lift doors shut him out of sight and then put both hands on my knees and bent over to catch my breath. It wasn't like I'd seen anything wrong as such, it just felt strange, out of place. Without seeing more, there was no reason why I would have guessed what he was up to.

I finished polishing the doors – thought I might as well seeing as I'd started – and got back in the lift, going down to meet Milo for a cigarette. I decided to pretend I hadn't seen anything. I wasn't meant to look in the rooms and I didn't know how Milo would take it if I asked about the woman. He might tell. At least grief gave me a reason for any strange behaviour. And the thought, no matter how fleeting, that the pain of losing Fran might be useful made me feel wretchedly guilty. I went down to the kitchen door with a heavy heart. I couldn't imagine anything bad could be going on. It was only the sick suspicions of an old, twisted bloke.

Sighing, I got there before Milo and lit up, not even thinking of waiting. When he came we had a half-hearted attempt at conversation, leaving me feeling sicker than before. I needed to do some hard, physical work, anything to take my mind off the morning's bleak thoughts. I couldn't stomach the idea of lunch, so I went back to polishing the ground-floor corridor.

More than you used to, you find yourself spending time by just feeling it pass. Sitting quietly at the kitchen table, you stare out over the sink into the garden, watching the leaves swaying in the breeze, looking out for birds, thinking about cloud formations. The attention to tiny, silent detail makes you feel consciously alone, like you're the only person in the world that can see the tap's slow drip, swelling until enough accumulated mass makes it fall blank and hard onto the metal of the sink. At those moments, you could reach out and feel time moving around you, you're that sensible to things passing, to solitude, even though you can hear cars outside and shouts from the street. It's then you wonder if love can outlive material death.

I'm not a religious man. If anything, I'd feel both angry and impressed should God reveal himself. It seems to me he would be the kind who'd build an engine and never check the oil. He'd keep running it without water or fuel until it overheated. He's not a maintenance man. But despite my rational disbelief, it's in the quiet that I find myself straining to hear Fran, almost certain of a hint of her perfume, or her shape beneath the apron on the back of the kitchen door. I can't persuade my heart of her absence. And when I feel like that, we talk.

Of course, it's me that does the talking, aloud, into the tense dampness, noises deafened by my breathing, by my words. I don't have to hear her voice to know what she would say to me.

Before Maggie was born, misshapen, tiny, when we knew she wouldn't live, Fran cradled her own belly, spoke to it. She said she would always love her. She would always be there for her. She didn't need to be told she was carrying a girl. And it's like that now. Like she is somewhere holding some part of me, rocking me, soothing me, telling me she'll always be there, telling me she loves me. And then I reach out, hold out my hands to the empty air and bring them crashing back down, useless, the simplest of grasping reflexes caught short, my fingers pressing in on themselves. And the loss pins me down, holds me, achingly lost and alone, anchored to the present, hard furniture beneath me, my cries drowned in the sea of empty space that makes up my home.

Oh, Fran, I miss you.

The day I saw the bald woman, I was determined to stay on into the afternoon. I'd been working longer hours since Fran died and somehow I felt like I owed it to the place that day. It would mean I'd be able to finish cleaning the ground floor and I'd decided that I'd like to aerate the lawn. I couldn't tell whether it had been done the year before, but I thought it wouldn't hurt to pack a few more nutrients into the soil. I'd always been keen on grass and used to keep ours tidy thinking James would get out there and play football with me, but he was never really into playing the game. The total opposite of me, he always preferred to watch it and became a huge Lions fan. He gets up all hours in America to watch Millwall live on satellite. But following football has never been a huge deal for me. I was too busy with the business. You have to dedicate yourself to that game. I prefer a bit of dog racing, maybe a boxing match. When I was a kid I used to sneak into ratting contests, grown men – soldiers on leave or those left behind like my dad – betting on which terrier would come off triumphant. Anyway, we didn't play much on our lawn. James was always more of an indoors boy, reading books well above his age range. I didn't understand it, but it made me proud. He's always been a clever lad.

Still, despite not using our patch of grass, I'd had the practice caring for lawns and I wanted this one to gleam. There's nothing quite like a healthy lawn. I thought it would be perfect for all those people stuck inside looking out their windows. A lawn they could enjoy from their beds.

So, as I was finishing up the corridors, I was planning the lawn, trying hard not to think of anything but the tasks ahead.

I'd started out near Tasty's office and was working my way towards the entrance hall. At first it was the same as usual, quiet, but after a few minutes there was more traffic than I'd seen the whole time I'd worked there.

Just as I was coming into the entrance hall, Tasty rushed past me, her heels clicking, and went straight to the buzzer behind the front desk, triggering the gates to open. A sleek BMW swung quickly round the driveway. A car door slammed and a thickset man – the rugby type – pushed through the doors. Tasty gave me a little smile, but didn't introduce me. She and her man rushed back past me to the lifts and disappeared. I couldn't hear them upstairs so I assumed they'd gone into Tasty's office.

A few minutes later, I heard Sour-grapes in the kitchen with Milo and then they both came out into the corridor and got in the lift with a trolley bed. I could hear them on the first floor. They trundled along a bit, there was a short pause and then I heard them moving back to the lift again. As they didn't reappear, I had to assume they'd gone right down to the basement, which was odd because the only things down there were the morgue and the incinerator. They must have needed the bed to help move a client, or maybe a client's mattress needed changing and then they'd taken the waste down. It was probably a waste-burning day. So I kept the machine running, focusing on the shine of the floor. Still, as I worked twice over the heel dents, I wondered whether Tasty and the man were in the basement too. I had to shake myself out of it. It would do no good to stand about imagining all sorts of rubbish, so I rushed over the last of the entrance hall, packed up the machine and went out to the shed to fetch the garden fork.

I was feeling hungry by that point and decided to have my sandwich sitting in the shed with Fran's photograph for company. The aeration would probably take all afternoon so I'd need some energy. I'd planned to start on the front lawn.

Twice that afternoon I heard the roar of Milo's motorbike and later on the BMW drive out of the grounds. I was just getting to the grass near the patio when I heard another car turning into the driveway. I wondered whether it was the blond man coming back again, but it soon became clear that it was someone else entirely.

Where I was working I had a clear view into the day room. Tasty showed in a middle-aged man in a tired suit. He slumped into the first chair he came across, his head hanging down. He looked like he'd been lamped by a bunch of kids. He was all twisted over and desperate-looking. I felt quite sorry for him, even from through the window.

I wanted to know what the hell was going on, so, picking up the garden fork, I moved closer to the edge of the patio. Even though the weather was beginning to turn cooler, it was still a warm late summer's afternoon, and one of the windows of the day room was open. I stood right by the wall, close to the window, stuck my fork in the grass and rested my foot on it, listening.

At first there wasn't much to listen to. The man sat there, alone, staring at the floor. He looked like he hadn't had much sleep lately. His suit was all crumpled, the knot of his tie too tight, and he was wearing trainers. I know it's the fashion for people to wear trainers and suits – you even see old rockers wearing them – but it doesn't look right to me. It's one thing James and I agree on. Why waste the look of a perfectly good suit by shoving trainers on the bottom?

Anyway, the long and the short of it was he looked out of it. I was just beginning to get bored, wondering what on earth I thought I was doing, when Sourgrapes strode into the day room.

'Would you like to follow me?' she said, using her client voice. It's like she turns a dial, which slows her down and lifts her pitch all at once. It sounds like she's blowing her words through a whistle. The chairwoman of the local Women's Institute used to talk like that. The voice seemed to go with the job, as I remember several different women who held the office talking over the Tannoy on the coach when we went on days out to National Trust properties or the theatre, all of them in that 'listen hard, I know you're half deaf and your memory's faulty' tone.

I was waiting for her to say something else, or for

the man to reply, but that was it. He got up and followed Sour-grapes out of the room.

I was disappointed. I was standing, a right mug, pressed up against the wall, hoping to uncover some mystery and all I got was 'Would you like to follow me?' Fran would have laughed, asked me what the hell I was playing at. He was probably checking the place out for his mum. And then I realised he might also be there for his mum in quite a different way. She could have died. And all of a sudden the image of the bald woman, her breast exposed, hung in my mind like a bad dream. Surely Milo or someone would have told me if a client had died?

I prised myself from the wall and carried on forking holes into the lawn. I didn't like to think of someone losing their mum, and I was getting behind schedule. Even though the forking was nearly done, I still needed to put down a layer of gritty top-dressing, let it dry a bit, and then work it into the lawn with my brush. I'd be here at least another hour or so and I was getting tired. I kept setting myself tasks, forgetting I was not the man I used to be. I didn't have the strength any more and I knew I wasn't eating right. If it weren't for the job, my waistline would have been out of control. I'd pass a fish and chip shop on the way home and it was all too easy to stop by and pick up a pie or fish dinner. It wasn't as if I needed to worry about dying, not with Fran gone.

So I kept at it. Taking careful steps over the lawn, shaking out my mixed bag of dressing front and back, trying not to think about the man in the crumpled suit. I couldn't do more than one task at a time, otherwise I would have put down the soil as I put in the aeration holes. Some of the holes in the front garden were closing in. Still, it would do the job. It would improve the lawn no end. And after the top-dressing was dry – the length of time it took to lay it all over meant it was dry as soon as I'd finished, as long as I went back to where I started – I worked it well in with the broom.

It was at that stage I saw the man coming out, Tasty trotting by his side. I stopped, drawn to him right away.

'Thank you, again, for all you've done,' he said. 'It's good to know she had someone with her at the end.'

'No thanks needed, Mr Brown. It's what we do.' She laid a soft hand upon his shoulder, gently guiding him towards the gates. 'As I said, let us know when her service is and we'll make her transit arrangements. We want to do as much as we can for you at this difficult time.'

The man shook his head in a sideways nod. 'Yes, thank you, you've been very kind. I know I should have made more time for her and now … at least I know she was in good hands. Yes. In good hands.'

He was looking worse than when he came in. He was shaking like a lunatic, the nodding turning into a kind of twitch. I'd been right though, the poor man had lost his mother. All that day, Milo and the rest had been running about because this woman had died. None of them had mentioned it. I couldn't understand why no one had said anything.

I watched the man walk out through the gate. Tasty shut it behind him and teetered back to the home, pausing briefly on her way.

'You've had a long day, Steve,' she said, peering at the lawn, her nose wrinkling slightly. 'What are you doing to the lawn?'

'Aerating it. Looks a mess now, but the grass will soon grow through. It'll improve the lawn no end.'

She smiled.

'Good, well, keep up the good work.' She turned to go and then stopped in her tracks. 'How are you, Steve? Keeping well?'

'Not bad, considering,' I said.

'Glad to hear it. Don't work too hard now, Steve, you hear?' She gave a little mock waggle with her finger, grinned and carried on back towards the home. I had to call out to her. 'I understand someone died today,' I said, stopping her again.

'Yes. Sadly, Mrs Brown died today.' She cast her eyes to the ground and sighed. 'It comes to us all, Steve, in the end.'

'Sorry to hear that,' I said.

She shrugged, coyly pressing in her elbows and pushing out her cleavage. 'You get used to it,' she said and marched quickly into the home, giving me no chance for further comment.

So that was how they did death at the home. It wasn't what I'd expected.

It was some time after that night that I had the dream. It didn't strike me as odd that Fran was still alive; no, the strange thing was that her parents were alive too.

In the dream we were planning to move to the country. Fran was pregnant. There was no James. The house we'd found was large with a good-sized garden and due to some quirk of the place when we moved in we had to inherit the previous owners' dog. It was a huge, great black hound dog, mature with a glossy coat and tail that turned brown towards the tip.

Fran's parents also gave us a dog. It was a golden retriever, not a puppy, but still young and bouncy. They'd been given it but didn't have room to look after it, so suddenly there we were in a house in the country with two dogs.

This is where the dream started to go off track. It was like the dogs had been entrusted to us, like they were signs of others' trust and that we should look after them well, showing how good we were at responsible loving, showing how much we cared for others, especially Fran's parents. But something to do with the pregnancy made us realise that we couldn't care for the dogs, that they had to be put down.

Of all the possible answers to our dilemma, we came up with a solution that while straightforward in the dream, terrified me when I woke up. We decided the best thing would be to cut the dogs into pieces. And the best tool for the job was a bread knife. The really nasty thing was, as I sawed through the flesh, it didn't fall off into separate pieces, but somehow held together so that the dogs, sliced from the bottom forwards, could still move around, turning their eyes to us, all moist and pleading. Even in the dream I couldn't carry on hacking at them. I had to hand the knife to Fran, who said dogs had a different nervous system and wouldn't be able to feel anything. I was scared that the dogs would hate me and I felt guilty. I was worried that Fran's parents would want to see their dog, would want to know where both dogs had gone. They would no longer be able to trust me. When I handed Fran the knife its teeth were clogged with shreds of bloody, dark, brown flesh and tiny clumps of torn, matted dog hair.

As Fran started to cut into the retriever the dream shifted and instead of the dogs being killed it was humans. There was an epidemic and I found myself thrown to the bottom of a large swimming pool, sunk amid a pile of rotting corpses, their arms and hair calling out to me, holding me down. Fran was no longer there. I could see healthy people treading in the waters above me, shoving down the sick with their feet. I was at the bottom, still breathing but aware that I would run out of air and become like the mass of flesh around me, all limbs and no identity, stuck to the bottom of the pool like rusting spare parts, forgotten by the healthy churning the waters above.

I woke up then.

I thought a lot about the dream, not enough, or in the right ways, but it haunted me. I thought partly it must have been because it was rare. I wasn't getting much sleep – not straight through the night, not since Fran died – and insomnia is a really aggravating, disorientating thing. It's like going somewhere new without a map, only you aren't going somewhere new but travelling the same old routes, doing the same old things, it's just they look different. It makes you uncertain of yourself. Like when I knew my driving days were over. First the coaches, then the car. I don't think I'd even put myself on a bicycle. I suspect I shouldn't have operated the polishing machine, or the lawnmower, but I couldn't give up everything. There were too many positive aspects to the job to admit defeat. I had to take more care, that was all. 'Know your own limits' was an old saying of my father's, something he grappled with after he hurt his leg. It had just taken me sixty years to hear him.

My limitations narrowed and not sleeping meant

more to work around. More work and less motivation. It didn't seem worth it without Fran. I kept at it, but I didn't know what it was all for any more. I was floating somewhere between the healthy swimmers and the sunken diseased bodies and no one had noticed, no one was on the sideline cheering me on. I just had to get on with it, one way or the other.

Some time soon after the dream, James rang. I kept thinking I should talk to him. All that killing of things in your care, the healthy kicking down the weak, had made me realise how suspicious I was about the standard of care at the home. He was a lawyer after all. He'd know what to do. But I couldn't bring the words out. He'd think I was making it up. He knew I'd not been sleeping. He would have thought I was hallucinating or something. 'Evidence, Dad. You need evidence.' He would have been right, too.

The phone call went the usual way.

'Hello, Dad. How's your week been?'

'Oh, the usual. Keeping busy. And you?'

'Yeah, it's been a good week. We won our case on Thursday so we've been celebrating, out most of Thursday night and then more drinks on Friday. It's been good to have a bit of a breather. I've got a new case starting up Monday, so I took the weekend off.'

'Sounds good. Your mother always said you should take more time for yourself. How's Michie?'

'She's fine, Dad, thanks for asking.'

I had to ask because I knew she listened to the calls. I could hear her breathing. I'm never sure if she thought I was deaf, or if she wanted me to hear her. Fran thought it was creepy, but tried to pretend Michie listened in because she cared about us. I've always thought it was because she's over-protective, paranoid and doesn't trust us not to bad-mouth her behind her back.

'Things are going well for her at work?'

'Yeah. Looks like she'll make senior partner before me.' He laughed. It sounded a little forced.

'Oh, well, you must pass on my congratulations.'

'Will do, Dad, will do.'

In the pause we both listened to Michie breathing.

'How's the caretaking going?' James asked, offering me the perfect opportunity to talk. 'Any thoughts on your second retirement? You don't want to wear yourself out.'

'I think I'm fine for now. I like to keep my mind off things.' Like being a coward, even with my own son.

'Maybe you could take a holiday? Come out here and visit us?'

It was a genuine offer, but I could hear from Michie's sharp intake of breath that James was going off the script. In the silence after the gasp, I wondered if getting away would be a good thing. Perhaps there I would be able to talk to James. But I couldn't get rid of the idea that it was all nervous superstition. I needed to face facts: I was an old man. James and Michie were in charge now. If I was uncertain, they would be doubly so. Until I had something concrete to say, it was better to stay silent.

'I'm too old for air travel. Don't you worry about me,' I said.

Michie sighed with relief. There was another pause.

'Well, don't let me keep you, James,' I offered. 'I know you've got better things to do than chat to your old man.'

'I like to touch base with you, Dad. It's good to

keep in touch.'

'Thanks, son. Well done on your case. Have a good week.'

'You too, Dad. Take it easy.'

'Bye, son.'

'Bye, Dad.'

I heard the click of the receiver at James's end as the line went dead. Slowly I replaced my phone on its hook. Perhaps if Michie hadn't been listening … Maybe I could have called James at work? But really, what did I have to say? I could have asked about standards of care, the kind of evidence I'd need to justify my feelings. It was a sad state of affairs. I couldn't even talk to my son. I had to either forget it, or look into it. Maybe then I could call James. Maybe then I would have something interesting to say, something useful to contribute and could float back to the surface, churning the water with the rest of the healthy. But I'd said, and continued to say, nothing. I'd seen one bald lady and had a bad dream. Was that really worth worrying about?

Milos – II

Before I go out to the garden, I nip into my room and download the images from my morning's work onto the computer. I'll be able to look at them later, and this way I can wipe the camera's memory, making room for more shots. I refix it to my belt and head out through the kitchen side door into the garden. Steve is there already.

He holds out the pack of cigarettes without speaking. I take one, put it in my mouth and he lights it. His is already lit. We both inhale, exhale, looking out over the grass. In the background sirens wail, the lights at the crossing beep, and there is the odd car horn. I lean back against the wall, one foot pressed against stone. It's not cold, but it isn't warm either and I bring one arm in tight around my chest, its hand holding the elbow of my other arm so that I can keep warm and smoke at the same time.

Steve breaks the silence.

'Getting colder, eh?'

I incline my head. We stand side by side, not looking at each other. It's hard to talk to Steve, not because he is nasty or stupid, but because he does not know what goes on here. It's like talking to a child. It's another thing that Sarah gets cross about. She doesn't approve of my half-hearted friendship with Steve. I tell her I know how to keep secrets.

'How's the weather in your part of the world?' Steve tries again.

'Still like summer,' I say. 'They have saying in my country that winter finds out what summer lays up.'

Steve hums appreciation and interest through a further intake of smoke. He is a lonely man. His wife died not long ago. His son lives in America.

'How is your son?' I ask.

Steve stirs, turns directly towards me, and drops his hand to his side, the cigarette forgotten for a moment, ash building at the tip.

'Good, thank you. Still not proposed to his girlfriend, but he's predicting a large bonus for the end of the year. Business is booming. Lucky for some, eh?' he smiles, genuinely proud of his little American. Who can blame him?

He goes back to the cigarette, ash flicking off as it travels to his mouth, his body turning to face the garden again.

I would send Jelena to America. Middle America. Imagine growing up without thinking about politics, food or water, but only the braces on your teeth and the latest gadgets. She would not even know the shape of any other country on the map. Total freedom.

Warmth from the smoke travels through my body. It feels good. Nicotine is rushing to my head, riding along my arteries and veins. I feel more relaxed as I draw out the last few puffs. Steve is already crushing his fag against the wall. He will hold on to the butt and put it in the bin. He's a proper caretaker. Never leaves a mess.

One last drag and I too stub out the end against the wall.

'Best get on, eh?' he says, walking in.

It's lunchtime though and we will both probably have lunch now. But routine does not make us take it together. He will go out on the fire escape. I will stay indoors. I check my watch. Lunch will have to be a sandwich. Theatre starts in twenty minutes and I need to get the old woman down there.

Steve walks through the kitchen, holding his hand out in a backwards wave and we part wordlessly.

The cigarette has suppressed my appetite somewhat and the sausage in the fridge reminds me too strongly of the old man's penis. I have to cut it fast and press it into the loaf without paying too much attention. I eat quickly. There isn't really enough time. As I clatter the plate into the sink, Sarah comes into the kitchen.

'Milo?'

I leave the dishes for later and follow her into the lift. She's already got the stretcher out.

It takes two of us to lift the old woman into place. Once she's ready I push the stretcher back to the lift. We go all the way down to the basement.

It's not cold down here, in fact it even feels quite warm, but the basement always makes me shiver. It's the underbelly, the bowels of the home. The walls are simple concrete, lights breaking their line rather than blaring from the ceiling. It feels like a ship or a submarine.

We push the old woman out of the lift and around into the morgue. One arm falls off the stretcher as I turn the bend and bounces slightly with the rotation of the wheels. Sarah is walking a few paces ahead and doesn't notice. I lift the arm back on, but it falls off again, seeming to point at Sarah, swaying to the rhythm of her hips.

The doctor is already there, in scrubs. I leave the old woman in one corner and go to unhook the cellar door. I pull it all the way back and then turn the crank that raises the autopsy table. We don't always put the table away – there seems little point. No one comes down here. Even though Steve makes the occasional visit to the furnace, he's not allowed to come in here. And anyway, a recently dead wife obviously tempers his curiosity. The morgue is meant to be a temporary one, so no one goes off before the funeral people arrive, but we put it to more permanent use.

The autopsy table looks amazing: it's made of gleaming aluminium and has raised edges and faucets to catch the blood. I push it to the centre of the room – where there are proper lights that twist from the ceiling and can be pulled down closer to the body, and a small drain has been installed in the floor – and replace the cellar door. I rearrange the room without offers of help from either the doctor or Sarah.

Of course the old woman isn't dead yet. That's where Sarah's gift comes into play. She's our anaesthetist. It doesn't really matter if she gets the doses a little wrong because we don't need the old woman to wake up.

'Let's transfer her,' the doctor says.

He is a bastard. I've never liked him. He talks at you rather than to you and enjoys ordering everyone around. He always scrubs his hands early so that he can just stand and wait, his arms held up, bent at the elbow.

Sarah and I move the stretcher next to the table and then lift the old woman out onto the metal surface.

'Blankets, please,' the doctor barks at us again. The protocol calls for all other voices to be silenced at times like these. Only the doctor speaks unless his questions require a response. 'We don't want her cold just yet.' He chuckles.

'Scrub up, Sarah.' I help Sarah into scrubs and gloves and make sure she is properly washed with her mask on. I keep to the edge of the room, watching Sarah attach a new drip to the needle still in place on the back of the old woman's hand. There is a heart monitor, and various other machines that blip with screens that display waves – all of which mean nothing to me. Sarah looks at them and then nods.

'Music!'

I switch on the music. The doctor likes opera. Today I play *Tristan and Isolde*. So many beautiful unresolved harmonies. I listen and pretend not to watch too closely, all the time clicking the shutter of my camera, snug against my waist. I can't know how the shots will turn out until later, but it's the only way I can take pictures in the morgue. I can't risk them seeing.

Sarah is assisting as well as keeping the patient unconscious. Sometimes we have Alexa down here as well – all hands on deck. But today it's Sarah who hands the doctor knives, scalpels and all the other strange instruments he asks for: rib cutters, scissors, an enterotome, toothed forceps, a bone saw, a skull chisel. But not all of them, not all at once. The huge incision down her torso makes it clear that some of the old woman's organs will be used in transplant. The doctor works quickly.

'Gloves, Milo, gloves!'

He has worked much faster than I anticipated. I'm supposed to get the special organ container ready for transfer. There are three ready on the side and I hold one out to him. He picks up the liver – its surface glistening beneath a fine network of veins – and places it in the box. I seal it up and get ready to leave.

'Wait!' the doctor yells. 'This is a three in one. You need a kidney and the heart.'

I have a strong stomach, but the morgue now smells like a butcher's. Despite the sucking tube draining away at the old woman's blood, and the clips and the burning rod that cauterises her flesh to minimise bleeding, I can see that the old woman is bleeding too much. Sarah won't need to increase the drugs. The old woman is going to die of blood loss before they even get to her heart. I watch the blood trickling down the faucets into bags beneath the table. OrganoMed will have that too. Use it to build the blood banks.

It doesn't take long for the doctor to remove one kidney and the heart – the vessels and arteries around it dangling like electric wires, the muscles still contracting though it no longer has blood to pump. The old woman's bowels are now resting in an aluminium basin behind me, her torso emptied out, ribs cracked open.

'What are you waiting for?' The doctor's shout knocks me back to attention. For a moment, I thought I saw my grandmother's body lying there.

'Get going, Milo. Now!'

I take the three containers, each clearly labelled, and put them in a special case that straps onto the front of my motorbike – well, it's their bike but I'm the only one who uses it. I go up to the ground floor, turn through the front entrance and out into the courtyard. There is no one watching. The bike is waiting by the gates. I strap on the case, pull on a helmet, turn the key and drive, drive as fast as I can to the drop-off. Sarah or Alexa will have called ahead. Round the back of an abandoned factory there is a man on a motorbike, waiting. He puts my case inside his own. He is dressed in Day-Glo, a special logo warning: 'LIVE ORGAN DELIVERY'. He nods at me. We cannot see one another properly under the helmets, but his eyes are strikingly bright blue and his face, squashed in by padding, is covered in heavy, greying stubble. Maybe I've seen him before, it's hard to say. We don't stop for pleasantries. I know he is going to the hospital, but I've no idea which one. He raises his left hand at me as he sweeps out onto the road leaving me behind, raising my hand in return. He is going to save people's lives.

When I can no longer hear the churning of his engine, I drive out back on to the main road, towards the home. They will need my help in the morgue. There will still be other parts to pack, and the body will need to be refilled.

Back in the morgue, Tristan and Isolde are hiding from the king's guards and pieces of the old woman lie all around the place in shiny aluminium bowls. Sarah and the doctor are still working on her, though all the machines, bar the sucker, are switched off. They have to be careful not to remove too many bits – the body has to be carefully resealed and made to look untainted. Sarah is removing toenails. The old woman's fingernails have already been pulled and are waiting in one blood-smeared bowl to be cleaned, labelled and packed. I am glad they removed the brain while I was out. I hate the sound the electric saw makes as it cuts bone and tiny flecks of skull tissue fly at you and lace your clothes. I see the brain has already been sunk into formaldehyde. They take months to preserve properly. This one will probably be sold to a medical school. I read up on OrganoMed clients.

This time I scrub up properly and set to work on the fingernails. I wrap them in cotton wool and place them in a box, using OrganoMed stickers to seal them in. I write 'Full set fingernails, both hands' on the box. There is also a right femur bone (no one looks under Granny's skirts), and the brain to be sealed and boxed properly, plus unfinished toenails, tendons and ligaments from the same thigh as the bone, and a patch of skin. All of it will be bought by the pharmaceutical and medical industries through OrganoMed International and we all get our little cut of the money. So much for no animal testing.

'Where is skin from?' I ask.

This breaks the quiet industry of the room. Isolde fills the pause, her voice swelling with desperate love for Tristan.

'Her arse,' the doctor replies.

I take care to note this on the outside of the box.

As I package, the doctor sews up. Sarah has finished with the toenails and moves on to the filling and stuffing of the body, replacing the missing tissue with rags and scrap metal. The head doesn't need stuffing as the skull keeps everything in place, so the doctor simply clips a couple of staples in place and lets Sarah sew the skin of the scalp together. The old woman will be wearing a wig, as I predicted.

It's amazing how light the body is without the brain. Apparently pallbearers notice the difference, mutter to each other about how light the coffin is.

An old length of pipe replaces the femur bone and is filled out with rags, which the doctor sews in, patting both legs in an attempt to maintain consistent leg shapes. It wouldn't do to have one leg slacker than the other. It's much easier when there is no one to see the body. The remains are just incinerated – the funeral home fakes a service in their books and everyone is happy. Vagrants are even easier – no need to account for anything. Alexa's hard men bring them in and we harvest them right away. They've had to cut back though; Alexa's men mustn't attract too much attention to themselves or leave too many street corners empty of all but old cardboard boxes. It's a side of things I know little about.

The old woman's bowels are pooled back in to her body. Like the skull for the brain, the ribs hide the absence of the heart, though they do have to be pushed back into place and thick black stitches sewn over the T-cut on the torso. The old woman looks almost normal now her wounds have been resealed. Sarah seals the blood bags beneath the table and nods at me. I've got to clean the old woman up. Wash away the blood. When I'm done I towel her and dress her buttock wound. Together, Sarah and I move her back onto the stretcher. We have a hard job stretching on support tights to hold the woman in place. We dress her in socks and place medicinal white gloves over her hands to hide the missing fingernails, and we give her a clean nightdress with a slip underneath that covers all signs of the stitching. Upstairs we will spray on lavender water and make sure there are lilies in the room. They hide the smell. Finally we fit on a wig. We will say she died after a visit from the hairdresser. It's a good wig. The hairs sparse and weak like natural old-woman hair.

The doctor smiles. He sees this as a job well done. He snaps off his gloves and cleans himself up, leaving his scrubs in a pile on the floor. We will burn them. As he leaves, he switches the music off. 'Good job,' he says. He never stays to tidy up. 'I shall go and sort out the forms with Alexa. We'll be calling Mr Brown in half an hour.'

The wide empty space of late afternoon stretches ahead of me. Sarah will deal with Mr Brown. I lack the required sympathy – or, at least, ability to fake pity. I don't want to sit with him as we both lie about how sorry we are. The fact she isn't even his mother would make it hard for me not to look at him with scorn. It surprises me they never notice.

I am standing in the corridor on the ground floor, facing the entrance hall, looking at the ugly flecked lino, shapes emerging, swirling with the energy of memory and laced with the vertigo of a hard day's work. I think I will drink some coffee in the canteen. If I'm lucky, Mr Brown will wait a while in the day room and I will be able to photograph his alone face. Concern will no doubt fade to a blank stare. His lips will relax, his brow uncrease and he will look through the entwined fingers of his hands and perhaps think of his mother, some moment in their past, or maybe he will breathe deeply and sigh out all the pressure of her living death (at no time did she acknowledge him fully when he visited, she seemed always half asleep) and the freedom that now waits to embrace him. I don't imagine him feeling guilty, though he is one of better relatives.

I am interested in this absence: the spaces that intervene between people; there is so much we guess at, assume. I always hoped that I would bridge it. That somehow I would find someone who I would want to embrace into my silence. It has not happened. I want it. I want a family. I tried to create a unit, that triangle of father, mother, child, but I couldn't do it. I can't trust Ana. I am in awe of her, but there is no respect. I know she ensnared me and now I am trapped by the beauty of our daughter, little Jelena, whose tiny fingers reach out and clasp away the breath in my heart, my chest, my throat. But I have to try to love Ana. It is this trying that marks the faces of the relatives in the home. The individualism and greed of capitalism have smashed their happy family portrait and shards of glass splinter through moments of connection. It's not about embracing, but about displaying affection. And broken glass is more beautiful in the light, glittering, flashing as the viewer moves around it, but the unity of the image is lost. Instead, you see a displaced arm here, an isolated smile there. Why reach out and touch your mother, give her the care she gave you, when you can pay someone else to do it and allow your life to go on as before? So I reach out and touch Ana, I try to reconnect through sticky meetings of flesh, but she uses her body as a battleground. I have to win the right to touch her. Maybe it's the same with all women. I hope to regain intimacy through our bodies, but she wants closeness of mind before she lets us touch. So I am here, earning money and sending some of it home. She is there, refusing to join me, wanting the comforts of home, family, weather and sea. She thinks my ambitions vain. But this is the place to be if I really want to make money from photographs.

I sigh and wend my steady way to the kitchen.

There is an American photographer called Evans who took pictures of people on the New York subway with a hidden camera. He fixed the shutter switch down one arm of his coat so that he could expose light on the lens without being seen. It meant he couldn't ever look at a picture he was taking until later. He liked the idea of a lack of human intervention in the shot, the viewer disconnected from the frame of the camera, the subject unaware of it. He shot faces that were naked in repose. I like this idea. It's like watching people's souls. I would like to see myself like that some time. Instead, like everyone else, the moment I catch myself in a mirror or pane of glass, I shift my face into one dependable expression. I only ever see a composition, not the fluid features of my unseen face. There perhaps I would find the true image of myself.

It's colder this afternoon. All the metal surfaces in the kitchen are devoid of heat. I set the coffee maker on the flame and stare out towards the garden. There is time for another cigarette. Even if Mr Brown comes straight away, he won't be here just yet and they rarely come quickly. Often there is a tinge of alcohol on their breath.

Patting my pockets I realise I've left my lighter in my room, so I bend under the coffee maker to light my cigarette from the gas flame. I feel heat wither my eyebrows a little and as I stand, still inhaling, I wipe a hand over my forehead, brushing across the tops of my brows. It's nothing serious, so I move quickly to the garden door and step out onto the concrete patio. The home is meant to be non-smoking.

Blowing smoke up into the sky, I remember how much Jelena loves smoke rings. I know it's bad to smoke in front of her, so I don't do it often, but it's hard to resist the laughter that peals out of her as she tries to put her fingers in between the rings of grey that evaporate outwards, dissipating ever wider into the air. Her joy is infectious and hope colours the past, making the future seem feasible, buoyed up by a sea of previous lives, not drowning under wave after wave of repeating mistakes.

I brush my hand over the rising smoke, breaking up the rings I've started to blow. I hate sentimentality. I'm turning into an old fool.

Behind me, a hiss of steam sounds from the coffee maker. I stub out my cigarette on the wall and carry the end inside – well trained – to put it in the bin. I've made the coffee so thick and rich that a dark grainy pool amasses in the bottom of the cup, and the flavour is pitted with tiny morsels of bean that lodge between my teeth. Beautiful. I slip into a chair in the canteen and stir in an extra spoonful of sugar, waiting, half hidden behind the open double doors, watching the day room. He will come and I will wait until the silence of solitude engulfs him.

When Mr Brown arrives at last, I hear him before I see him. Alexa is on the front desk. She feels this is the best way to make people feel at ease; they like to see the manager out on the front desk to welcome them. She wants people to see that it is a family business – God knows what that makes me. A cousin? A brother? She'd like me to be her lover but, as I've fucked her daughter, I suppose I'm more like a son-in-law. This wouldn't please her at all.

I hear the front doors opening with the familiar sound of that ringing bell. Feet shuffle on the lino floor. Short, sharp gasping breaths are clearly audible from where I'm sitting in the canteen.

'Mr Brown,' I can picture Alexa rising from her chair, 'I'm so sorry for your loss.'

Now she moves across the floor, her heels sounding on the lino. Steve finds it hard to remove the tiny round black wedges made by those heels.

'Let me show you into the day room. I'll get Sarah to take you up to her room. You'll see she looks very peaceful.'

Her voice grows louder as they walk towards me. His gasping is unnerving.

'Can we get you a glass of water? Tea or coffee?'

'No, no, thank you. I'd like to see her. Straight away if I can.'

'Yes, of course. Sarah will be here shortly. Please, do take a seat while you wait.'

They are in the day room now and I can see them through the door. I edge back slightly. I don't want Alexa noting my presence. She will find something for me to do. If she can think of nothing, she will decide to sit and flirt with me. It's pleasant enough, but I would rather not encourage her, especially since Lily. Alexa is all too clearly the older version of her daughter. Too old for me, the weight of her flesh is sexy enough, but it's beginning to hang south or spill too thinly over the edges and waistbands of her clothes. Deep down she knows I won't sleep with her, but her fantasy still suggests otherwise. It's best to avoid her, leave her daydreams intact.

Mr Brown sits down close to the corridor, but far enough into the room so that I can see him. Alexa abandons him to phone for Sarah.

He looks tired. Something in the way his hair falls back from his face – pale lines of scalp showing where a comb has ploughed over his head – reminds me of Linus from Charlie Brown. We used to watch that show on cable. There were the glowing colours of democracy with lemonade stands, baseball and young Beethovens in the making. Perhaps this is what grown-up Linus would have become: defeated, the skies closing above his head. I did not see negative possibilities back then.

Because the front of the home gets sun in the afternoon, most of his body is shaded in the strange grey-tinged light of the garden, though one glint of light passing from reception through the open door reflects off the sweat on the right-hand side of his forehead. He looks waxy, drained and, as I imagined, he lets his head drop down but looks instead between his knees, not at his hands. And then I see why. He is dressed in an ill-fitting suit, its colour matching his name, but it seems he could not find his shoes. On his feet he wears a pair of trainers by a brand I do not recognise. They look like proper running shoes: dirty white, their soles worn by the pressure of his particular pair of feet inside. I turn the camera lengthways and take a portrait shot of a man in a suit staring at his running shoes, the sweat on his forehead catching the light. I keep clicking as his face relaxes, looks through the shoes, the floor and on into his own mind. His breathing slows, his lips hang partly open, the smallest string of saliva linking the corners of his mouth and bubbling gently as he exhales.

When Alexa's heels return, their clipping matched with other footfalls – Sarah's – both Mr Brown and I jerk together. A thin line of spit falls to the floor between Mr Brown's feet and he rubs his hands up and over his face, dragging the skin back to life. He looks up at the women and climbs to his feet.

'Would you like to follow me?' Sarah asks.

Mr Brown nods and they leave the room. I hear them calling the lift, its doors open and close, and then they are gone.

I sip more coffee, rolling the grains over the front and back of my teeth with a meditative tongue. I wonder about those shoes.

Back in my room, I download all the images onto my computer. Something about absence, about gaps between things, Mr Brown's inappropriate shoes, has got me thinking beyond what the camera can see and take by how I arrange myself, and more about what darkness might thrill the eyes if I arranged what I saw. On the screen I see the dead woman Mr Brown thinks is his mother. I see pieces of her flesh, taken in secret, cut from her bones, some while she still breathed. I see Mr Brown's hands, caught in each other, never able to touch the flesh of his flesh long since gone. I see pieces of her and pieces of him, forcing themselves together, the edges blurring. And then I can't get two images out of my head: Diane Arbus's 'Masked Woman in a Wheelchair, Pa. 1970', and Joel-Peter Witkin's 'Interrupted Reading', 1999.

The woman in Arbus's picture faces the camera, but her features are obscured by a witch's mask, the nose and chin imposing, the eyes nothing but black holes. She sits in a wheelchair in front of a building that looks like some kind of home or boarding house with lots of windows and evidence of further buildings behind. Despite the number of people those buildings could hold, she is alone. You wonder if she is stuck where she is until someone helps to push her chair. The light is such that a tree on her left is clearly depicted in shadow across the building behind her, its branches beautiful but creeping dramatically across the photograph, like a carefully created gel used in stage lighting or some gothic fantasy. The seeming brightness of the day reminds me of pictures of Auschwitz: the world seems full of dappled sunlight, of happy order, and yet there is some silence or darkness lurking behind the buildings, or behind the witch's mask, that we cannot see.

Witkin's photograph might make you sick. Is it a trick of light? Is it real? You stare at the woman sitting at a table covered in velvet pile cloth, one finger of her right hand marking a page in an old hardback that rests there. She is decadently dressed, wearing a shimmering ball gown in satin or silk, tight around her midriff and overhung by exposed breasts that fall flat against her bony chest, flesh and nipples spilling onto the dress. She has a pearl necklace around her neck and her left arm is raised, the fingers curling around a forwards-facing palm as if she knows someone is looking, as if she has arranged herself like this. But she cannot know. Half of her head is missing, cut off or blown away. And her arm, the hand raised to her shoulder at such a commanding and coquettish angle, is severed above the elbow and only remains upright because it has been balanced against her body. It is so well done that you almost don't notice the gap in the flesh. Her only intact eye is focused downwards, out of the photograph's frame. One long, ornate earring, hangs from her ear, balancing against her neck. Then, across the closed book, is a note or handkerchief, I don't fully remember, that has fallen on top and rests there as if waiting for someone to come and pick it up, to place it in her amputated hand, not noticing that reading will always be interrupted.

These pictures corrupt, like negatives in flames,

one atop the other in my mind, casting against the dead woman and Mr Brown, and I find that more than anything, I want to compose a picture of their meeting, of the gaps and darknesses they cannot see. She will be laid out on the bed. The photograph will be taken from above. She will look up into the camera, but her face will be obscured by a crudely cut white mask, mimicking bandages. Mr Brown will have his head hanging down, his hands tightly wound around hers. As the viewer looks closer, closer again, they will see her hand is not attached to her body, but cut above the elbow. Light from the window will cast tree-branch shadows like ugly fingers across the bed sheets. The implication will be that Mr Brown has not seen the gap in her arm, where the flesh is broken.

I am so excited by the image that I begin to sketch it out on a scrap of paper next to the computer. I feel inspired. I plot out another of Mr Brown in profile, the whole of his body in shot, capturing the incongruity of suit and shoes. He holds nothing but the severed arm, its wrist clasped to his chest, the dead fingers stiffly caressing his cheek. I can feel more and more shots flowing through my mind, everything else on hold, breathing arrested while I work them all out onto torn pieces of scrap paper.

When the telephone goes it makes me jump. At first I think I will ignore it. I am busy. But the second ring reminds me it is probably Jelena on the phone. I answer, my voice somewhat hoarse, 'Hello?' There is a pause, in which I hear myself echo down the line, then, *'Tata.'* It's Jelena. Immediately I see her thick curls, silky and unusually blond (it's a mystery to both Ana and I, though my mother tells us I had blond hair as a child), her hazel eyes shining from beneath a cloud of eyelashes, her lips and cheeks pink, her chin dimpled. When I think of her, she is always laughing.

We only talk for a brief moment. She is too young for a proper conversation, but I'm glad she recognised my voice. I tell her I love her and she replies, the echo of my voice louder than her answer, and then she hands the phone to my mother. I can hear her scrambling off Mother's knee, rushing out somewhere, perhaps into a different room, distracted, looking for something, someone to play with. As my mother begins to talk, I can hear her squealing at the cat. I imagine her dangling a piece of string in front of it, waiting for the cat's paws to reach up, scratching out at the string, only for Jelena to pull the string higher, jumping as she lifts her arms.

'Milos?' my mother has noticed I am not listening.

I reassure her and she goes on, telling me everything: how Jelena is doing at school, how they still have a few tourists making the most of the last gasp of summer; how good Ana looks, how well she is doing at work. She always tells me how good Ana is. I know she thinks this will heal things between us.

I ask her if Ana is there, but she is working. She is milking those last few tourists, working at a beach bar, making good tips. And I see her, her broad back encased in lycra that snugly twists in at her waist, smoking at the bar, cracking the tops off beers, making the odd cocktail. The way she holds her elbows close together, pushing out her cleavage. The way she lifts her chin to blow out cigarette smoke, lips pouting. She will twist and wiggle in the tight Levi jeans I sent her and she will make tips from these poses. Maybe some nights she will even kiss men on the beach, sand rubbing into the sweat beneath her breasts and curling tight within her belly button. I imagine pulling sea-changed jewels from those sandy crevices and all too quickly I feel myself pulled under again, her siren's call drowning me, crashing my brains against the rocks. I have stopped listening to my mother again. Eventually, I tell her the line is bad. I send her my love. I tell her I will call soon. And then the line goes dead, the connection broken, and I hold the receiver to my chest as I imagined Mr Brown might hold the dead woman's severed arm. But it's only for a moment. Embarrassed, I put the phone down and run my hands through my hair. I push it, curl it back from my forehead and behind my ears, rubbing off the past. Mother used to say that life is like a game where God shuffles the cards, the devil deals them and we have to play trumps.

Soon it will be time to eat.

There is a knock on my door at 9 p.m. The home is already shut for the night – just me and the old people upstairs. It is too early for the OrganoMed pick-up so I assume it must be Alexa's daughter, Lily. Since we fucked, she's been keen to hang around. I put my beer down on the table and get up to open the door. It is her.

In some ways it's a good thing. It will be a long night and now she can fill it. I look down at her standing in the corridor. She returns my look, keeping her head down so her eyes filter up through the heavy, angled fringe. She has stuck a sparkly jewel high on her right cheek and her eyelids are carefully lined and edged with silver-blue shadow.

I open the door wide and she dips into the room under my arm. She drops the keys she took from her mother on the table and melts down onto the sofa, taking a swig of my beer. I close the door behind her and get another beer from the cooler. It makes a sweet hissing sound as I crack off the top, a slight haze forming around the rim that is soon enveloped by my lips.

Lily takes a pack of cigarettes from her bag and puts one in her mouth.

'Want one?' she says, talking around the cigarette, maintaining her pose, eyes still blinking through the fringe. She holds the packet out towards me and I take one. Moving closer to her, I lift the lighter from the table and hold the flame under her cigarette. She sucks and draws the tobacco to life, her eyes half closed. As she blows the first exhalation of smoke out over her tongue, her lips parted and purposefully seductive, I light my own, cupping the lighter flame, enjoying the rush of nicotine. When it's lit, I look back at her. She has settled into the sofa, her shoes discarded and feet tucked up, knees by her chin. She smokes with her elbow resting on the arm of the sofa. She is all angles and charm.

I sit on my computer chair.

'How are you?' she asks.

'Good.' I am pleased I haven't printed the photographs yet and that everything is put away. 'You?'

'Fine.' She lets her knees fall into a cross-legged position and nurses the beer bottle for a while. Her jeans are tight and slithers of stomach bulge plump and hard between her belt and T-shirt. A tiny bead of sweat has formed at the uppermost crease of her cleavage. She is wearing a small, sleeveless top with a scooped loose neck that falls in folds across her breasts. 'Just had supper with Mum. I told her I was going out for a drink with a friend.' She smiles at me, the edges of her hair brushing against her shoulders as she moves. Only the fringe is short. She tries to look like a rock-chick from a fashion magazine. She is doing a good job. I say nothing.

'I went to that exhibition you mentioned?' Her speech will now be full of rising terminals. It's nerves, I know, but it's irritating all the same. 'I was thinking about it and I'm not sure you're right, you know? All that post-modern stuff? I mean, irony doesn't mean anything, does it? If you do something or say something tongue in cheek then either you are saying nothing at all or you want to say the thing you pretend you don't want to say. Do you know what I mean? It's bollocks, that's what I think.' She waits for me to respond, taking another drag from her cigarette, another sip of beer.

I smile and push the hair from my face, twisting it over my ears.

'So, feminism,' I ask, mainly to keep her talking, 'you think is dead or not?'

'Well,' she looks into the right-hand corner of the room, concentrating, her face suddenly years younger than the make-up suggests, 'it's like, post-feminism is, well, it's like pretending feminism is over, that we don't need it any more.' She looks back at me, her cigarette millimetres from her lips. 'But I don't see equality.' The cigarette makes the final distance to her mouth and her eyes half close with the effort of breathing in the smoke.

We have had so many of these conversations before. It passes the time. She goes away, learns a few more things, comes back and tries them out on me. It is as if she thinks I will not fuck her without these conversations, as if they form some kind of bond. But

I will always fuck her. I like the idea of fucking Alexa's daughter. The symmetry of it pleases me. Besides, she has a good body, not too thin, firm, her tits heavy but pert. She's beautiful.

'So nudes exploit women or don't they?' I ask, letting a swig of beer lull over my tongue, cooling my throat as I watch her thinking about what answer will please me most.

'Sometimes,' she says, shaking her head to twitch her fringe out of her eyes. She is only nineteen.

'What about if I photograph you?' I ask, stubbing my cigarette out in the ashtray, my hand and face drawing closer to her, heightening the tension through proximity of flesh.

She looks at my hand, its long fingers, and up my arm into my face. I hold her gaze, a smile playing on my lips.

I think she is a little afraid, but only of herself. She takes a final drag on her cigarette, stubs it out in the same ashtray and takes hold of my hand. She half pulls me, half pushes herself, so that my hand caresses her breast. Now she is on the floor, kneeling on the floor by the table undoing her belt.

'You can photograph me,' she says.

I take my fingers from her breast, grasp her hand and lead her to the bedroom. She takes a condom from her pocket and watches me put it on. Then we make love. I fuck her on top, from behind, I make her bounce on me, I twist her legs around her head, then crush one leg beneath my knee, sideways on. I watch her arch her back. She sucks my fingers, my balls, licks hard circles around my anus. I keep at her, silently fucking on until the shuddering takes over and I feel a final surge of relief.

Pulling back, rolling onto my back, away from

Lily, I feel the sweat turn cold. I pull the condom from my dick, tie it tight to check for leaks, then lurch to my feet. I want to throw it away. I go to the edge of the room, leaving her lying on the bed. I can feel her following me with her eyes. I drop the condom into the rubbish bin.

'You okay?' I ask. She sits up. I can just make out her nodding. She has grasped the sheet around her, suddenly modest.

'I'm just going to the loo,' she says.

I watch her go, then slip out of the bedroom behind her and fetch my camera. I will photograph her now. The shots will be better now her make-up's smudged, her hair is tangled, her body subdued.

She comes back to bed and we stay there for at least an hour. As it gets later, we both grow colder. I have not stopped to put on clothes and when I begin to see her shiver, I suggest some coffee. I do not want her sleeping here.

We get dressed and move out to the kitchen. No one will see her, there's no one here, but it still feels risky being with her out here. It adds a certain frisson. Fucking Lily could cost me my job. Alexa would not be happy about it.

I cut some bread and cheese, offering slices to Lily, and we sit and eat waiting for the coffee to boil.

'When does she expect you back?' I ask, hoping to push her away.

'I said I would stay over.' My heart sinks.

'I can't do tonight,' I say. OrganoMed are coming later. Besides, I don't want her to stay.

'Oh,' Lily says. 'Why not?' She has borrowed one of my T-shirts and sits engulfed in cotton, her mussed hair creating a halo around her head as she eats her sandwich.

'Business.'

'Business? So late at night?' She pauses mid-chew, half-masticated food visible inside her open mouth.

'You know,' I say. Conveniently the coffee starts to whistle and I get up to pour it into two cups. I place them in front of us and stir in spoonful after spoonful of sugar. OrganoMed won't be here for another two or three hours. I have to stay awake.

Lily sighs and stirs sugar into her own coffee. She shrugs and asks, 'Do you have a fag?'

I nod, pull a crumpled pack from my pocket and the whole ritual of smoking and drinking begins again. I watch Lily sipping coffee, smoking and wonder how much she knows, how much Alexa has told her. Alexa may have said nothing, but still Lily could work it out. Perhaps she does not want to know. Sometimes you can see things and not want to know and so you pretend you are ignorant. It can be easier to live that way.

When all the cheese, bread and coffee is gone, and Lily has quietly smoked yet another cigarette, I scrape back my chair. But she is not ready to go yet.

'You will show the photos to me, won't you?' she asks. God, I fucked such a child. She looks so young in my T-shirt, sitting on the cold plastic chair.

I nod.

'Promise?'

I nod again and she seems satisfied. She too pushes back her chair.

'I can make you, you know?' She says this under the screech the chair makes as it scrapes against the floor, but she knows I heard her. It's like a whispered dare.

'I will show you, Lily,' I say, clearing things into the sink. I start to run hot water and pour liquid soap over the sponge.

She moves in behind me. Her closeness shocking, too close, her breathing in my ear. She wraps her arms around me and kisses the back of my neck. She squeezes. She kisses again and then she lets go.

'See you,' she says. Pulling my T-shirt over her head, she walks off down the corridor. I hear her go into my rooms and then, a few minutes later, she comes back, shoes on, bag ready, keys jangling in her hand. She waves at me, blows me an ironic, post-modern kiss. I nod, see her go out of the front door and sigh, turning back to the washing-up.

Fucking her again was probably a big mistake. Women always want to get closer.

By two thirty they still haven't come. I can feel my eyes growing heavier. I am listening to music – hoping sound will keep me from sleep, but I cannot trust myself any longer. I will have to set an alarm. I missed them once before and Alexa was so angry I have not been allowed to forget it. Only through charm and the hinted promise of fulfilled flirtation did I keep my job. Apparently they got out of the car and rang the buzzer at the gates. They don't like to get out of the car. The whole thing is meant to be quick, seamless, quiet. If I set an alarm for 3:00, then at half-hour intervals after that, I should be okay. There's some statistic about it being harder to stay awake at three or four in the morning. It's when we get our deepest sleep.

I set the alarm and curl up on the sofa, my head resting on the arm with a cushion pushed underneath. My phone is on the table, in my direct line of sight. All I need do is reach out. Satisfied, I shut my eyes.

Quickly I begin to dream. My father is alive, the insignia of government office printed across the briefcase on his desk. I peer in at him through a crack in the doorway. He has been reading but now he has his head in his hands. He is sighing deeply, his hair sticking up from his head in strange patterns, where his fingers have clenched and released it. He was often like that. I was fascinated by these signs of weakness he would never have shown in public. If he heard me, or caught sight of me there, his whole posture would change immediately.

In the dream, I can go into the room and walk right up to the desk. He does not change posture, or try to stop me. He does not even notice me. I come right round and stare at him, into his face, his eyes. And as I look, I see his vision blur, whiteness creeps in over his irises, and lines crease his withering skin which shifts in colour and texture, breaking out in red veins, turning sallow grey, a dark pallor growing beneath his eyes, under his cheeks. He starts to smell of nesting mice and, seamlessly, his ageing slides into decay, his lips tightening, blackening and receding over teeth that dangle from his jaw, some falling right out. His eyes sink into his skull. Skin melts into muscle, tendon, then wastes away, until my father is just shining white bones, his suit still intact around his skeleton as if he could go on, could return to the papers on his desk, all those work proposals. I reach out a hand to shake him, still believing he can be brought back to life, but the feel of his empty clothes, the rattle of the bones that remain, sets me screaming in short sharp angry bursts.

It's the sound of the alarm, waking me back to the sofa and more waiting.

I shut off the alarm, think about resetting it and

then decide not to bother. I do not think I will sleep again just yet. It's been a long time since I've allowed myself to remember my father. In the wrong place at the wrong time, overseeing government business, he decided to take a short walk and was shot by a member of our own army. Sniper fire doesn't recognise the rank, position or beliefs of a lone wanderer. Gun, bullet, flesh: war has rules that overcome people, that peel back layers of civilisation to reveal one early, ugly grunt of survival. Such is the true language of all peoples.

He was fifty-four and minister for the environment: forests, plants, wildlife, rivers, trees.

I do not want to think of this any more. I climb to my feet and start to pace the room, checking that everything is ready and all the boxes are by the front door. I will get a little extra cash in hand for this night watch, but fuck it, it's not a pleasant job, stuck here within these closed walls thinking about the misjudgements of history. The memory of Lily's body already feels distant. As if our touch lasted only a moment, not solid hours. I feel disorientated, uncertain, so I walk to the bin in the bedroom and pick out the condom, checking again for holes or leaks. The latex has hardened slightly, but falls loose as I pick it up. It's fine. There are no holes. Lily will not be walking back in here her belly swollen with our child. I could not bear it. If Jelena has a sibling, I want it to be one of the same flesh and blood. These fucks with Lily mean nothing, nothing at all.

I feel suddenly very angry and kick the chair by my desk. All of it feels pointless. Even the photographs are a waste of time. I could look at them again, could check Lily's curves, but I cannot concentrate. I could drink coffee or beer, or smoke a cigarette, but it's all just time-wasting. Snatching my phone from the table, I decide smoking is the best option. I walk past the kitchen, day room and front desk and unlock the front doors. I lean against one of the pillars that bolster the overhang and light up, watching the gate and the street through clouds of my own smoke. The pillar feels cold, cutting right through the clothes and flesh that rest against it, and I suck harder on the cigarette, my fingers closed tight around it, my other hand in my jeans pocket. I should have put on a coat.

Despite the time of night, cars are still passing on the road. They go faster than normal, headlights like streaks of colour. The odd person walks past, visible through the metal-barred gate. People are awake, but only a select few, and those few are wrapped up in themselves. You can see it in the way they walk, their heads held in, shoulders hunched. They do not want to see or be seen. They dodge orange neon pools that melt into purple clouds in the night sky. One man coughs into the folds of his hood. The noise rings around the buildings, bouncing back and forth until a speeding car shatters the echo with its engine. Even the street cleaners have come and gone, the beeping of their flashing light sounded ages ago, around midnight. It's a pitiful scene. Heat from the cigarette smoke fills my lungs only briefly, the next breath cold, then warm again, then cold. I consider lighting another, but feel too sorry for myself to stay out and so I walk back into the lobby, the cigarette butt crushed out by the pillar. Fuck it. Steve can clean it up. It isn't my job.

As I walk inside, the smell hits me. Living here has made me almost immune to the fug that seeps from every wall and fabric of the home. It's the smell of age, of rusting blood, of heat and closed windows and of disinfectant. It is stale and close. But it is warm. I crouch by the front desk and lean my back against it, resting my arse on the hard lino to wait out the rest of the time, my eyes trained on the gate, phone in hand.

Finally, gone three thirty, my phone rings. It's OrganoMed. With relief, I get up and press the buzzer to open the gates. They drive up to the entrance and I rush about filling the car with the packages full of pieces of human tissue and bone. The car engine is kept running. The two people inside have their faces covered with balaclavas. It used to trouble me that they know who I am, but then I realised that they would know anyway. They know the place, they know the staff. Any face covering would be false modesty.

Once everything is neatly packed into the boot of the car, I slam down the door, smile and raise a hand in mock salute.

'Is everything,' I say.

I get a nod in return, which I catch in passing as they drive out past me. With a foot held above the gas pedal and the car kept in gear, the turnaround is less than five minutes. I walk behind them to the gate and watch them drive off. Then I check that the gates have locked back in place, go back inside and check the entrance doors as well. Now, finally, I can go to bed. The trouble is that when I get back to my rooms, I find the hours of waiting have taken hold and my tired eyes won't shut. I decide to lie down anyway and imagine that rest is as good as sleep. Isn't that what they say?

*

The nature of this place allows several months to pass in one blink of an eye. My days are regulated by the caring, or half-caring, clock: coffee, cigarettes, patients, visits and photographs. Lily is becoming a more frequent visitor, which is fine for sex but nothing else. She wants more and my holding her off is only increasing her desire. Even at nineteen she is full of feminine wiles.

Because it has been a while since a crossover has taken place, these months have been lazy ones. Autumn has come, trees paving the ground in colour, which has since turned to mulch and been frozen over or washed away in the drains of winter. It's nearly Christmas and I have presents to buy, so I have a day off. Drago, a friend from home, is going back for Christmas and has promised to take my gifts. He will come over later, and in the true spirit of the season – it is the pagan festival I choose to celebrate – I've invited Steve as well. Drago is bringing *rakija* and I'm pleased that, at last, Steve will get a chance to taste it.

But before then, I have to buy all my gifts. Lily has insisted she come and is meeting me in the centre of town. I grab my thick parka jacket and gloves, wave Sarah goodbye and jump on a bus. Sarah will fill in for me. I haven't left the home for a whole day in a long time, but already Sarah looks pissed off. I couldn't help but smile at her. The crispness of the air outside is like a promise, sharp, exciting and fresh.

On the journey through town, I check over my list. There are certain things I'm expected to buy: stockings, face creams, hair dye; certain brands are only available here or are cheaper. I will get Lily to help me pick underwear for Ana and then there is Jelena. She wants roller boots, Barbie if possible, and I want to send her English DVDs.

When I get to the designated meeting place, Lily is there before me and the day progresses as expected. We do Jelena first. Lily seems to enjoy it. We find little pink roller boots with Barbie printed even in the plastic of the wheels. Lily says nothing about what Barbie might do to Jelena's self-esteem. The lessons of feminism are easily lost in pretty shops with girly, pink things and sunny memories of roller-blade routines, which I am treated to as if this were intimate information. And despite knowing that this sharing is dangerous, I like her here, warm on my arm, her enthusiastic youthful face passing on a sense of contentment.

With the boots we buy several DVDs, all bright, colourful and hopeful. My mother tells me Jelena is already copying English words from films. She wants to talk like *tata* can.

Then we move onto the underwear, lacy and under-wired. French knickers. I see Lily's eyes light up and wonder whether to trust her suggestions. Then I realise that she wants a pair for herself. When Lily turns her back, I buy two sets: one for her. I wonder if I should worry about buying the same gift for Ana and Lily. But at least this way, I will get to see the underwear, get to feel it against my skin. I'm unlikely to see Ana until the summer. It's a long way away. And given that I haven't seen her in months, I am buying underwear based on how she used to look. For all I know she may now be fat. It happens to girls sometimes. I know she is unhappy. If I knew how to solve it I would, but she won't come and live with me and she won't get divorced. The underwear I buy for her and Lily is even in the same colour: fiery red.

Finally we get down to the less interesting items, mostly for my mother. We buy stockings and face creams, hair dye, hairspray, hair-removal creams and perfume. Mother loves the smell of expensive perfume. Drago knows what to expect but he will be taking a whole suitcase from me. I will leave everything unwrapped because of customs, but I'll include a letter to Mother explaining who is to get what. I might even go the whole way and buy gift tags so that I can write personal messages on them and get as close to Jelena as possible on Christmas Day.

Shopping takes all morning and by lunchtime we are starving. I take Lily to a Moroccan restaurant I know where the food tastes exquisite but is cheap. We have wine with the food and Lily grows giggling drunk. Over coffee and cigarettes we decide to take the shopping into a film. We can squeeze the bags between our feet. We do not care. We are carefree. I enjoy the looks men give Lily as they walk past us on the way to the cinema, in the queue for tickets, as we take our seats, and I lean over and kiss her. She doesn't expect such a public display of affection. Too late I realise I'm leading her on, but fuck it, fuck it all. Darkness descends on the theatre and a series of photographic stills, like a large flick book, stutter into life on the screen.

After the film Lily and I go our separate ways. We are not to be seen together. I take my shopping back to the home, then go out again for beer and olives, bread, sausage and cheese, good solid party food. I play music through the computer and cover the table in plates of food. Then I sit back and crack open a beer, waiting for Drago and Steve to arrive. I'm already feeling tipsy and buoyant with the joy of a consumer-rich day. This, I think, is life as one expects it to be.

I sip my beer and look up at the ceiling. Just letting my thoughts run always brings me back to Jelena and I turn to look at her smiling from the computer. How much bigger will she be now? Would I even recognise her? It's so hard to know, so hard to be far away. I stretch out my left hand and imagine how much of it would be covered by hers. Last time, even with her fingers stretched wide, her hand did not nearly fill my palm. I know she will not understand this separation, will not even think of it perhaps. Not thinking of it seems worse. Every day that passes makes me more distant, more alien, the features of my face less familiar to her.

Allowing nostalgia to get the better of me, I pull out the family album. Photographs of Ana and me as Ana's belly grows. Photographs of us with smiles on our faces. Little Jelena growing every couple of pages. I discard my beer on the table and pore over the images I have already fixed in my memory. Then there is a knock at the door.

'Eh, Milos.' It's Drago. Sarah must have let him in through the entrance doors.

I put the open album on the computer table and go to open the door. Drago comes rushing in with Steve a few paces behind, slightly embarrassed. Drago can have that effect. Though infectious, his enthusiasm is so bright it knocks everything else into the background. He thrusts a bottle of *rakija* in my hands and throws his spare arm around my back.

'Let's drink,' he says, patting me and pulling himself away.

'You've met Steve?' I ask, in English, for

Steve's sake.

'Yes, yes,' Drago says, throwing a companionable punch in Steve's direction. Steve smiles.

'Merry Christmas, Milo.' He holds out a Tupperware box. 'Mince pies. Made them myself.'

'Eh, we have chef in our midst,' Drago adds.

I put the *rakija* on the table and take the mince pies from Steve.

'Thank you,' I say.

'It's my wife's recipe.'

I nod. Drago keeps smiling.

'Make yourselves at home.' I gesture to the sofa, then open the Tupperware, placing the lid beneath the box so the pies are easy to take. Then I go into the bedroom. I know I've got some small *rakija* glasses somewhere under the bed. I don't know why I didn't think of them before.

'Good spread,' Drago shouts to me.

'Please, help yourselves,' I shout back. But Drago won't eat yet. You should really wait to drink *rakija* first and he enjoys tradition.

The glasses were a wedding gift. Six tiny coloured glasses with delicate stems and gold rims. They are a bit dusty, so I blow on three of them and wipe them with the inside of my T-shirt. Drago and Steve will never know. Suitably presentable, I push the cardboard box back under the bed and carry three glasses back into the other room. Steve is sitting on the sofa and Drago is by the computer, still standing, checking out the playlist on the screen. When I come in he cheers.

'Hey, party is starting. Let me.'

I put the glasses on the table and let Drago open the bottle and pour out three measures.

'Is homemade *rakija*. Made on grandparents' farm.'

He hands a glass to each of us.

'Will knock your socks off.' He picks up his own. 'Now, we say, *nazdravlje*.' He looks at Steve who lifts his glass and frowns. 'Naz-drav-l-je,' Drago says very slowly.

'Naz-drav-l-je,' Steve repeats.

'Yes, *nazdravlje!*'

And after Drago we all join in, cheering, lifting our glasses and downing the *rakija* in one warm draft.

'That's good stuff, that is,' Steve says, smacking his lips.

'And another,' Drago replies, pouring a second round into our glasses.

'*Nazdravlje!*' We all shout again, and as we breathe around the liquid chasing through our chests there is another knock at the door.

'More guests?' Drago asks.

I shrug and walk to the door to find Sarah standing there.

'Well,' she says, 'aren't I invited?'

From behind me, Drago can see Sarah at the door. He clambers to his feet, calling out to Sarah.

'Hey, welcome, welcome. Milos, another glass for lady, please.'

Sarah comes in.

'Sarah, Drago,' I say, introducing them.

'I believe we met at door and, I think, we have met some time before, no?' He takes Sarah's hand and kisses it.

I leave them getting acquainted in the Drago way and go to fetch a fourth glass. And so rounds of *rakija* are repeated. Sarah's accent is surprisingly good. When Drago tells her this, she laughs.

'I listen to Milo all day, what do you expect?'

'Milo's English is bloody good,' Steve offers in

my defence.

'Oh, his English, yes,' Sarah says, trying to look coquettish through her greasy fringe, 'but his accent is terrible.'

'I do not try to speak like Englishman.' I want her to understand this point. 'I speak with accent because you understand, but you hear I come from different place. Is closest way to speaking my language. Is closer to real me.'

The room goes slightly quiet, so Drago fills our glasses for one more shot.

'I try to sound American,' he jokes.

'And you do, you do,' Sarah says. Oh, yes, Sarah has eyes for Drago now, poor man.

Steve, trying to change the subject, points to a picture of Jelena.

'That a picture of your little girl?'

We get into a conversation about Jelena, and I show him the album, left open on the computer table. We share anecdotes about bringing up babies and laugh about mothers. He says it took him and his wife a while after their son was born to balance out again. He remembers working long hours back then, just to keep away from home. It's an interesting conversation and beside me I see Drago and Sarah are happily chatting away. They have moved onto beer and Drago is slathering butter onto bread then piling the bread with sausage and cheese. His hands are all over the place, now and again brushing against Sarah's arm. Watching him, even from the corner of my eye, makes me laugh. Soon he will accidentally brush against her breast. He has some crazy theory that subtle touching builds a subconscious desire in women, making him irresistible. But the fact he is trying it with Sarah says everything.

By the time all the *rakija* is gone and we are down to the last few beers, my room is cloudy with smoke and crumbs litter the bald carpet. I decide we need more booze and get up to head out for extra cases of beer. Steve offers to come with me, but I insist. It's my party, I am the host so I should provide. Rather unsteadily I go out to the off-licence, returning with as much beer as I can carry.

When I get back, Sarah and Drago are laughing on the floor, leaning against one edge of sofa, and Steve is on the other corner of the sofa still looking through the pages of the album. He closes it abruptly as I come in through the door. Deep lines crease his forehead and his hands seem to be shaking. The snapping sound from the closed album makes Drago look back at him.

'Mate, mate,' he says, affecting the local lingo, 'have another beer. Looks like you need one.'

I pull a bottle from the pack and hand it over. Steve manages a weak smile, rubs his hand over his brow, wipes the sweat off on his trousers and takes the beer.

'Think this better be my last,' he says. 'It's getting late for an old man like me.'

This knocks Drago into action. He decides a change of music will liven Steve up and goes to fiddle with the computer. Steve lights up and quietly drinks his beer between drags. Sarah doesn't smoke, but she is so far gone and so keen to please Drago that she has not once remarked on the smell or even coughed. She has a dazed look on her face. Her head is resting heavily on the arm of the sofa.

Drago finds some dance music and tries to get Sarah up. She is reluctant at first, but Drago drags her to her feet and they begin to dance. I sit next to Steve and watch them silently. Sarah is very drunk and keeps losing her balance. Drago is always there, in the path of her fall, catching her lilting with his arm, his torso. It's like watching a master at work. I turn and smile at Steve. He winks.

Just as Steve is finishing his last glug of beer, there is a further knock on the door.

'I will go,' Drago shouts, leaving Sarah twirling around the middle of the floor.

He pulls the door back.

'Oooh,' he says, 'Milos, for you. Beautiful young girl.'

Sarah stops dancing. Steve puts his empty beer bottle on the table and stands up. Before the door opens any wider, I know, we all seem to know, who it is. Drago steps back into the room, pulling the door with him. It is Lily.

Whether Lily thought it was just me and Drago, that Steve would have gone by now, I'm not sure. Certainly, she cannot have expected Sarah, whose halted position stiffens, her arms falling to her sides. There is jealousy in her eyes.

Lily somehow manages nonchalance. She holds out her hand to Drago, who is the only person unruffled by her arrival.

'I'm Lily,' she says.

Drago takes her hand and kisses it, drawing her further into the room.

'Drago,' he says.

Lily moves towards Sarah, whose jaw has fallen open, and nods at her and Steve. 'Sarah, Steve.' Then she turns to me. 'Milo, a party and you didn't invite me?'

I don't know what to do so I kiss her three times,

from cheek to cheek. It's as if I'm watching the scene from somewhere outside of myself. Everyone is still, there is no talking and the music, still pulsing from the computer, is the only sound. After the kisses the awkward pause continues, pregnant with unasked questions.

Thankfully Steve chooses this moment to leave, saying it was about time, and other such phrases, wishing everyone happy Christmas, moving faster than I have ever seen him move before. The door slams shut behind him.

Sarah's eyes have narrowed and her hands have moved up to her hips. Only Drago remains bright.

'So,' he says, 'where have you been hiding this beauty, eh, Milos? You are dark horse, no, Sarah?' He slaps his thigh, seeming determined to get the happy atmosphere back. His laughter dies in the air between us.

'I think,' Sarah says, 'I'd better be going, too.' She does not look at Lily, but at me. I can hear her words berating me, slapping at me like a teacher talking to a naughty schoolboy.

'Oh, Sarah' – Drago tries to hold her back – 'don't go yet. The night is young!' He slips his arm around her waist, but she twists out of his grasp.

'It was lovely to meet you, Drago.' The way she says his name makes us both wince. Even though her accent seemed good earlier, she draws out the vowels of his name, making it almost unrecognisable. 'Milo' – again that inner voice speaks through her eyes – 'thanks for a lovely evening. I'll see you in the morning.' Then she turns to Lily and says nothing, just nods.

'Are you going back to the desk?' Lily asks.

Sarah nods, primly.

'It's just, I thought it was odd, you know, the lights being on and no one there. I thought I'd better come and check it out.'

Lily manages to mingle a threatening tone into her explanation.

'Well, I'm just shutting up,' Sarah replies, reaching for her cardigan which is draped over one end of the sofa.

'Right,' Lily says. 'Well, I suppose ...'

We all know she is making this up, but Drago obliges.

'No, no, you must stay. Have some beer. Sit down.'

Lily shrugs and drops onto the sofa.

'See you, Sarah,' she says.

And Sarah leaves, throwing a tight-lipped smile over her shoulder.

Drago hands Lily a beer. He looks like he is trying, or hoping, the evening can recover. But it's desperate. We sit for a while and quietly sip beer. Drago answering Lily's rather polite questions about his family and when he is going, and that prompts him to ask me for the presents. I take him into the bedroom with me, leaving Lily with her beer. I don't need to talk him through the gifts, I just want a chance to explain Lily. Drago gets it pretty quick. He raises his eyebrows and smiles, then whistles out a long, exaggerated breath, showing both his admiration and disbelief at how much of a mess I am in. Like the good friend he is, he carries the suitcase into the front room and says he has enjoyed meeting Lily but has to go, would she like an escort to the station.

Lily turns from aligning the spines of the photograph albums and smiles.

'What a gentleman you are. Milo, you should learn

from your friend.' She ticks her finger at me.

'Sarah is probably still there,' I say and Lily takes the hint, thank God. Lily takes a long swig of beer, slams the bottle on the table and stands up.

'An escort would be perfect.' She takes Drago's arm. 'Goodbye, Milo. Thanks for the beer.' She pecks my cheek, once, twice, her arm staying firmly inside Drago's. 'Take care.'

Drago is now helpless. Shrugging as much as he can with Lily on one arm and the suitcase in the other, his eyes gleam at me.

'I take good care of her, Milos, don't worry.'

They go. I don't have the energy to see them out to the front desk, but I hear sounds of conversation with Sarah. I slump across the sofa and wonder how fucked I am. Would Sarah say anything? I'm not worried by Steve, but Sarah? Bloody Lily. She just can't leave me alone.

Loud dance music is still coming from the computer. It sounds even more out of place playing to a nearly empty room. I sit up and switch the whole thing off. In silence, I hear the sound of Sarah locking the front door. I strain to hear her walk down the driveway to the gate, but her shoes aren't spike-heeled like Alexa's and her footsteps fade into the darkness.

Steve – III

The autumn seemed to pass without incident. The lack of sleep was wearing me down and I didn't have the energy to question the things I'd seen. I thought I was probably exaggerating. I was old, sleep-deprived and prone to invention. Fran always said that was why I got on with all the old women we took out on trips. I was the only man they'd known who would listen to stories about their postman's sinister habit of bending mail rather than ringing the doorbell and nod at their theories behind the unpredictable rubbish collection and the rising price of gas.

I had a routine established and moved through the days like clockwork. I've always had a good work ethic. Never taken a sick day in my life.

I found the build-up to Christmas unsettling. It would be my first Christmas without Fran and I wasn't looking forward to it. Jean had asked me round to hers – she was having her kids and grandkids round – but I wasn't sure. I thought I might be better off on my own. When Milo asked me for pre-Christmas drinks, on the other hand, I was happy to accept. He was offering new things, different traditions, rather than the old, and that seemed perfect. Besides, I knew Fran would have been keen for me to go. She was always up for a party, especially when foreign alcohol was on offer. She loved Christmas parties even more because she could bake for them. Her mince pies were the talk of the staff back when we had the business. Every year the drivers and the fleet engineer, his assistant, the secretary, they'd all start talking about Fran's mince pies from November onwards. The secret, Fran said, was making your own mincemeat.

It was probably a crazy idea, but Christmas didn't feel the same without the smell of Fran's baking and so I thought, in her memory, I'd try my hand at some mince pies. Her recipe was where she always kept it: on a shelf beneath the spice rack, tucked into her favourite cookery book, the edges crisp with old bits of butter. I made a list of the ingredients I would need, bought them on my way home during the week and then the day of Milo's party, I left work early and went home to make the mince pies.

Something about it made me feel festive. The weather had been bitter cold for weeks and somehow I couldn't get the house warm. But once the oven was pre-heating and I was chopping up nuts, dates, candied peel and glacé cherries, mixing sultanas, raisins, currants, ginger, nutmeg and brandy, I began to get up a bit of a sweat. It smelt lovely. If I closed my eyes, I could see Fran, her back to me, preparing the pastry with her apron on. I could see her and hear her chatting as she cooked, talking about all the gifts she was planning to buy, what was light enough to be able to send to James. It was beautiful. She made everywhere we lived into a home.

Eyes open, even with the smells of the mincemeat, nothing looked the same. I had covered the kitchen with bowls full of ingredients – measured and chopped – that now sat in messy piles. The flour that Fran would have contained in one corner was spread all over the kitchen table and down my front. But it felt good all the same. Something of Fran was kept alive. It felt like a kind of ritual or homage, doing everything as precise as I could.

When I clapped the pies in the oven, I sat down at the table and waited the ten minutes with my eyes closed, thinking of her.

The pies didn't turn out quite like Fran's – the pastry was harder and darker with blackened bubbles of mincemeat around the edges where I'd stuffed them too full – but she would have been proud. I laid them all out on cooling racks and waited until they'd cooled down before putting some in an old bit of Tupperware to take to Milo's party. I'd made enough to give some to Jean – who, it turned out, was so moved by the pies that she burst into tears – and left hers under a tea towel. Fran would have laughed seeing me squeezed into her old apron, breathing hard and frowning my way through a recipe she knew by heart. I was never much of a cook and I couldn't help chuckling myself when I caught sight of my reflection in the hall mirror. I looked more like a butcher than a cook.

I tidied myself up and went back up to the home with my mince pies under my arm. I was rather pleased with myself, I should add, and for once I was feeling light, chirpy even, which was lucky given the course of events.

When I got to the home, I was thrown straight into the party. Milo's friend Drago was just going through the doors ahead of me. We shook hands in the entrance hall, Drago patting me on the back like we'd known one another years. Sour-grapes was behind the desk, smiling in a way I'd never seen before.

'Lovely Sarah,' he said, pointing to her and grinning in a smug 007 leer, 'will be joining us later. I tell her she must come and drink *rakija* with us. Is homemade. Catch you later,' he said winking at Sour-grapes. Even though he was flirting with the most sullen woman in the home, I couldn't help but like the man. He had a brash kind of charm and he certainly knew how to get a party started.

We went down to Milo's rooms and Drago turned up the music and poured the *rakija*. It tastes like any strong, homemade spirit – gives you that warm burn as you swallow it. Bloody good stuff. Milo's table was heaving with party food, sausages and bread and crisps. And there were my mince pies. It was getting off to a good start, all of us downing shots of *rakija* and saying cheers in their language. It was the most fun I'd had in a while.

Then Sour-grapes knocked on the door and even though it looked like Milo hadn't invited her, he let Drago kiss her hand and get her *rakija*, turning to me and rolling his eyes in their direction. We continued to exchange looks throughout the evening as the pace of the Drago and Sour-grapes flirtation increased.

We drank more *rakija*, then had some beer, and Drago and Sour-grapes started to dance. At some point, I asked Milo about his daughter. There was an album of photographs open on his desk and we had a look at them, talking for a while about bringing up children, about women becoming mothers and how strange it is to share affection. I didn't know he wasn't getting on with his partner, but it wasn't really a surprise. I would have hated to live apart from Fran and didn't know how he could do it. It turned out I didn't need to worry. It was all about to be made clear.

After a while, Milo ran out of beer. I was taking it slow, but Sour-grapes and Drago were drinking a lot. He decided to go to the off-licence and left me tucking into my own mince pies, a bit of a Billy no-mates with Drago and Sour-grapes laughing at the other end of the sofa. I wasn't bothered by it, but didn't quite know what to do with myself to keep from staring at them. Milo's photo album was still open on the side, so I picked it up again and began to leaf through it.

I'd seen most of the photographs before, having already looked at it with Milo, and though I was now noticing different things, checking for resemblances, looking at the landscape behind the people, I was soon feeling bored. Album in my lap, I turned my attention to Milo's flat, wondering why he didn't have a telly. He had quite a few books and DVDs, and in a cluster at the foot of a shelf near his desk, there were a series of albums like the one on my lap. With nothing else to do until Milo got back, I thought I might take a look at a few more.

The first one I picked up was more of the same – more baby pictures, more beaches, mountains, smiling faces. The second album, however, was totally unexpected.

The early shots, laid out quite differently to the family snaps, weren't so bad: sepia shots of the day room, or odd reflections off urns in the kitchen. It was when I started to see old people's faces, their hands, their arms and their bodies, that I began to feel uncomfortable. My throat started to feel dry but when I tried to swallow there was no saliva in my mouth. I was gasping. I was knocked flat with shock.

As I continued to turn the pages, the images I saw were indescribable, degrading, frightening. There were pictures of clients naked on their beds. Shots of their bruises. Harsh pictures of their ageing bodies in bright, unnatural light, with weird shadows playing across them from doors, tables, Milo's own body. And once I'd seen a close-up of a client's face, their eyes gleaming pits of despair, I couldn't help but see my wife in every shot. As I've said, I'm not a religious man, but these pictures were sacrilegious. The pain of those silent limbs was shouting from every page. And then, just when I thought it couldn't get any worse, metal urns became knifes, needles, and all the living flesh was turned grey as blood ran from it into grooves along a metal table. The pictures were half operation, half autopsy, but I recognised all the features from earlier shots. I didn't want to look, but it was too fascinating to turn away.

In the background Drago and Sour-grapes continued to laugh, occasionally dancing then flopping back to the ground again, happy, absorbed, the modern computer music jangling, while a world of ugliness opened out before me. I had no seasonal cheer left. I was so stunned I didn't think I'd be able to move.

Then Milo returned. Without thinking, I slammed the album shut. The noise caught us all off guard and everyone's eyes turned in my direction. There was a moment's pause. I swallowed hard, and, perhaps in response to this, Drago offered me a beer, breaking the silence and reawakening the party atmosphere. After a sip or two, I felt a little better. I needed a chance to put the album back on the shelf. I wasn't sure what I'd seen. I know you can do things to photos these days. Computers can change things. But my instincts were telling me to pretend I hadn't seen anything. My gut reaction was to be afraid. Fuck, what would Milo do if he knew I'd seen them? I wasn't much younger than some of the people in the photographs. Would he strip me too? Take pictures of my wrinkled flesh, my grey chest hair, rough me up for it?

I started to roll a fag and thankfully it set off a chain reaction. Milo and Drago both pulled out their own cigarettes and lit up. Drago leapt to his feet 'to find music to liven you up' and both he and Milo turned their backs on me. It wasn't the best time, but I shoved the album back, pretending I was also looking at the computer, slipping it behind their calves. Leaning forwards, I felt my shirt peel off the sofa, slick with cold sweat. I had to get out of there, go home.

At the sound of the new music, Drago and Sour-grapes danced again. Milo smiled at me and, not wanting to seem different, I winked back. I couldn't see why Drago was bothering with Sour-grapes, but it would have been very amusing if I wasn't desperate to get the hell out of there. It was like being back in an army training exercise, only this one wasn't fun. The enemy felt real.

Then there was another knock on the door. Drago let Sour-grapes twist from his arms, leaving her wobbling alone on Milo's carpet, and answered the door. I thought it might be Tasty. Milo hadn't said that she was invited, but if she was around she would have heard the party, might have wanted to drop in. But it wasn't Tasty, it was Tasty's daughter, Lily. I put my empty beer bottle on the table and stood up. Lily is only a teenager and it seemed the perfect opportunity to leave, saying it was all getting a bit young for me. I've always thought it's easier to leave when someone else is arriving and because I was so keen to get home, I didn't really have time to register the strangeness of Lily being there. It wasn't as if she helped out with the home. She was hardly ever there. In fact, I'd only met her once before, when she'd been visiting her mother and had stepped out into the garden for a smoke. It was only as I left the home and was no longer right up close to Milo that it all became clear. He was shagging her. No wonder he wasn't planning on going home for Christmas.

Once I'd seen the photographs, I couldn't pretend my suspicions were an old man's delusions any more. I'd have to do something. I still didn't feel I could talk to James and Jean had enough on her plate. Besides, she was really Fran's friend. I didn't have anyone to talk to about what I'd seen. All my friends were business connections. Fran used to keep us in touch with everyone, remember birthdays, invite people round. I'd never been good at all those things. And suddenly I was alone, living under the weight of those terrible images.

I tried to ignore the responsibility at first. It was Christmas. I decided to go to Jean's. She and her family were all very sweet to me and we had a good day. It was a relief not to be alone in the house. I couldn't thank Jean enough. But then there was Boxing Day and the long wait for New Year, Fran's absence and my latest discovery lurking in the shadows beneath the sofa, catching my eye in the bathroom mirror as I brushed my teeth. Flashes of the images kept and keep on returning. For the first time in my life I understood Dad's shell shock. I felt too old to be visited by waking nightmares, but it didn't stop them coming.

A bald head, empty eyes staring up at me. The wrinkled flesh of an old penis, half-erect. Grey, labelled toes. A shaven, tired vagina. A flat breast, pooled under an armpit. And then, Fran's chest: the flatness on one side, the scar still angry and jagged; radiation burn marks in perfect symmetry; the tiny mole that sits above her nipple, the one remaining beauty spot. Fran's body lost in the filth of Milo's images – one more old maid among the rest – hurting like someone is squeezing my chest, hugging me so tight I can barely breathe and my ribs are aching, cracking with the pressure.

Sometimes I imagined hurting myself. Just as a release. Maybe banging my head against the wall or pushing a nail into my palm. But I don't have it in me. I could punch, slam my hand down on the table or the bed or the arm of the chair, but it's only ever a jolt. I might get the odd graze on my knuckles, nothing more. It goes against my instincts. I'm too attached to life not to worry about mistakes, especially at my age. I don't heal the way I used to.

The worst of it was that the thing that kept me going was work. When I was sat at home, the images came more frequently. Before Christmas I would have given anything to get some sleep, but since then, I've avoided it. Trouble is, an unrestful night leads to napping. I'd drop off in the day for a few minutes here or there. Always I went back to the photographs and woke less easy than I was before. Being at work helped to keep me going. I couldn't just take a nap when I was busy in the garden or polishing floors. Fran knew I'd need occupying and until Christmas the caretaker job had been just right, but since Milo's party, despite needing to work, the home was the last place I wanted to be. I was trapped between waking and sleeping, fearing and mourning, necessity and disgust. It was like the walls of the home had been stretched out, remoulded to hold me in. The home became my world – a world in which I do not want to belong.

At first, I thought I could hide away somehow. It wasn't a bad instinct. The less I'd known probably the better things would have gone for me. The garden was useful. Even over the winter months there were plenty of tasks to keep me busy. I'd spend a lot of time working on the soil, digging in organic matter. And there was always some tree and shrub pruning to do. There wasn't much snow, but when it came, I went round knocking it off the trees and hedges, minimising frost damage. I repaired a few bits of fencing in the back garden and there were bulbs to prepare for the spring display and that.

I was doing all right. I was just keeping the panic at bay, telling myself Milo was a computer whizz kid, beginning to think I might really have imagined it all. Then I went into a client's room for the first time. I didn't intend to go in. I'd been avoiding the clients' rooms more than I had done before Christmas. I didn't want to think about them. It was the only way to get the job done. But there was no avoiding it that day.

I was polishing the ground floor again, working back over Tasty's heel marks. I'd really taken to whistling when I worked. It was another trick to keep the mind alert but focused away from those images. I concentrated on the tune and held off other thoughts as best I could. It's tricky to hear certain noises over the machine, so I liked to whistle hard, really belting it out. It was a great release.

I had no idea what everyone else was up to, but I'd seen Sour-grapes and Milo going up and down in the lift with the trolley, probably checking on clients, doing bed baths, that sort of thing. I wasn't bothered though. If I left them alone, they left me alone. That suited me fine. I'd been avoiding Milo.

I was working from the entrance hall down the corridor that day. I liked to change which direction I cleaned in, to give the job a bit of novelty. I'd been at it since I came in to work, going over the bad patches several times, and was about to turn into the corridor. The lead on the machine is quite long, as you'd expect, but not long enough to take me from the entrance to Tasty's office door, plus I didn't like the idea of leaving a long trail of wire across the front hall. I'd never seen floods of visitors, but it's a health and safety risk I liked to avoid. So I had switched off the machine to move the plug to a nearer socket when I heard the shouts from the first floor. It was lucky for Sour-grapes I'd turned off the machine because I'd never have heard her otherwise.

'Steve,' she was yelling. 'Steve, come and clean up this spillage, please, quickly.'

It wasn't normal for them to boss me about. I didn't particularly like being summoned to do Sour-grapes' dirty work, but it was my job to take care of the place.

'It's all right, keep your hair on. I'm coming up.'

'Quickly,' she yelled back.

So I left the polisher, shoving its wire in a heap beside it, well out of the way, and went to the storeroom for my bucket and mop. I filled the bucket with a bit of cold water and disinfectant, grabbed some paper towels and got in the lift.

It was immediately obvious where the spillage was, but Sour-grapes was there pointing to it, like a small child pointing to dog shit. I nodded at her, to stop myself saying something I shouldn't, and took a look at the mess on the floor. It looked and smelt like a mixture of shit and urine. It was still spreading outwards, creeping towards one of the doors to a client's room.

'Have you got the container it spilled from?' I asked Sour-grapes.

She held out the plastic bin with a gloved hand.

'I was leaning over the trolley,' she explained. 'I must have tipped it off balance.'

I told her not to worry, I'd get it cleaned up, and she left me to it, guiding the trolley around the mess and to the lift. The wheels of the trolley left slick tracks behind her. I'd have to clean the whole corridor again.

I snapped on a pair of latex gloves from my pocket and dropped paper towels down, soaking up the worst of it. I dragged and dropped the towels, dripping piss and crap, into the white bin and put down more towels until most of the puddle had gone. But because the towels pushed at the liquid before they began to soak it up, the mess had continued to spread slightly and some of it had welled under a client's door. I had no option but to knock and go in. Still, it made me feel nervous. Before Christmas I'd probably have jumped at the chance to get a legit look at a client's room, but right then I felt more fear than curiosity.

I did know roughly what to expect, having seen into the rooms before, and the architecture wasn't surprising. It was sparsely furnished: the bed in the centre of the room towards the rear wall; a window on one side; two bedside tables, one on each side; a chair; and one of those tables that twists round over the bed. There were no flowers or cards. The sun was shining brightly through the window, casting shadows across the bed, and the person in the bed was attached to a drip. They had a huge bandage across their face.

'Don't mind me,' I said and continued to clear up the mess with the door open.

Something about the face was familiar. I had another peek around the door, finding the eyes above the bandage, staring down at me. I smiled, not wanting to be rude or frightening. I recognised the poor woman because I'd seen her photograph in Milo's album. I could feel the blood flushing my face, making my ears tingle. I knew this client was a woman, not because I could make out her curves from the prone shape beneath the sheets, but because I'd seen all of her, naked, stretched out and photographed on that very bed.

My head started to pound with the extra blood rushing round my system. I cleaned up as quickly as I could, mopping the floor with disinfectant all the way back to the lift, disposed of the crap and the gloves, put the polisher, bucket and mop back in the storeroom and made off home. I couldn't stay. I had to get home and think. It was clear that I could no longer pretend Milo's photographs were fakes.

Steve – IV

Fran wasn't the only one who saved things until later, only I don't store objects or food; I save memories.

When I was nine, I had a thing for shrapnel. It wasn't just me, loads of us kids built up collections of it. We'd go out looking for it after air raids. Some kids even got burns from picking up the hot metal too soon. That day I'd gone quite far from home and was walking along a deserted street of office blocks, no shelter in sight. When the siren sounded, I wasn't afraid because I was too busy thinking about something else. I could see a piece of shrapnel glinting in the sunlight ahead, embedded in a lamppost. I had that childlike belief that I would live forever, having survived so many air raids with not even a scratch. I was excited about how envious all the kids on my street would be. It was a really big piece of shrapnel.

I remember half skipping, half running along the pavement, my arm reaching out towards the post, not even thinking about the whine of the buzz bomb, until it fell silent. I didn't count to ten. I didn't think anything, but felt held somehow in time, my arm still reaching out. There was no noise when the impact came, just an angry sweep of air that threw me towards the office blocks, knocking me down a flight of stairs leading to the basement. When I came to, I felt a bit knocked about but nothing was broken. I brushed myself down a bit, my ears ringing and hurried right back up to the street, hoping the shrapnel would still be there.

Back on the pavement, surrounded by rubble, the lamppost was bent in half. There was no sign of the shrapnel. I ran right up to the post, but the shrapnel had been blown free and was nowhere to be seen. I looked for quite a while, kicking up rubble, but couldn't find it. There was no prize object to take home and share, but the story of the experience itself – the day Steve nearly died collecting shrapnel – became a favourite. It wasn't that it was significantly different to lots of Blitz stories told back then, but it was mine. And in the end the memory lasted a lot longer than my shrapnel collection. I used to tell Fran – before she got ill the second time – that memories, stored in little tales, always last longer than objects. I told the shrapnel story right into my coach-driving days, amusing old ladies and schoolchildren, and making Fran groan.

Around the time I saw the old woman, I thought a lot about that sweep of hard air, the temporary deafness. The photographs had a similar effect on me, like I was lying at the bottom of the stairs hoping I'd soon wake up, climb to the top again and see the new lay of the land. But I wasn't bouncing back up, I was afraid to look and see what else had been flattened. I didn't want to see the damage, but what choice did I have? Would I really stand by, hidden in the dark, while Milo, and maybe the others too, coolly tore up their clients' lives? Fran wouldn't have wanted me to. People aren't things you can save for later, or things you can collect. They can't be stored in a loft gathering dust. Inside every client are the stories and memories that make them people. Fran would have wanted me to tell their stories, and I've failed. I like saving memories, but the home likes saving other things. You can't say they let things go to waste.

It was thoughts of Fran, the old woman and story-telling that started me thinking about the content of the photographs – something I'd tried to avoid up to this point. As well as pictures of naked people on beds with sunlight dappling their skin, there were pictures of pieces of people on metal tables, toes with tags on. The naked woman on the bed had been a true image – I'd seen the woman. It stood to reason that the metal tables and toe tags were real too, and if they were, they could only have been taken in the morgue. I didn't like the idea, but if I was to find out anything about what was going on, I was going to have to go and take a look in the morgue. There might be further bits I recognised from the photographs. I didn't think about what this would prove to anyone else, it was more about proving something to myself. Despite the bad pun, I couldn't stop thinking about seeing it all in the flesh. I started to imagine rows of dead bodies. Perhaps that was where all the clients were really kept. It would explain why the home was so quiet.

Because I had no business down in the basement but for the occasional waste-disposal visit, I'd never been in the morgue. Tasty had made it very clear that I was only ever to go downstairs to the furnace if there was no one else to get rid of the waste for me. This had suited me fine until then. Normally, when I'd no choice but to go down, I'd walked straight past the morgue, avoiding the double and then plastic doors that held in the cold. If I wanted to go in, I was going to have to work out when would be the best time.

After a couple of days of watching everyone's routines, it became clear that early morning would be the ideal time to get in there unnoticed. I reckoned I had a window of half an hour in which to get down there, nose about and get back to work without being noticed by any of them.

I picked a Friday, because no one wants to work early on a Friday if they can avoid it, and left home at six o'clock. I didn't want to be there too early, otherwise they might be suspicious. I thought six thirty, though early, was a potentially reasonable time to be at work, especially for an old insomniac like me.

There was no need to take any props with me, because if I was caught coming out of the morgue or coming up in the lift, I could say I'd dropped off some waste. If I was caught in the morgue, there would be nothing I could do to excuse myself. I wasn't meant to go in there at all.

It was a biting cold day and dark. I could see my way to the bus stop, but only barely. It took me back to my childhood when we'd be walking through fog half the morning, me and my dad squinting our way to the canal, listening out for the sounds of the horses.

Mr Raja hadn't opened up yet, but I felt I could do without my paper for one day and sat on the bus counting stops until I could press the buzzer and get on with it. It wasn't quite like a military operation, but I had the nerves of those years of service, the early-morning drills, the excitement and fear. Of course I never had to fight anything, but we all took it serious like. Wars were close to home in those days.

As predicted there was no one about when I got in. I lost no time fiddling about and went straight down to the basement, pausing only to drop off my packed lunch in the storeroom.

If I'm honest, I was scared. Last time I'd been in a morgue had been at the funeral parlour. They'd asked me lots of questions about Fran's make-up, what colour eye-shadow she used to wear and that, and even though I brought in her make-up bag, unable to say exactly what she used, they picked a colour I couldn't ever remember her wearing in life. It was all golden and shimmering in the harsh morgue light. She looked shrunken and painted, like a stuffed animal. They'd fixed down her eyelids, but somehow I could imagine her eyes hard and round like the fake amber plastic ones taxidermists use for foxes and badgers, stags and bears. Something about her face was simply wrong. It wasn't my Fran.

At the first set of plastic doors, I shut my eyes and pushed through. Already the air was cooler. I walked through the heavy double doors and then paused again, eyes tight shut, taking a deep breath before moving through the second set of plastic doors that swished beneath me, scraping against my shoulders and arms as the temperature drop caused tiny mountain ranges of goose-bumps to form all over my body. With my eyes still shut I could picture early mornings back before central heating. Sometimes it was so cold the frost would grow up the inside of the windows. And in the morgue it was like ice was forming inside my chest, each breath drawing the dry cold into my lungs.

I counted to three and opened my eyes. I'd forgotten to flick on the lights and couldn't see anything, so I had to fumble about a bit slapping the walls until I tripped the switch and the room was flooded with harsh, blue-yellow light. I could see every freckle, hair and vein on my hand, every tiny fold of skin around the wrist. To say the light was bright would be an understatement.

Blinking, I looked about. I'd almost expected to see Fran as she was that day, taut and shining and unreal, but of course there were no bodies at all. The room was almost empty but for a kind of filing cabinet of drawers and a metal table. I'd seen the drawers on television. If I pulled one out I was sure I would find a stiff in there, blue-grey and staring. I didn't have the courage to try one just yet because I recognised the table. It was the gleaming sheet of metal upon which I'd seen the bodies. In Milo's photographs blood had run down the curved rivets surrounding the table like gutters. But an empty table didn't prove anything. The table existed, but that didn't mean the bleeding bodies did. I knew I'd have to open the drawers.

I had no idea how I would feel if there were bodies in the drawers, but if I wanted to get to the bottom of things, I'd have to look. Of course, even if there were bodies, it wouldn't prove anything. Nothing would be proved unless I could get those photographs back and even then Milo could say they were – I've checked this since – digitally enhanced, like what they do to Page Three Girls' cellulite. No, I'd just have to slowly figure things out, build up a pattern of what was going on. I had to find out for myself initially and then work out how to take it further.

I decided to do drawer checking methodically and pulled open the top drawer on the left-hand side first. It was empty. I'd pulled out a long metal drawer with nothing in it. The second drawer was the same, and the third. By the time I'd made my way to the bottom right-hand drawer, it was clear that all of them were empty.

I looked at my watch. I'd only been in there ten minutes and I'd found nothing. There was nowhere else to look. Despite having been so afraid, I was actually disappointed. The morgue, if it had secrets to hide, was keeping them well out of my sight.

Before anyone could catch me down there, I switched the lights off, left the morgue and got back in the lift. I'd have to look elsewhere for signs.

Even though the empty morgue made me feel I could be making things up, there was at least the likeness of the metal table and the old woman to go on. I'd decided I wasn't going to hide away any more, but I couldn't work out what to do next. I was unsure of how to play detective. I suppose I could have got hold of one of Milo's albums, maybe taken it to Tasty, but I had a hunch that they were all in on it. I needed to think of something else. Because of the difficulty of sneaking into clients' rooms, I was still staying clear of the upper floors. I was, however, on red alert for any unusual activity, which meant I was prepared early one morning in March when the whole team started to rush about.

That they were starting work shortly after me, just after seven o'clock, was strange in itself, but the general air of frustrated panic, the running about, made me curious to find out what was going on.

I was back in the flowerbeds working on the

perennials, weeding and such like. I had the wheelbarrow with me round the front at first and it was quite a shock when the doctor turned up. He isn't a regular. When Tasty ran out of the building to meet him, I was even more surprised. She was never in work this early. I knew something had happened, so I moved closer to the bed by her office window. But she wasn't having any of it that morning. She was at her window, looking around the garden for me. When she saw me wheeling my way towards her, she opened the window.

'Steve,' she said, pretending to be glad to see me. 'We've got some very private matters to discuss this morning and we don't want to be disturbed. There must be some work you could do in the back garden? Would you mind?'

'Not at all, Mrs Tace, in fact I was thinking of coming inside to polish those floors.' I hadn't been thinking this at all, but I wanted a way to get closer to the action.

'We're going to be very busy today. I'd rather you stayed out of the home. You do have enough in the garden to keep you busy?'

I nodded and she smiled, reining herself back into her office. Just before she closed the window, she turned back to me.

'Off you go then,' she said, making an odd gesture with her hand that was a cross between a charming wave and a dismissal. Then she drew across the curtains.

I turned the barrow and pushed it round to the back garden, trying to come up with things that needed doing that would allow me to overhear and witness the unfolding events. I felt I'd missed a chance by saying that I was planning to polish the floors. If I'd said nothing and just done it, I was certain to have found something out before she turned me from the home into the garden. I saw no other option but to watch closely. There probably wasn't much else going on outside of that office and there was no way of getting in there anyway.

By eight o'clock Milo was up making coffee in the kitchen. Sour-grapes had come into work only ten minutes or so before that, and as Milo watched his kettle boil I heard the doctor's car engine firing up out front. This was an unusual amount of activity for a normal weekday morning.

Whether it was the noise of the engine or something else, Milo came to the kitchen door and lit up a fag. I had to turn away. I didn't want him thinking I was looking. Already I could feel this was going to be a long day. At least I would get the flowerbeds sorted.

One crushed fag later, Milo headed back indoors to prepare a tray of coffee. Before the kitchen door swung shut I could see him making his way towards Tasty's office. Something serious was afoot.

Not knowing where to go, I felt I could only wait. I moved my way slowly round the garden – taking care to do the beds thoroughly so as not to attract attention to myself. For some time, there was little noticeable activity in the home. By the time I'd made it round towards the day-room windows, it was about ten fifteen and I'd only seen a flash of Milo rushing past the day-room doors. I knew I'd need to take these beds slowly, so I was leaning back on my haunches, having a bit of a breather, when Milo showed an old couple into the living room.

I think I'd seen this pair before. The woman is very shrewd-looking, a busybody Miss Marple type, her hair neatly bobbed and her eyes sharp as tacks. She strode purposefully towards the day-room window and gave me a little wave. I couldn't hear, but I could see her husband was saying something to her as she turned suddenly, the smile falling from her face, and walked towards him, taking his hand in hers.

Her husband looked rather upset, not in a womanly way, you understand, but sort of put out. He must have been sighing a lot or nervously puffing out air because his cheeks and lips kept filling out, his moustache dancing as they resumed their restful shape. I just knew someone must have died. It seemed the only conclusion to make.

Both Sour-grapes and Tasty turned up in the day room and led the couple out of the room, the wife peering round behind her as she went as if on the lookout for something. I didn't see them again, even though I took my time over the beds around the day room. But I had my coffee break shortly after they arrived and might have missed them.

When I got back to the flowerbeds, I'd assumed the show was over. I mean, if someone was dead, the relatives had come in now and that would be that. There might be a car to pick up the body and take it on to the crematorium or funeral parlour or wherever, but nothing else. So when another couple turned up at noon, I was a bit shocked. They were totally different to the first lot. They didn't look upset, they looked inconvenienced. They were in the day room for a good ten, fifteen minutes and one was on the mobile and the other was tapping away at one of those mini-computer things with a plastic pen. They weren't too different to James and Michie. When Sour-grapes greeted them, the man finished his phone call, but the woman held her hand up for a moment and kept Sour-grapes waiting until she'd done whatever it was she was doing.

I had to look at them sideways because I didn't want Sour-grapes to think I was nosing. Luckily, she was too busy looking pissed off with the woman to notice me. Milo came in with some coffees just as they were getting up to go and the woman took hers along. I didn't like the idea of visiting a dead relative with a mug of coffee in one hand. They showed no respect at all. But then again, I wasn't sure they were there for that. Perhaps they were just looking around the home, prospective clients. They weren't very old, much younger than the previous couple – I'd say early fifties.

Anyway, I did catch sight of them again on their way out. Just a flash, and then once they were outside, I heard the man on the phone again.

'Sorry, John, it's been a difficult morning … Yes, yes, we've seen him now. He had a good innings, that's what we feel. Anyway, I'll be back in the office this afternoon … No, no. He'd been on his way out for a while. It's sad, but it was expected … Yes, yep. Thanks. I think I'd prefer to keep the mind occupied … Okay … Yeah … Bye, John, and thanks again.'

I heard the slamming of car doors, the engine start up and the gates open to let them out.

With two sets of couples, I started to think maybe two clients had died. I mean, it must happen sometimes. You don't know when your time will come and who is to say whether you might share your last breath with someone lying next door.

I thought by now it must be all right to move to the front of the house. I'd finished with the beds in the back garden. I thought I'd give it a go and see if

Tasty objected. So I wheeled the barrow round, set all my gear up and ready and went round to the fire escape for lunch.

The fire escape gives a great view of the driveway and I was just taking my first bite of pork pie when another car drove in through the gates.

This was unheard of. I'd never seen so many visitors all in one day. It was another couple. This pair were all suited and booted and climbed out of an Audi TT convertible. Nice vehicle, but a bit girly.

The woman was in a red trouser suit and heels as high as Tasty's. The man was in a soft pile jacket and jeans with pointed boots. I saw them go in and then come out the back, onto the porch area outside the day room. The man was pacing up and down, a thick cigar wedged between his teeth. He looked like an arsehole. A show-off type. If they were also relatives or maybe if someone else had died, this pacing was feigned grief. It almost put me off my pie.

Some time later, after I'd read my paper and had another smoke, I headed back down into the front garden. The flashy couple were in Tasty's office. The curtains were now open, but the window was still shut. I could see them signing forms. I began to wonder whether these people were coming in response to a recruitment drive – maybe the home had been advertising itself in the local rag. There couldn't be three dead clients could there? Maybe these people were all related, but then why not wait around for one another? Something fishy was going on and I wanted to get to the bottom of it.

Once this couple had driven off, I went inside the home, taking care to clear the dirt from my boots, and knocked on Tasty's door. She called for me to go in. She was wearing pince-nez, peering at paperwork in a very uncharacteristically serious manner.

'Oh, it's you,' she said, taking off her glasses and leaning back in her chair. 'Well?'

'Sorry to bother you, I was just wondering if I could polish the floors now. Only, they need doing and that.'

She sighed and brushed invisible dirt from her jacket.

'I'm sorry, Steve. Can't you leave the corridors until tomorrow? There will be quite a few more visitors today, I'm afraid.'

'Right you are. Any reason?' I ventured.

'Reason?' she queried back. 'If you must know, a client passed away last night.' She put her glasses back on and turned her attention back to the papers on her desk.

'Got a lot of family, haven't they?'

She peered up at me over the rim of her glasses, a document in one hand. 'I dare say. Now if you don't mind, I've got rather a lot to do.' She smiled at me and I left. She's good at refusing to answer questions. It struck me as very odd that only one person had died. Why weren't the family all coming at the same time? Even Michie had made some kind of effort for Fran and she isn't even properly related. No, unless the modern family was even more warped than I'd imagined, it didn't make sense at all.

Still, there was nothing I could do. I had to get back to work. I'd thought about repairing the grass again, like I did this time last year, when Fran was still alive, but there wasn't any damage to repair. No one had been walking on the grass and it was only me that ever went near the flowerbeds. They didn't even cut roses or anything. I didn't much fancy sitting about all afternoon, but I couldn't leave just yet. I wanted to get a look at the other visitors, pick up some clues. So I made some tea in the kitchen, filled my Thermos to the brim and went out to the shed. There was an old pair of binoculars on the shelf and I decided to balance my chair on one of the work surfaces, focus the binoculars and watch the home. Fran would have called me a stupid bugger because I had a right time of it trying to get up on the work surface and the chair was a bit precarious up there, but I had my heart set on it, stupid bugger or not.

At around three o'clock another pair of visitors arrived. They were probably only just younger than me – late sixties, their hair white and the man's eyebrows bushy. At first, I thought there were two men together, but when I fiddled with the binoculars, I saw the woman had a fairly thick batch of grey bristles growing across her upper lip. Fran had started to get the odd chin hair, but she plucked them out. I thought it weird that a woman wouldn't want to get rid of those hairs. She looked like the sort of woman who kept cats. I think perhaps they weren't a couple after all. They could have been brother and sister.

I could see them in the day room while Milo made them instant coffee in the kitchen. Maybe he thought his own coffee would be wasted on them. He probably couldn't be bothered. Once he'd handed them their coffees, it was only a matter of minutes before Sour-grapes and Tasty collected them and took them out of the day room. They reappeared on the first-floor corridor. They must have gone into one of the rooms either on the other side of the home or into the room with the curtains drawn because I didn't see them again until they appeared back in the corridor. Then they were out of sight for a further half an hour or so. I thought they were probably in Tasty's office and took the opportunity to pour myself some tea.

They left just before 5 p.m.

Because Tasty had said there would be quite a few more visitors, I wasn't ready to go home just yet. I thought I'd sit it out for a bit longer, but by six o'clock I was beginning to question my sanity. It wasn't as if I was gaining anything from watching them. I couldn't even see which room they were going to on the first floor. I was simply watching for the sake of it – turning into a curtain-twitcher, as Fran used to say. There was nothing going on to suggest that bad things were happening to the clients, it just felt wrong to have so many visitors arriving separately for one dead person. Fran would have wanted me to stop being a stubborn so-and-so and get home for some tea. But I had started so I was going to finish.

About an hour and a half later, I was rewarded by the arrival of another set of visitors. They looked well to do, the woman in a good coat and gloves and the man all in black. They didn't take coffee and didn't once sit down in the day room, but apart from that the routine was the same. They went up to the first floor and returned some time later to the ground floor and eventually left.

What was different about their visit was Milo. I saw him photographing the day room once they'd gone upstairs. This was the first time I was conscious of him photographing anything – having thought back to the measuring he seemed to be doing to the bald woman that day I'd first seen into a client's room, I'd decided he must have been photographing her – and it made me shudder even though he was only taking a picture of an empty room.

When this couple had come and gone, I felt a real

urge to go home. I wasn't sure any more what I was waiting for or what I hoped to see. I was tired. My whole body was aching. My legs were going numb with sitting idle. My back was tense and twisted at an angle from staring out of the window and my arms could barely lift the binoculars. But I would be going home to an empty house and the possibility of further nightmares. If there was any way of finding out what the hell was going on in this place, I had to stay. I owed it to all those people in the photographs and to Fran. So I stayed put, jiggled my legs a bit and rested the binoculars on my lap. I thought I might just as soon hear something as see something, especially as it was very dark by then and I'd only be able to see into rooms with lights on.

Just before nine, I recognised the doctor's car engine. He was back. I didn't see him, but I knew he was there. I picked up the binoculars and was immediately drawn to the first floor where Milo and Sour-grapes were wheeling a stretcher towards the lift. I assumed they must have been taking the dead client down to the morgue. I wondered whether Milo ever took pictures of the clients with other staff around. In the photographs I'd seen, there had been no evidence of anyone else in the pictures, just the clients. It suddenly struck me that if Milo had taken those photographs – and it certainly looked like he had – he probably wouldn't want the home to know what he was up to. I wondered if this might give me some bargaining power. The trouble was, the photographs weren't the only fishy thing going on. There seemed no point in bargaining about anything until I had hard evidence. I wasn't even sure what I'd be bargaining for.

The home was quiet then for several hours. I must

have drifted off because I woke cold and stiff, my face pressed against the pane. It was half eleven.

I rubbed my hands over my face and through my hair and, yawning, picked up the binoculars. There were lights still on in the home. It was the kitchen light, and with a few adjustments I could see Milo moving about quite clearly.

I was still groggy but it looked like he was preparing a meal. There were bits of meat laid out on chopping boards and that. But when I looked closer, I realised he wasn't cutting anything up or putting anything in a pan or a dish. Instead, he was photographing the meat. It was hard to see clearly, but I remember shaking my head. That Milo really is an odd bloke. I couldn't see why you would bother to photograph your dinner. But then I've never understood art. Those people just talk bollocks as far as I can see. The only art I ever liked was a good straightforward watercolour of a country scene. Something pretty to look at. If Milo had taken those photographs in the album for his art, he was one sick man.

I watched him snapping away. He'd taken the meat from boxes, which lay strewn about the kitchen, boxes of metal and plastic with seals and lettering that I couldn't quite make out. I was just trying to zoom in on what looked like an Italian sausage when the kitchen door was flung open and Lily walked in. Her mouth dropped open and though I couldn't hear I could see her gesticulating at all the boxes and meats. They started to have an argument, him still kneeling on the floor from where he'd taken his last shot, her in the doorway, her mouth moving fast, her shoulders up by her ears as her hands flew wildly about the kitchen pointing first at this and then at that.

I was sad to see Lily there. I'd known they must have been seeing each other since the Christmas party, but in my eyes it was wrong. Milo had a wife and child back home, and here he was flirting with a teenager. That sort of thing is criminal in my mind. If we'd had a daughter, I'd have clung to her like a bad smell. You can't be careful enough these days. Young men aren't what they used to be, what with drugs and knives and gangs and that. No such thing as discipline any more. They've no respect. Fran always said it was because they had nothing to do, stuck in ugly tower blocks with nowhere to go where the police wouldn't follow and accuse them of loitering. She saw the good in everyone, did Fran.

After a few minutes, Milo seemed to calm Lily down. She left the kitchen and turned the lights on in Milo's rooms. I saw her standing by the computer, staring, waiting probably.

Milo began packing all the meat away in the boxes, stacking them all in a pile near the door. Then he went through to Lily and they started another row, which ended in kissing. I stopped looking when they went to the bedroom. Part of me wanted to see, but it wasn't right to look. I put the binoculars down and wondered what the hell he was doing with all that meat. It didn't seem right. In fact it was downright doolally.

But I'd had enough for one night. I'd seen enough to know things were not at all right in the home and I knew I needed to keep a strict eye on things. Those people they were caring for deserved the peace that Fran got. We all do.

Woman – III

After my visit to the day room, when I met the Jameses and saw the old man, it felt like I was alone for days. Their lack of interest in my welfare frightened me. For the first time I realised how totally alone I was. I had no control. For what seemed like days at a time I would be ignored, my bags unchanged, no feeding or new drugs administered. I could feel my circulation breaking down. I couldn't remember when I had last been moved. I longed to see a kind, friendly face. All I had for company, apart from the sound of traffic and the occasional birdsong, was the distant whistling that sometimes echoed down the corridor.

In the middle of this lonely time, I heard a loud crash in the corridor. Someone swore and started to yell for Steve. They must have knocked something over or dropped something. However it happened, the spillage began to seep in under my door. I could just make it out, a dark patch gurgling over the lino.

They sent someone to clean it up. I heard him coming. It was the whistler. I listened to him slapping the mop on the floor, turning and twisting it so the liquid emptied into the pail.

I knew he'd have to open my door to get it all. I heard my door handle turn in time to the whistling.

'Don't mind me,' he said, peering around the door. I couldn't remember ever seeing a cleaner in my room before. He was a big older chap with white hair around his ears and a cap on his head. Now he was so much closer, I could recognise the tune he was whistling. It was a popular tune I must have heard on the radio. He whistled it slightly off-key, but it was loud and comforting. He absorbed most of the liquid with paper towels and then mopped up the rest, filling the room with a strong smell of bleach, keeping the tune going throughout, the trilling continuing out of my room and into the corridor. The sound only faded when the lift doors closed.

He must have been Steve. I was pleased to see him.

I've been thinking about Ann, lying here listening to the traffic, musing on the muted shadows of a grey midday. Ann's situation interests me. I wonder how long she has been in a wheelchair. Judging by the state of her legs, as thin as bicycle spokes, I would say a long time. I think if I were Claire, I would resent Ann. The little tragic sister: so brave in the face of adversity.

The last time they came to visit I was having my nasal feed changed. The noise of the dripping is one of those other intermittent constants, if you can have such a thing. When it's on, gravity drops the stuff down into my stomach. Normally they do it at night. It saves bothering during the day, but they aren't that regular. I think they don't mind if my weight fluctuates, they can always get the pump in when they feel like it. When they do it that way, quickly, it's more like having a meal. You fill up. But at night I can't sleep. You're not supposed to feel it, but it keeps me awake. I wonder what they are putting into my body. Claire, when they came the time the feed was being changed, said I should always be informed even if I can't reply. I was surprised. She didn't strike me as the caring type. She smiled at me and said, 'A moment on the lips, a lifetime on the hips.' But she isn't always here and as she rather bitchily suggested, if there are no lips involved, there is no monitoring of the hips at all. I can't regulate any of it. They come and they do it for me. It's a hideous feeling, that plastic up my nose and down my throat. Even with the drugs numbing the pain, I can still feel it, like a thick knot of hair tickling my larynx, or a toothbrush shoved too far back in my mouth.

That time they came, Claire asked a lot of questions about my force-feeding. She annoyed the nurse. Spotty's neck and cheeks turned a mottled red and she suggested that she and Claire discuss my feeding outside. Pathetic really. I could hear them through the door, but Claire would have known that.

'I've been reading,' Claire said, with Ann all the time stroking my hand again, her eyes glazed and distant, 'that you have to get a signature for the nasogastric tube.' She paused. It felt good to learn the name of my feeding tube. 'If my mother couldn't respond to you, due to her health, you should have asked for one of our signatures.'

'I can show you the file,' Spotty replied. 'She signed all right.'

I could hear Claire breathe heavily through her nostrils in contempt.

'I'd like to see it,' she said. 'I'd also like to talk to her doctor about other possibilities. She could be fed more directly into the stomach, isn't that right? A PEG? She's been fed with this tube for weeks now and, as far as I understand it, that isn't advisable.'

'A percutaneous endoscopic gastrostomy isn't always best for the patient,' Spotty replied. There was a hint of a sneer in her tone. I could tell she'd used the medical terms on purpose. They were like badges of authority, keys she used to keep out trespassers.

'Yes' – Claire raised her voice – 'thirty days after a PEG placement mortality rates can be as high as twenty-five to thirty per cent.' She had done her research. I was enjoying the exchange. I felt important, each of them squaring off, throwing health-care punches over my prostrate form.

'Well, as you know the risks—' Spotty started to say, but was interrupted.

'I'd prefer to discuss this with her doctor.'

'Of course.' She's a clever one that Spotty, agreeing with Claire. As far as I knew, they didn't have a doctor. I couldn't remember seeing one. 'I'll see if I can arrange it.'

So Spotty left to find the mystery doctor and Claire came back into the room. Ann continued to stroke my hand. Claire stood at the bottom of the bed.

'It looks horrible, that stuff, doesn't it?' Ann said, nodding at the liquidised food they drip down my throat.

Claire raised her chin a little in response.

'Do you think she can taste it?'

Ann looked up at her sister, who was now staring out of the window, and stopped rubbing my hand for a moment, waiting. Claire didn't reply so Ann turned her attentions back to me.

'How are you, Mum?'

Of course I said nothing.

'All right? Blink once for yes and twice for no.'

I blinked. She resumed the hand rubbing.

'If they gave her a PEG she might die quicker,' Claire said.

Ann said nothing, only rubbed my hand harder.

'They'd inject food direct into her stomach through a tube on her chest. How would you like that, eh Mum? Just a little operation. Only half an hour.' She wasn't looking at me, but still out of the window.

'She's doing fine as she is, aren't you, Mum?'

'Just because she made you suffer, doesn't mean we have to put her through the same.' Claire's voice was very quiet now.

Ann stopped rubbing my hand again. Her voice dropped to Claire's level.

'I got better,' she said.

'You'll never walk again,' Claire whispered back.

Ann stared at her sister's broad, strong back. Her lips tightened in on themselves, disappearing into one thin gash across her face. Her nostrils quivered. She squeezed my hand so hard her knuckles turned white.

'I'm alive,' she breathed.

My bowels chose that moment to move, but not with faeces, with wind. Ann started to laugh. She let go of my hand and clutched her sides, bending forward with the effort, pushing herself backwards from the bed.

'I told them to put in a wind filter,' Claire said, unmoved.

I farted again. A long-drawn-out blast of air that ended in a loud popping and a foul stench. Ann was crying with laughter.

'A wind bag,' she wheezed. 'Get it? You see? Fun, even in this.' She glared at Claire. 'I'm alive, she's alive. She smells' – she paused to wipe her eyes – 'but she's still alive.'

I could feel burning down on my left side, near the hip. It was the stoma. Something was wrong. Hot wet shit was seeping into the wound around the bit of bowel they'd stuck through my abdomen. I would get an infection.

Ann was still gasping for breath, trying to control, and then trying to encourage, ripples of laughter. She looked up at Claire.

'We still have a good time, don't we?'

Claire turned to face her. 'Evidently,' she said, pushing her glasses up the bridge of her nose, 'you do.'

Ann's forced hysterics stopped abruptly.

'Fuck you,' she said, the words articulated carefully but tumbling out in a rush that was almost a whisper.

They glared at each other, malice in the open. All the time my runny diarrhoea crept, gurgling, over my torso, gathering in pools where my body met the bed.

'Fuck you?' Claire asked. 'You're telling me to fuck off? That's rich.'

Ann gulped.

'Without me, you'd be the fucked one, and now you want me to deal with another dependent,' she paused, gesturing with wonderful effect at me on the bed. 'Well, fuck you, Ann, fuck you.' She glowered a little longer and then, quite calmly, still playing to her audience, she pushed her hands needlessly back over her hair, brushed dandruff from her chest and strode to the door. 'Nurse,' she called, 'nurse. We need help in here. There's a problem with Mother's colostomy bag.'

When I came to think of it, I didn't recall signing anything. There was no contract, no paperwork of any kind. I'm not sure if I'd be able to hold a pen. That would be evidence in my favour. But how can I be certain? It's as if someone went in and cleaned away my mind. Can I be Mrs Smith if I'd have to ask what happened to Ann's legs?

Ann and Claire left when Spotty returned. No one needs to see the mess, if they don't have to. It's why I'm here. They all pay someone else to wipe me up.

It is growing brighter this afternoon. A flock of birds flew past, high above the window. I couldn't see them, but I saw their shadows like darting butterflies filling the room with graceful, busy wings. I wait for them to come past again.

I've started to enjoy not speaking. I'm a silent witness to my visitors' lives. Without my own memories of them, Joe, Ann, Claire, Ron, Lynne, they are all so insubstantial. They shoot through the room like the bird shadows playing across the walls and the eiderdown. Their grievances shade the sun from my eyes, break the day into cooler, more distant chunks. I lie and watch them twitter through my life, shake me up, add layer upon layer of confusion, and leave me in the tatters of the various women they think I am. And I remain almost unaffected. They can cry or shout, squeeze my hand to pieces, but I feel untouched. If I do not know who I am, why should they claim me? It's almost as if I am achieving a meditative calm. It surprises me. And this surprise in itself is pleasing because it attests to memories of not being calm. I cling to such tiny certainties.

Perhaps I like Joe because even if I could

remember him, there would be limits to our acquaintance. People may say you know a child's character from the start, but I think everyone is revealed slowly. Like a photograph in a tray of chemicals, the picture is there from the beginning, but it takes a while to see. Sometimes you have to develop your image over and over and even then it might be blurred, or you might choose to filter different colours over it, scratch at the negative, paint it with distorting oils. I keep staring at the different images of myself, searching for the true picture, waiting for my edges to sharpen.

Sometimes I think pain will do it, shock me into myself. When the drugs aren't strong enough, pain takes me over, reminding me of the body I try to forget: my nose itches, especially around the edges of the bandage; the skin around my stoma is cracked and sore; my throat is dry and the pain along the nasogastric tube has been eased into dullness by a callus of skin grown thick beneath the plastic that in my most lucid moments I can feel bristling against my tonsils. But then I imagine my flesh spread like liquid in cellophane over my skeleton and onto the mattress. I meld into the bed, a puddle of dying nerve endings. I am undistinguished, one body among many, useless without clarity of mind.

Then the visitors come again – Joe and his family, Ann and Claire, the Jameses – and they nudge at me, nagging at corners of memories. They exhaust me. They throw emotions over me like blankets, holding me down under a weight of cottons and silks, wools and polyesters, and then they go and their blankets go with them and I'm cold again. I think I am freed by my passivity, but I am part of this. I collude in the charade because it brings me warmth. And however proud I may be of my distance, it costs me my health. If I could properly connect with just one of my visitors, I might get out of here. I might be able to get to the bottom of why I am here, of who I am. Instead, I give myself to Spotty and the male nurse, gloating over their carelessness. Escape has taken a darker form. I've begun to feel that it would actually piss them off, dying. I don't know why. It makes me happy to continue letting things go to waste.

Milos – III

Something about that Christmas night marked a change in my time here. In some ways things continue as before: weeks of photographs, bed baths and waiting for Jelena to call. But other things are more difficult now. Lily is more difficult. It's as if she thinks I owe her something. And my smokes with Steve are quieter. And now, on top of this growing discomfort, as tiny buds begin to form on the garden trees and daffodil bulbs grow out yellow and green around the edges of the home in time for Easter, the old man goes and dies. It wasn't in the schedule. He just died of natural causes, lucky bastard, but still, we will have to clear him up. Back home there is a saying: fear the man ready to die without much complaining. Alexa and the doctor are not afraid as such, but his death will have cost them. They had a lot of money riding on fresh organs, but a live transplant was simply not possible – he died in the night.

So here I am making Turkish coffee for everyone. They called an emergency meeting after I rang them all. As always, the bringer of bad tidings was the first to get the blame. They tried to push the heat my way, trying to claim that I should have been going in there every couple of hours to check up on him. As if. I didn't say anything, just shrugged. They made the rules. This place doesn't run like a proper home because they don't want it to. Eventually, they gave up trying to blame anyone and decided to do an autopsy after getting the family in. That way they can sell more tissue. No one looks as close at funerals.

As there is no other old man ready to replace him, they may have to haul in all the old-man relatives on their books. It's what they're working on now. Who is unlikely to visit in the next month; who would come on a visit unannounced. Playing God requires caffeine and so it is me they send to make the coffee.

Once the coffee is bubbling nicely on the hob, I walk over to the patio door. The garden looks beautiful with the spring flowers and the trees dripping with pink and white blossom. It's a strange time to die. Makes me think of exchange and renewal: one dies, one is born. Everything making way for youth.

Steve is weeding a flowerbed at the far end of the garden. He always makes me think of cigarettes. Like Pavlov's dogs but with fags. I think I will have one while the coffee is brewing, so I open the door slightly, pull the cigarettes and lighter from my upper pocket, light up and lean against the doorframe. It's cold out. I wrap my arms tight round my chest, smoke and watch Steve weed. He is dropping discarded plants into an old wheelbarrow. Despite the boots and tough gloves, there is something timeless about the image. I feel like a feudal lord watching his peasants. As Steve straightens, one hand pressed into the hollow of his back, a shaft of sunlight breaks through the foliage above his head and he is momentarily singled out, illuminated like the dusty statue of a saint in a medieval church. Quickly I try to catch the moment with the camera at my waist, but Steve's annunciation is brief, the light beam flicking on and then off like a torch. He seems not to have noticed. He stands, leaning back, for another moment or so and then bends again to pick up stray weeds, throwing them into the wheelbarrow.

Behind me, the coffee pot is whistling slightly and rocking with steam. I stub out my cigarette, dump the butt in the bin and turn off the gas. I put the coffee on a tray, with four cups, shut the patio door and take the tray through to Alexa's office. The doctor has gone. Only Sarah and Alexa remain, their heads lowered over the desk. They do not look up as I come in.

'Mr and Mrs Leadbeater should go on the list,' Sarah remarks. 'The wife likes to chat. She's talked at the old lady a few too many times.'

'Yes, I made a bad decision on that pair. Fine. Let's put them down.'

I start to pour coffee.

'Don't bother pouring one for Graham. He's gone back to the surgery.'

Only Alexa is allowed to call the doctor Graham. He is such a pompous wanker. Still, I listen to Alexa and just pour three cups. Sarah likes hers with milk and sugar. Alexa has hers black, no sugar at all. I place the cups in front of them and Alexa goes straight for it, grasping the handle without looking up from her records. She blows on the coffee and takes a tentative slurp, still keeping her eyes fixed on various clients' names.

'The Turners never visit. They haven't been in over two years, despite complaining about the bills. So we're safe with them.' Alexa lifts a second hand to her cup, so she is now enfolding the coffee in her fingers like a sacred object. 'I think we should keep the real relatives on the books. They've only visited once and spend half of the year in the Caribbean. They'll be good for another few years. I'm sure we'll have found a replacement old man before they're back again.'

I go and lean against the windowsill. I have nothing to add to the conversation. It makes no difference to me whose relative will have died. I watch my coffee cup, still on the tray, feeling the cold sill against my buttocks. Steam is rising in a swirling storm above the cups. They do not seem to see it, but must feel it like a warm cloud around their faces as they lift the cup to their lips. Sarah sips without thinking and has to flinch back from her cup, her lips probably scalded. The shock of it breaks her concentration and she must feel me looking at her because she turns her head towards me briefly, blinks, and returns to the papers on the desk. Alexa has seen nothing.

They continue to talk, calling out names, and I look away. I am not interested. Alexa's window looks out onto the front garden, the driveway and the wall along the roadside of the property. I can't see much over the wall, but there are rooftops and behind them raised train tracks where every now and then trains pass, carriage after carriage covered in half-hearted graffiti. The noise of their passing does not register; it has become part of the fabric of this place. The trains are not as loud on my side of the building, but even here I only note the sound when I see the carriages rushing past. Not that the trains are quiet, they are just one of many background noises, the way washing machines or radios, or traffic on the road becomes unheard because it is anticipated. It is strange to think of all of these machines forming a soundtrack to our lives.

At home, having your own washing machine was a big thing at one point and my mother's pride in ours has never fallen away. She runs it constantly, even though she still washes delicate fabrics by hand, and the sound and smell of washing is constant. Then there is the ironing. Everything is pressed carefully and folded just so. Even Jelena's clothes have creases ironed in along the sleeves. For a long time, that was the smell of family for me – clean clothes, either on the line or in piles for ironing. Starch or vinegar water stiffening collars. Heat and detergent thinning clothes, wearing out their colours so that even the brightest shirts became acceptably muted. Lily taught me the English phrase, it will all come out in the wash. I keep meaning to pass it on. Mother would love it.

One fleeting thought of Lily is enough to drag my mind down different paths. She drives me crazy with her neediness, but it seems worth it just to be able to run my hands over her body. She has that perfect spring to her flesh.

'Milo? Hello!' Alexa's voice shatters the image of Lily, reforming it into an older mould. 'Are you with us?'

I wonder how long I've been ignoring them.

'Yes, yes,' I say.

'Good. We're going to need to contact five families and try to co-ordinate their visits. We're going to phone them now and we need your help to work out how we can fit them all in. Okay?' I nod at her. 'Take a seat next to Sarah. She won't bite.'

Sarah squints at me, in a very unfavourable way.

'I think we should start with the Leadbeaters. They'll probably be able to come straight away,' Sarah says.

'Right. What's their number?'

Slowly, Alexa works her way through all five. Her bedside manner should be applauded. She keeps up the same sympathetic voice for all of them, as if this were the first time she has had to pass on this distressing news. She asks what time they can get here and then suggests the most convenient time for them to arrive. If they question her, she mentions something about making him look presentable and by the end of it, we have a day organised in hourly shifts. It's going to be a nightmare.

'We simply have to do it all today,' Alexa says in response to my incredulous eye roll. 'We could try to stretch it out to tomorrow, but the longer we leave it the older that body gets and we don't want a decomposing corpse.'

Lucky for her, each family she contacts can make it when she suggests. It always amazes me how death finally rallies disinterested families. They always remember their relative too late.

'In order to make this work, we are each going to have to pull our weight. Right?' Sarah and I nod. 'Milo, I want you on the front desk. You will greet families, show them into the day room and contact Sarah. If we can, both Sarah and I will take them up to the old man's room. You must make sure of the families' names so that we get the right people at the right time and the right name for the old man. If a family turns up early, get them coffee and say that we'll be with them as soon as we can. Both Sarah and I will have our pagers on and you will inform us straight away. To avoid any crossovers, Sarah and I can then split up. I will try to take each family to my office so that Sarah can greet the new arrivals. I will explain the need for a regulation autopsy, as death was unexpected albeit unsurprising. They will sign the forms and we will try to get them to arrange a funeral through the usual channels. All of these families should comply, we think, which means the body can be brought back round the curtains a few times before it is finally cremated. We have to keep our fingers crossed no one wants a burial. Okay.' Alexa sighs and pours herself more coffee, draining the last dregs from the pot. 'The Leadbeaters will be here at ten thirty. Milo, I want you to make sure the old man looks presentable. We need to keep the glasses on – any plausible excuses?'

Both Sarah and I look blank.

'Shit,' Alexa says.

'He looks quite bruised,' I offer after a moment's silence.

'It'll have to do.' She puts her coffee down and runs her hands through her hair, clasping them at the back of her head and looking up at the ceiling. 'Well' – she sighs again – 'what will be will be.'

'It's only the Leadbeaters we need to worry about,' Sarah says. 'The others only come for appearances' sake. They would probably pretend to recognise him even if he was a different colour.'

Alexa smiles and sits forward, placing her hands firmly on the desk, her red nails gleaming. 'Sarah, you're a gem. So, Leadbeaters ten thirty, Hunters at noon, Naylors at one thirty, Cowans at three and the Wolfes can't make it until seven thirty. They're flying in from Brussels.' She looks earnestly at me, then at Sarah. 'Graham will be here at nine. He's organising the arrangements with OrganoMed. We'll let you know about those later, Milo.' Finally she finds time for flirting, throwing this last remark at me from under her eyelashes. The corners of her mouth twitch ever so slightly and I smile at her. Sarah looks decidedly sour.

'Right then.' Alexa waves her hands over the desk. 'Clear this lot up and get on with it.'

Sarah and I start to move.

'Not you, Sarah,' she says. 'I want you to help me organise these autopsy forms.'

Sarah sits back down and they watch me leave, holding their tongues until I click the office door shut. Such conspiracy worries me. But so far, Sarah seems not to have mentioned Lily turning up at my door. It's like she's holding off, waiting for the right moment. It gives her far too much power. Anyway, I can't think of that now. There are other things to occupy them both today. As for me, I might have to add some bruising to the old man's face. I'm not sure what would happen if someone tried to prove he wasn't their relative.

The old man's room is warm when I return. This side of the home catches the morning sunlight and despite the probable chill in the air outside, it's like a greenhouse with the window closed.

I shut the door and stand with my back to it, just looking. Sunlight casts window-shaped patterns across the bottom half of the bed. Long oblongs creep up his legs and over the lump of his torso. Though I pulled down his eyelids earlier, they have popped back up. It looks like the lights and shadows are holding him prisoner. I lift the camera from my waist and start to click.

But there isn't lot of time for photographs today. The visitors will be here soon and I will have to play out the drama at the front desk. My present task is to make this man invisible.

I walk closer to the bed. Luckily, I shaved him yesterday so his face is clean enough, but I will have to close his eyes again. Maybe even put in a couple of stitches. It's a trick of the funeral trade. A couple of stitches keeps the eyelids closed. There is nothing more disconcerting than a corpse whose eyes keep gliding open. Also, even though a thin milky cloud forms over the irises, we don't want visitors looking too close and noticing their father or grandfather's eyes have changed colour.

His face in general is sunken, his cheekbones exposed. He is not wearing his false teeth. I slap my forehead in frustration. I should have put them back in when I found him. It might be tricky now. Although rigor mortis does come and go in two waves, so his face might just be pliable enough. Thankfully he died lying down. If people die in odd positions, sometimes, even if you move them, the muscles can still pull back into their first rigid position. It's as if they want to tell you something.

I put the camera back on my waist. I've taken enough shots of teeth floating in water, of light, of vacant staring, of peace, which surprises me. I find it hard to believe that peace is possible here.

I test the movement of his jaw and I think I can probably move it enough to replace his teeth. It will make his face much more presentable. Though, of course, presentable is not really what we go for. He needs to look both bad and presentable at the same time.

I take the teeth out of the glass and rest them on his chest. It takes both hands to prise open his jaw and I have to keep it propped open with my knee. For moment, I wish someone else were with me to photograph me doing this. Holding his mouth like that, I take the teeth and push them in place. They don't seem to fit quite right, as if those twenty-one grams you lose in death have been taken solely from his gums. I push them about in his mouth, which is still moist, until they look good enough and then drop the jaw and the face back into place. But I do it too fast. A piece of his lip gets trapped between the incisors of his false teeth. I have to pull the lip loose. There is a tiny bit of blood and the lip looks like it might swell slightly. There's nothing I can do apart from wipe away the blood and hope it looks okay.

As for the rest of the face, something will have to be done. He is too individual without his bee glasses on. It has something to do with the bridge of his nose. It falls away, thin and deep between his brows, in a most unusual way. The glasses normally cover it up. How do I hide such a feature? I decide to sew his eyes closed while I think. A couple of stitches is all I need to do. There is very little blood. His eyelids are heavy and thin, full of excess fatty tissue. When he was alive the weight of his eyelids meant his eyes could only open to slits. No one had bothered to remove any of this excess. He couldn't see anyway, or that was the story we told. There certainly wasn't much for him to see here. It was probably easier for him if everything he did see was squashed oddly out of shape or squinted at. He might even have been able to imagine the people who visited him were his real family.

Leaning, touching, feeling him under and around me, is like moving a very lifelike doll. He is not cold, especially where the sheets have covered him during the night, his body retaining heat like a hot water bottle, but neither is he warm. He is simply inanimate, energy seeping from his skin like a biscuit on a cooling tray. There is still some heat somewhere deep inside him, but his surface has gone tacky and hard. He is meat. It continues to shock me that all we are comes down to this heavy, useless flesh.

I decide the best thing for the bridge of the nose is swelling. I take off my shoe, work out the best place to aim my shot, avert my head and hit him. A brittle snap confirms the broken nose. Though there is no flow of blood, enough is held there for this movement to push liquids about. Already his nose looks both less and more strange: flatter, some bone pushing up to fill the empty narrow bridge. With his teeth in and his nose squashed he just about passes for any man. It will have to do.

I rearrange the bed sheets, smoothing them over his torso but under his arms. They always like to hold hands with their dead. Then I quickly take a couple of shots of my handiwork, grab my things and head downstairs. I need to be on the front desk in twenty minutes and knowing the Leadbeaters, they will be early.

The rest of the day seems to go smoothly. The Leadbeaters do turn up early and the wife is her usual self, peering behind doors, disappearing while her husband says goodbye to his father. We will all be happy to see the back of them. She is here, there and everywhere, sticking her nose in. Probably a good job she has a husband. I would not put it past them to haul her in here. She is old enough. She has a funny way of talking, leaning in at you, her shoulders held high, peering through her glasses with a silly smile on her face, which is eager, meek and patronising all at once. She calls me dear.

They kept Alexa talking for a while, but once they were gone, all the other visitors were straightforward. I've just been sitting here, surfing the net on the front desk computer. Sent some emails. Made instant coffee for visitors when asked and took a couple of cigarette breaks out front, ready to dive back to the desk when needed. It has been relatively relaxing.

As I've sat, I've thought about the old man. They will cut him to bits tonight and I will look after those bits, waiting for OrganoMed. I just wonder what I could do with them, whether I could use them, not in simple object photographs, but as part of some more bizarre collage. I could set his nails beside a half-eaten fruit: five bloody fingernails stretched out like a reaching hand. Or maybe I could push them into the flesh of an apple, or an orange. I could lay his skin across some bone – they are bound to take some bone – and put it on a plate surrounded by raw potatoes and cabbage leaves. If they take out his brain and pickle it in formaldehyde, I could sit the jar in front of an open book, shelves of volumes in the background. I could even go down to the morgue and use the old man himself, prop him up in provocative positions. His body is an object now, the shell of a man who had already lost himself. Once his, then ours, now, possibly, mine.

One of the things that interests me about these body parts is that recent studies of memory claim we store memories in other places as well as our brain. I wonder if people who get these old hearts and livers (though not this man's, of course, death having cheated him of reincarnation) also get feelings, smells, emotions. The flesh carries ghostly whispers of the past into new bodies, turning good all that negligence and greed, creating hybrids – people who suddenly develop new tastes for black pudding or whose dreams are filled with memories of previous world wars. A friend once told me that someone they knew had to take pig insulin as they were allergic to the human kind. They said that, all of a sudden, they were drawn to pigs. When they went for walks in the countryside they would lean against the fences of pig enclosures and the pigs would come to them, slowly moving from all corners of the field to be close to the strange man-pig. I'd like to depict this, but I don't quite know how I could.

The light is fading. We're still waiting on the Wolfes.

I drop my head down and back, cracking vertebrae. I will be totally empty one day, just a collection of organs and flesh. The thought is frightening – more than that, it brings with it the sense of hollowness that will mark me then. I feel my throat constrict. Of all places, I do not want to die here. It would be the emptiest death, all those memories seeped into foreign soil.

I rub my hands over my face, through my matted hair, pushing everything back, and wait.

At 7:34 the Wolfes arrive. They are embarrassed about being late. Apparently their train was delayed. It's Mr Wolfe who does all the fluster and discomfort – Mrs Wolfe stands behind him, slightly to one side. It's curious. She looks like someone sheltering from a strong wind. It's obvious that it has been this way for so long that they do not see anything odd in it. It makes me wonder which of them instigated and nurtures this physical statement of subjugation. It could be meant to suggest one thing while being another. Perhaps it's Mrs Wolfe who is really in control.

I tell them not to worry, they aren't late at all and show them into the day room. They do not sit down. There is a strange air of excitement about them, which makes me wonder why, after all this time, they felt it important to come now he is dead (well, as far as they know – their real relative was farmed of organs long ago). As I go to call Sarah, I see Mrs Wolfe brush imagined fluff and dandruff from the shoulders of her husband's coat. Her hand is gloved. When I turn away, and picture her in my mind, I see her wearing a hat. Yes. She looks like she should wear a hat, like a middle-aged woman of the 1950s perhaps.

Both Sarah and Alexa come to fetch them and they go up in the lift, their voices drifting through otherwise empty corridors. I do not hear what they say. Though clearly enunciated, their voices are hushed.

I get up from the desk and walk to the edge of the day room. I take a photograph of where the Wolfes just stood. 'After the Wolfes' would be a good title for a photograph of a deserted room. The daylight is still strong enough to cast eerie contours from the garden windows, turning time backwards, picking out wooden framed chairs upholstered in textured orange and brown, or green and brown fabric set at odd angles from one another and the cold metal tea trolley idle against the flat of the wall near the entrance to the canteen. A flash of reflected light sparkles off a curve in the trolley, making a diamond in the bleak expanse of faded décor.

This room alone would be enough to put prospective relatives off, those that cared at least. Even at Christmas with tatty bits of tinsel draped around the walls, the room absorbs and deadens all feeling. It is unbelievably depressing. It looks like all those abandoned houses they talk about back home. If you woke up one day and realised that despite living next to your neighbours for years, your origins put you in the minority, you left – either you were rounded up or you simply ran into the countryside to escape. Whole villages did it sometimes. They left everything to live in the woods and watch while enemy soldiers slept in their beds and ate what they couldn't carry from their cupboards. If people stayed in the village, people who were once your friends but were now completely different to you, then your house was looted. Neighbours stole your television, your treasured antiques, your furniture, your cooking pots. Rooms were left empty like this one, light illuminating shafts of dust hanging over discarded, disjointed objects. Such places are ghosts on the modern landscape, desperately and quickly sold or appropriated in order to forget, sometimes left to rot, the taint of previous ownership too much for prospective families to overlook. Just like those houses, this home is a place to forget.

As I am about to turn away, I hear a noise from upstairs. The Wolfes are making their way down to Alexa's office. This has been a very short visit. It is clear to me that they only wanted confirmation of his death. He was probably a burden to them. I slip quietly back behind the desk before they reach the bottom of the stairs. It's been like this all day – up in the lift, down in the stairs. It's a wonder the relatives haven't questioned each other, or at least noted the number of conversations they overheard about death. Maybe they think such conversations are normal in a place like this. Death is an everyday activity.

Sarah leaves the Wolfes and walks round to the front desk. I am to bring coffee and biscuits to Alexa's office. 'Real coffee,' Sarah stresses.

'All going okay?' I ask, standing up, readying myself for the kitchen and more coffee making.

Sarah nods. 'Fine,' she says. 'I'll cover the front desk. Just in case. They shouldn't be long with Alexa.'

She is clearly in no mood to chat, but I mock salute her anyway. Things between us have felt fragile since the Christmas party. I cannot trust her. She responds to my salute with a firm nod. 'You are dismissed, Milo,' she says, unable to hide the movement at the corner of her lips. It's a relief to have teased a smile from her.

'Aye, aye,' I say and march towards the kitchen, swinging my arms stiffly and raising my knees at each step.

She grins and I go on appeased. Things are not so bad.

By eleven o'clock, the Wolfes, the doctor, Sarah and Alexa have all gone. The autopsy is over. I have boxes ready to hand over to OrganoMed and am preparing myself for the usual long wait. Tonight I want to use the time properly. I want to try out a staged photograph. First, as Sarah and Alexa assisted in the autopsy without me, I need to see what I've got to play with. I like the idea of using the kitchen as a backdrop, so I carry all ten boxes into the kitchen and start to unpack them, one after another.

I pull out the heart, liver and kidney, probably for medical use. As predicted there are full sets of nails from the fingers and toes, both femur bones, the brain is in a jar of formaldehyde – like they say, one ounce of good luck is better than brains – and there is a large patch of skin, which the label describes as 'skin section from client's back'. It is spotted and mottled with moles and age and I have no idea what they will use it for. The final package contains his eyes. Despite the glasses we made him wear, his eyesight was good. Apart from the milky film of death, there are no signs of disease. Sarah told me there is a big market for eyes in Russia. I have no idea why. The old man's eyes are floating in some kind of saline. When I poke them, they feel curiously springy, like rubber bouncy balls. I'm tempted to throw them on the floor to see if they bounce.

I stand back and stare at this haul for some time. I'm not sure how best to arrange it all or quite what I want my picture to say, but then it comes to me suddenly. I push each piece of old man, except the skin, heart, liver and kidney, into a heap. I cross the bones around the brain and eyeballs, and scatter the nails over them like nuts or petals. Next to the pile I lay out the biggest chopping board and put the organs and skin on it, overlapping each other like meat in a busy butcher's shop. I take a large chopping knife from the magnetic wall mount and wedge it into the chopping board so it looks as if it is cutting into the flesh. By happy chance, enough blood pools on the white of the board to show that this was all recently alive. I step back, wash my hands and start to photograph my still life from every angle I can.

*

This is how Lily finds me, crouching on the floor, my camera turned up at the butchery above.

'What the fuck do you think you are doing?'

I do not answer. I simply turn to look at her. She is standing in the doorway, half in, half out of the corridor, her arms stretched out and braced against the doorframe. It's an imposing stance, judging, blocking my exit. I see she is wearing a new pair of tight black jeans.

'Well?'

'What do you want me to say?' I ask, standing up. There is no way out of this. 'You can see for yourself.'

She looks at the old man's severed bits and pieces, the chopping board, the knife, and back at me.

'You are one sick fuck.'

Her words hang in the air between us. Her eyes are narrowed, lips trembling.

'Oh?' I say. I have no patience for this. 'Mummy didn't tell you how she earns money?'

She drops her arms from the doorframe and frowns.

'Fuck off, Milo. I mean, what the fuck are you doing?'

I don't know what her response implies. It's like someone has pressed pause, only the whirring of our minds is audible still. After a few minutes, I start to pack the old man's parts away in their boxes. Lily watches me.

'Have you done this before?'

I do not answer.

She walks closer to me.

'Milo?' Her voice is angry without being loud, tension growling out at the back of her throat. It is curiously sexy. I do not know how to play this.

'Actually, is first time,' I say.

'Really?' There seems to be some relief in her question. She grabs my wrist. 'I need to know.'

'Why, Lily? Why do you need to know?' I cannot continue to wrap the organs and bones when she is holding my wrist, so I whisper to her, feeling strangely calm. 'Does it matter?'

It has a good effect. Lily speaks more calmly in response, her grip starting to relax, 'I just need to know, Milo. I'm not stupid. I've seen your photographs.'

She says these words as if she is talking to a child and the tone and words together instil me with fear. She has seen my other photographs. Which ones? Why has she not said anything before now? But I don't know how to ask these questions yet and all I manage is, 'Oh.' I feel her eyes on my face. I haven't turned to look at her. 'Alexa?' I say.

'I haven't told Mum. Not yet.' She takes a deep breath. 'Milo,' her voice is louder, more commanding, 'you tell me why I shouldn't tell her. What the hell are you taking these pictures for, anyway? Who are you going to show them to?'

'Okay,' I say, trying to bide my time, 'I will tell, but first let me put all this away so there are no problems with delivery later.' Without turning to see her reaction, I feel her consent. Slowly she drops my wrist.

'Go to my room, sit down, and wait.' Now I'm the one with the commanding tone. 'Should take no more than couple of minutes, okay?' This is when I turn to look at her. She is staring down at her hands, avoiding the old man's flesh as well as my gaze.

'Fine,' she says, turning. 'I will wait for you to pack all this away, but it better be a bloody good explanation.'

She leaves. I listen to her walk down the corridor, open my door and go in. She does not close the door behind her. Probably she is listening to me too, so I decide to work quickly. I just needed a little extra distance from her to think up my strategy. There must be reasons why she hasn't told anyone about the other photographs. I think she believes she loves me. It's the obsessive, possessive love of a nineteen-year-old, but she wouldn't know any different. I regret having started this affair.

When everything is packed away and the boxes are stacked neatly on the kitchen counter, I have no choice but to go to my room. I find Lily standing by the computer staring at the picture of Jelena. I need to smoke.

'Cigarette?' I offer Lily my packet.

She declines with a shake of her head. It's the first time I have ever seen her reject a cigarette.

I light up and inhale nervously, the smoke giving me a false sense of stability. I take several drags, holding off the moment when I will have to talk.

'So?' she says. She is leaning against the computer table while I stay standing.

'Pictures are aesthetic. I take for sake of composition, comparison, beauty. Yes, is part of body of work I hope to show, but never, never have I thought of saying from where they come. Will say are fakes, or maybe taken in different country. Why should they not believe me?' I suck on my cigarette. Lily does not move. She is waiting. I will have to go on.

'First, relatives interested me. Seeing nothing, inventing feelings. Way they do not care.' I pause again to inhale, then blow out smoke as I talk. 'Was all part of wider feelings about this country –

individualism as disintegration of social responsibility. Is how this place runs, you know that.' Again I need the nicotine from the cigarette. Lily keeps watching, unmoving. 'Then, am more interested in old people. Is what I do all day, so I take photographs of daily routine. Photographs are not all without pity, no, I take pictures with humanity, invest feeling in emptiness. I want to show old people are already dead, already objects. So, yes, becomes kind of documentary of this place, but still, am not looking to expose home, no. Please, Lily, believe me.'

Feverishly, I continue to smoke. I don't know what else to do. I light another from the end of the first and then push my hair back from my face, curl it behind my ears. I look at her, my turn to wait.

'I saw them at your Christmas party,' she speaks into me, poking words through my face. I hug my chest with one arm and continue to smoke, listening. 'I was looking for the photographs you took of me. It looked like someone had been looking through your albums because all the spines were at different angles and I didn't like the idea that Steve or Sarah might have seen naked pictures of me, so I started to check, looking at the albums that seemed hastily shoved back on the shelf.' Standing up, she begins to walk slowly towards me. 'As soon as I saw pictures of the preparation of tissues for trade, I clamped the album shut. I stopped looking. I had seen enough.' She continues to walk very slowly towards me. 'I know what goes on here. I'm not stupid. I worked it out years ago, and I've worked through my disappointment, the way I saw my mother fall from the pedestal I had created for her. I see it's just business. And when I saw your photographs, I knew they could be used as evidence against the home, against my mother. They were dangerous, but I didn't think you were working to expose us and so I decided to stay quiet. Instead I thought I would follow you, check up on you, see what you were up to. I love you, Milo, but I don't trust you.' She has reached me and stands as close as she can without touching me, delivering her lines up at me through her fringe. 'I saw you were pursuing an artistic rather than legal ideal, as much as you can follow an ideal. Everything is broken for you: your family, your home, your baby far away, your dreams of being a famous photographer. You are a bitter man, a cynical man, and I was naïve to you, an intellectual and sexual plaything, but I am more than you think. You are too afraid to love again, but I think you do love me, underneath all that bullshit. And I want us to be together. I want to heal your broken dreams. I want you to start again, with me. I want you to tell my mother about us. I want you to divorce your wife and live with me, marry me. We can have our own family.'

I take a step back from her. I can't say I'm surprised exactly, but her tirade feels like an assault. I'm unnerved.

I manage to stumble out one word, 'Jelena.' The force of her name sums up everything about why I cannot do what Lily asks.

'Jelena can come here. She can live with us. I can look after her. I would love her because she is yours.' Lily is not moving any more, she stands watching me walk backwards. She puts out her hand to touch me and I dodge it. She lets it fall back to her side, her eyes now filling with tears. 'I could tell Mum. I could have told her months ago.'

She doesn't need to say more. I could run, of

course. But what then? The Home Office doesn't need much to consider deporting me and I'm not the only one who takes photographs. They've recorded enough bedsores and minor infections to make it look like I neglect patients, or they could claim I stole off with something. The only place I could run to is back home, but then all this work would be lost. Who would look at it? No, I need to plan. I need to make her think that this could work, that I love her. With time, I could work out a way of escaping, I could finish the photographs, even take pictures that make the home's culpability clear – then I can go anywhere.

'And then what you did tonight, well' – she sniffs defiantly – 'she might want to hear about that too, tampering with tissue samples, contaminating them, behaving as if you have no respect for the dead.'

'Is not like that, Lily. You know.' I take a step towards her and brush some hair from her face. Her tears fall faster.

'You scared me. Playing with dead body parts like that. I don't get it. I don't get what all these photographs are about. I just don't.'

Despite her professed disgust, she falls into my arms, sobbing, and without warning her hands run over my chest, my back, my buttocks. She turns her face up towards me, lips expectantly parted. I kiss her.

We do not talk again that night. I let her stay with me, through the OrganoMed exchange, and on into the morning, sharing my bed.

I wake early the next day. Lily is still sleeping. I will have to wake her, get her out before Sarah and Alexa arrive. I need to persuade her not to tell.

Gently, I stroke her face. I can see it nudging her

from sleep. I bend over her and kiss both of her cheeks. She moans and pushes her mouth forwards, her eyes still closed, and I kiss her lips. Halfway through, she opens her eyes.

'What time is it?' she asks.

'Seven thirty.'

I stroke hair from her face, turning my hand around as I sweep the backs of my fingers over her cheek. Her forehead crinkles with what looks like worry, so I kiss her again.

'I will tell Alexa,' I say, 'but not yet, not like this. Let me organise things at home, first, okay? Can you wait?' I keep on stroking her.

She nods.

Steve – V

Over the next few months, I slept, or avoided sleep, in the shed a number of times. I brought a warm blanket in from home along with a tin full of chocolate biscuits. It wasn't that I was seeing anything – even on that first night's vigil I must have fallen asleep again, because when I woke in the morning the boxes in the kitchen had gone – it was just that I couldn't let it rest any more, and it wasn't as if I was sleeping at home. But I wasn't built for nights spent sitting in an old wooden chair, occasionally nodding off at odd angles, and my work started to suffer. I just can't bend as much any more. I have to take things more slowly and that. I keep finding myself out of breath, pausing with my hands on my lower back while I snatch some air into my lungs. It's not pleasant but I know it must be a fraction of what Fran felt, so I keep going. Slow and steady wins the race.

Nothing suffered at the start. I kept up with all my jobs. But I started to sneak around in the day as well. I wanted to get a picture of where all the clients were, figure things out a bit better. So I began breaking the rules and looking in rooms. And once I'd started that, there really was no looking back.

Most of the rooms were empty.

The day after my first vigil I woke frustrated and confused. Something was going on that I was missing. I was damned if I was going to be fooled by the bunch of human wreckage running the place. Tasty had said I could do the floors that day, so I decided that was just what I would do. Only this time, I wasn't going to stick to my remit, I was going to look in the clients' rooms. If I couldn't see anything in the morgue and I'd seen nothing yesterday, despite all the running about, the clients' rooms were the only places left to look. It didn't occur to me to check the morgue again. The client was dead, after all, and probably already sent off to the crematorium.

I thought it made sense to work my way down the building. Start on the top floor and work down. Because I hadn't gone home, but had woken in my chair in the shed, it was very early. I reckoned I'd be all right exploring the home at this time in the morning, especially after a day like yesterday. If the body left last night, there'd be little for them to do today, except for the normal routine. It seemed likely to me that they would have a bit of a lie-in. I'd managed to get in and out of the morgue without being seen and though this would be more time-consuming, it would be easier to break off my inspection and I'd have a plausible excuse for being close by.

So I went inside, unlocked the storeroom and got out the polishing machine. It always cheered me up, that machine. It's a beauty. I wheeled it to the lift and went right up to the top floor. I thought it was important to use the machine to cover my snooping. I was planning to set the machine going and then peer through each of the clients' doors as I passed. I plugged in the machine and set to work.

The rooms were just like the one I had seen on the first floor a few weeks previously: empty but for a bed, two side tables, and a chair. The only difference was that there were no side tables, no drips, and most importantly no clients. There were no people at all in any of the rooms on the second floor. I was polishing the floor of a deserted corridor.

When I'd finished I went down to the first floor. I worked my way along the corridor, going left out of the lift and then back up past the lift to the other end and back. On the left side of the lift all the rooms but the one with drawn curtains were empty. Only the room I couldn't see into from the shed showed signs of recent occupancy. It wasn't the way it looked so much as the smell. There was a distinct scent of tired breath and antiseptic soap, even though the window was open. On the floor, by the far end of the bed there was a tiny fleck of what looked like dried blood. I could only imagine that this was the dead person's room.

I moved on up the corridor along the right-hand side of the lift. There, in a room facing towards the street, was the old woman. She was still there, sleeping this time. It seemed unlikely that she knew she was the only client in the entire home. I was glad she was asleep. She looked comfortable enough. There wasn't time to go further into the room because I could hear Tasty arriving early for work again.

And just like that I gained a new routine. Every day I cleaned the floors, I checked on the rooms and the old woman. There were no new clients. It was odd, yes, but there was nothing criminal in having only one client. No one mentioned it. I still got paid. But it made me interested in Tasty's records. I remembered that plan she'd had on my first day, with all the rooms marked up with different names. I wondered what it looked like now. Still, as I said, having one client was odd, not illegal.

At first, I kept up my garden work. I made sure the lawns looked okay with the advance of spring and kept the flowerbeds relatively tidy. I'd been getting used to living on no sleep for weeks, but as spring turned to summer, the night vigils began to take their toll. My daytime dozing, which had been increasing since the onset of insomnia, was at a peak. I never felt myself falling into sleep, I only seemed capable of catching myself asleep. It happened most often on the fire escape, when I'd been having a break, but it could just as easily happen while I was leaning on something, a mop or a broom. They were tiny naps, like sighs of sleep, and they were as useless as they were brief. I woke startled and confused and even the idea of sleep started to haunt me.

That was when the floor-cleaning cover had to change. I was worried I would do someone an injury with the machine, so I switched to mop and bucket on every floor but the ground, where Tasty's heels required industrial cleaning – she had obviously never felt the need to make many personal checks on the clients. The mop and bucket made it harder to check in on the rooms, though. There was no longer the whirr of the machine to cover the squeak of opening doors, or to disguise my lack of work. I had to take snatched glances into the rooms, sometimes even through keyholes, just to check rooms were still empty. And because my back was playing up and I was wheezing something horrid, I wasn't putting the work into the floors I should have been. Particularly on the first floor, where their only client had her room, I started to notice an increase in flies. I think I was leaving the corridors wet, letting pools of stagnant water sit for too long, and because of the heat of the summer larvae were breeding like mad. They were all over the day room too. I just couldn't clean as well as I used to. I remember it happening to my mother, bless her. She'd been a proud housewife, but in her last years she couldn't see well enough and dirt gathered in the seams of tables and the cracks in crockery. Hardened dirt built up on cutlery. I knew I was doing it to the home – unable to keep a whole building and its gardens shipshape any more – but I wasn't going to admit it. Someone had to keep an eye on the situation, had to work out what the hell was going on.

So every day, even when I was meant to be in the gardens, I made sure I popped in on the old lady. I didn't stay long. I looked in on her is all. There wasn't time for anything else. I could see she was being ignored. I tested it. Went up there all times of the day to see how often and when they monitored her, but it seemed to be totally random. Sometimes Milo, sometimes Sour-grapes would go by, but mostly I could get up there, pop my head round the door and get away without even being seen in the lift. It broke my heart. When I thought of how well everyone looked after Fran, of how wonderful all the nurses were, it didn't seem right at all. It was an outrage. Still, I had no idea what to do other than check on her. I was nervous of calling the police. Given the choice of believing me or Tasty, I didn't think they'd struggle to decide against me. I still needed more proof.

And then the weather worsened. I could barely move without getting a sweat on. All my clothes reeked of worn socks. The grass was going yellow and the flowers were dropping unchecked onto the flowerbeds. There were weeds everywhere. Even on the grass. I knew I couldn't be kept on much longer. I'd virtually given everything up but monitoring the old woman. I think I was going mad. Even when I dozed, images of Fran's scarred chest came back to terrify me. It was no place for an old man.

I had started out at that home feeling like I'd had a second wind – back at work, limbs moving like a well-oiled machine, something to distract me from Fran's death – but somewhere along the line I'd taken a turn for the worse, like a switch had been flicked off or on. I was fading. When I got home I couldn't make it up the stairs. I would sit in the living room with big mugs of instant hot chocolate and watch the television. Didn't matter what was on. I liked the sound and the movement. I didn't watch it; it was just a background to hours of drifting, not really asleep or awake. If I was someone else watching me, I'd have been crying myself to sleep late at night, knowing the end was coming. Like when Fran was nearing the end, you try to stay bright, but you feel someone's punched you in the stomach. You're all doubled up, struggling to breathe. Then what starts as a cold turns into a chest infection and slowly all the body's functions begin to collapse.

In some ways this memory was a comfort when I looked at the old woman in the home. I might have been on my way out, but she was okay. I had to keep going for her sake. The thought of her being left alone made me more determined. I'd have to plan something new. There was nothing else for it. I'd have to break into the files in Tasty's office.

Once the idea took hold, there was no shifting it. The only problem was to work out how I would get in. Of all the staff, Sour-grapes had grown the most suspicious. She seemed to know what I was up to. Even in the mornings, she would be there, waiting for me. It slowed me down. I had to try and work. I didn't want her catching on until I had something to show for all these months of nosing. So, I dead-headed the roses – less back-breaking work, but something that made me look busy – and in the evenings I started watering the lawns again. But I'd left it too late. Sour-grapes didn't stop checking on me, and the grass was already parched and instead of nurturing it I was drowning it. Bald patches of cracked, loose soil appeared all across the lawns out front and in the back. I was grasping at straws, trying to hold onto a sinking ship.

Knowing I was being watched, and feeling so tired, I had to plan carefully. Going home didn't seem like much of an option any more. I picked up a few changes of clothes and just hoped they'd put my appearance and smell down to old age. None of them talked to me if they could help it anyway. It was only beady-eyed Sour-grapes who seemed to keep track of me. So I holed up in the shed, wrapped myself in a blanket for warmth even though the nights were hot.

Seeing the dawn from the shed was lovely. The rising sun casts rays broken by the laburnum and the shed. Their shadow shapes stretch long and dark across the yellow lawn, and flashes of light reflect off the windows of the home. It was almost worth the discomfort of a night spent staring up at the dark windows, sometimes lit up by Milo and Lily – normally she left at first light – Milo shooing her out. I felt sorry for the girl.

I still wasn't sure what I was watching for, but I could use the nights to think. The time to get into Tasty's room would have to be early morning, once Lily had left Milo's bed. But before I could get into Tasty's room, I'd need a copy of her key. I'd have to invent some reason for seeing her and then steal the keys. It seemed so far-fetched. I'd never been the stealing type, had no idea how to play the sleight of hand. The only other way would be to break in, but I couldn't see how to do that without waking Milo.

I was thinking this over one morning – I'd woken with the birdsong – when I saw the usual Milo and Lily routine. I wasn't really interested in watching, only this time I noticed something different. It was later than usual and Lily, instead of walking past the day room and out the front entrance, seemed to disappear. Worried about bumping into someone, she must have left some other way. As far as I knew, the only other way out was through Tasty's office. She had her own en-suite bathroom off a little corridor behind her office. The corridor also led to a side door, bringing you out onto the gravel of the driveway not far from the outhouse. If she was going out of that side door, Lily had keys to Tasty's office. If I was lucky, getting the keys from Lily would be a lot easier than getting them from her mother. The game, as far as I could see, was on.

My plan was simple. Find a way to hide in the day room. Wait for Lily to come over and hope – this was the risky bit – that Milo would be in the kitchen making supper or coffee or whatever, so that they would sit there first. I'd noticed, sometimes – and mind you, it really was only sometimes – Lily would meet Milo in the kitchen and leave her jacket slung over a chair in the canteen. She always wore revealing tops under her jackets and seemed keen to give Milo an eyeful as soon as she saw him. Sometimes there would be a handbag, sometimes not, but if the jacket stayed in the kitchen, so did the bag. If I could keep from coughing and got lucky, I'd be able to sneak off with her keys.

As far as I could see it, she would think she had them on her when she left. She normally went through the main entrance, Milo closing everything behind her. As long as she didn't oversleep, she wouldn't miss her keys until later and then, hopefully, she would think she'd left them at Milo's place. In the meantime, I could tiptoe into Tasty's office and have a good look round. If I found anything, I could easily nip out to a locksmith before Lily came back.

The plan seemed reasonable enough. The only problem was that the whole thing relied on chance events and I'd have to move my vigil from the relative comfort of the shed to some awkward corner of the day room. Still, there was nothing like the present and I would have my first stab at it that night.

During the day, as well as trying to get a chance to see the old woman, I made an effort to clean the day room, scouting the place out. As luck would have it, there was one armchair whose back faced the canteen. I felt certain that, given the size of the chair and the relative darkness of the room when Lily and Milo would be eating and drinking in the kitchen, I'd be able to sit there unseen. All I had to do then was wait till nightfall.

There were many problems with the plan in practice, not least the fact that during the first two nights I fell asleep. Far from being more uncomfortable, the armchair was much cosier than the chair in the shed, and as I had to keep so still, my body seemed to think there was nothing for it but to sleep. Especially as I'd had my evening fag, trying to stave off the coughs, fairly early so as to get into position.

On the third night, when I finally managed to keep my eyes open, Lily didn't show. On the fourth night, Milo had already prepared food and coffee and they had no need to visit the kitchen until later when Lily had already shed most of her clothes. I was sad not to see that, I can tell you. I just heard Lily go on about how huge his T-shirt was on her and would he mind if she kept it. He said no. He took a certain tone with her that I didn't like. I'd have been happy to hit him, if I felt it would help, but somehow she seemed to ask him to talk down to her. She was needy, whiny like a child. I couldn't see them, but I could hear him pushing her away. She kept saying things like 'Don't you want me to' do this or that, or making excuses to touch him, 'I think you should let me do your hair.' It was pitiful.

It was on the fifth night that I had my chance.

Tasty and Sour-grapes had been gone about an hour, maybe two, and I'd been sat in the old armchair since then. I wasn't feeling too positive, I can tell you. Fifth night of waiting and I wasn't even sure exactly what I'd look for if I got into Tasty's office. I was certain there'd be records, but they would probably be locked up somewhere. I'd just have to hope she wasn't overly worried about the authorities and that. Then, if I found anything – maybe financial records would be good? – I'd have to think about how to use them. I would be breaking in, so I wouldn't be in the best position with the law myself. But, feeling the thin carpet under my feet, the armchair stiff even in its old age from lack of use, I had to try and find something. If I found even the tiniest bit of evidence that they were doing something different to what I could see around me, I could call the police and they could get a search warrant. I couldn't believe no one would look into a call like that. But then again, what did I know?

I fell back on the cushioned headrest of the chair and closed my eyes. No light remained; I'd shut out the dim glow shining in from the garden, my lids too heavy to allow even that faint tinge of pinky-red to mar my thoughts. No stars, no lingering flashes from what I'd last seen, just cool comforting darkness. I thought of Fran, like in the old days, young and laughing, playing hide and seek with me – lights off and under the covers. Life had been good once, full and happy. And then I saw her in her last days – head mostly bald, her kind eyes small and moist shining out through all that dull paper skin – and I couldn't help thinking of the woman upstairs. This wasn't a game, a laugh, a prank – this was for real. Real lives, real people shut away into an early grave.

I opened my eyes and shifted in the chair, turning my ankles round. It was mid-twist that I heard the kitchen door handle pulled down. I kept my leg in the air, hoping to time its fall with the click of the door when it closed. The door creaked open, the lights clicked on and I dropped my leg. I was moments too soon. The loud crack of my bending ankle snapped through the day room. I held my breath, waiting. Had Milo heard? It must have been Milo.

I heard the door close and then a few cupboards open, pans lifted and placed on surfaces – metal on metal. I was safe. It must be Milo. All I had to do now was keep quiet, stay awake and wait.

Having listened to Milo cook before, I wasn't surprised to hear him start to hum and mumble words under his breath. Foreign words that chopped and cooked the food by magic. I could smell freshly sliced onion, crushed garlic, a spicy herb. I could hear water boiling, objects bouncing against the sides of a pan and then eggs cracking and being beaten, the fork or whisk scraping hard and fast on the sides of a bowl. It smelled wonderful. I'd had nothing but a sausage roll for my tea and the hours seemed liked days, my mouth watering and then my stomach growling.

Like the sound of the ankle, the noise of my rumbling tummy caught me short, my breath held again, fear curdling into the acid hunger making the noises louder. What would I say if he came in and found me here – I fell asleep after a long day in the garden? Would he buy that?

But before I needed to test any excuses, I heard footsteps out in the corridor. It would be Lily.

The kitchen door burst open.

'Hey,' she called.

Milo's humming mumbling singing hadn't stopped.

'Hey, hello,' she said. I couldn't see her but it sounded like she was waving at him.

'Sorry,' Milo said, 'listening to music.' Finally I allowed myself to breathe more easily. All this bloody time, he'd had headphones on and wouldn't have heard anything. I was such a fool.

'So, what you cooking?' Lily asked, zips unlocking, tiny chinks suggesting a jacket dumped on a surface, possibly a bag.

'Spanish omelette.'

'Smells great. I'm starving.'

'Should be ready in twenty minutes. Coffee?' Milo asked, their conversation unusually wooden.

'No, thanks. I don't fancy it. But make some for yourself. Don't worry about me.'

They didn't talk for a while. Someone, Lily probably, scraped a chair back in the canteen, its legs lifting and falling. I could imagine her rocking there. Smells of rich coffee mingled with the garlic and onion.

Then another chair was dragged across the floor.

'Will be ready soon,' Milo said. I could hear liquid being poured. 'Sure you don't want coffee?'

Lily must have made some response as there was no more pouring liquid.

'You look tired,' Lily said. 'Hard day?'

'Same old,' Milo said. I heard him slurp at the coffee.

'I was reading Nietzsche today.' Lily said this like she was flirting. 'Yeah,' she said, after a pause, 'some of the things he says are beautiful.'

'You should read Heidegger,' Milo said. 'Is more interesting. Nietzsche is superego not superman.' He slurped again and then scraped his chair back once more. I could hear him walking and then the oven door opening, releasing warm, rich smells of fresh omelette.

'Yeah,' Lily said, 'I suppose so. Like that thing he said about truth being like a woman, you know? Enticing and elusive? Always just out of reach? I mean, it is kind of romantic, you know? But also, it's just misogynist, isn't it? Like only men can chase the truth, like women are some weird other species or something?'

Lily always seemed to talk like this. It didn't matter what she was talking about. Every sentence went up at the end. Her sentences sounded like open arms, begging to be completed, held. Not easy stuff to listen to. Still, it was keeping me awake tonight and that was something.

Milo grunted and then said, 'Prefer to eat in room tonight?'

Lily stood up, the chair scraping once more. Food was cut and served and knives and forks balanced on plates. The kitchen door opened.

'Don't you think, though? Not just arrogant but misogynist?'

I didn't hear Milo's reply. The light snapped off and they were gone.

As I've said, my hearing isn't quite what it used to be, so I just waited a few minutes until I could be sure they'd got into Milo's flat. Pushing myself up from the chair by my arms, I clambered to my feet. Sitting still so long had made me feel stiff, so I held onto the back of the armchair and shook my legs a bit, getting the blood flowing and that.

When I was ready, I walked as slowly as I could through to the canteen and kitchen. Being so long in the dark had made my eyes sensitive and I was easily guided by the light coming in through the windows. Milo must have had every light in his rooms blazing.

I was hoping to find that jacket I'd heard unzipping. Or possibly a bag.

There was nothing in the canteen; instead a black leather jacket, the kind only men used to wear in my day, was dumped in a bundle on a kitchen counter.

Hopefully, if there hadn't been a bag, I was in luck.

I lifted it gently, but still the zip pull made a scratching sound as I took it off the surface. I thought I would be safe, though, as Milo and Lily had put music on next door. I could hear the bass beats buzzing through the wall.

My fingers aren't quick any more. They are swollen with time, but after several attempts I managed to unzip every pocket until I felt the cold touch of metal. She'd left her keys in the jacket. It was just what I'd hoped.

Putting the jacket back down on the counter, I walked closer to the kitchen door, listening for sounds. They'd still be eating, I hoped, but I had to be sure they weren't about to come back for more of something. I could hear nothing but the music, so taking a grip on the door handle, I whispered, 'Here we go, Fran, wish me luck,' and opened the door into the hallway.

The lights were blazing. I should have seen them under the door, but I'd forgotten I'd been in the darkness so long and for a moment I stood still, blinking my way back to sight.

When I could finally see again, I walked down towards Tasty's office, moving fast but quiet past Milo's door. Tasty's office wasn't far from Milo's rooms, so I'd have to be quick with the keys, but there were several of them on the ring and I'd have to work my way through them, trying them one by one.

The lock on the office door was quite clearly for a latchkey – there was no heavy keyhole, so that ruled out a few of the keys. After trying the brass one, and then the silver one, I struck lucky with the dirty-looking key, which slid easily into the lock and opened in one clean turn to the right. Taking one final look over my shoulder, I pulled at the door, removed the key and slid into the room, closing the door quietly behind me.

I stood by the door for some minutes, catching my breath. I felt relatively safe away from the corridor and needed to collect myself. There was still much to be done. Given this was a planned operation, I'd not thought this part through. Here I was in Tasty's office without a torch. I'd have to put on a light. So first things first, I needed to close the curtains.

I didn't spend much time looking out of the windows onto the front lawn, flowerbeds and driveway, but the view from Tasty's office seemed different, unfamiliar. I peered out, saw no one, and drew the curtains shut. They weren't heavy enough to block out any light coming from the room, but they would mask it and that would have to do. I wouldn't be able to find anything in the dark.

With the curtains closed the room was hard to navigate. I pushed my hands out far in front and slid my feet slowly ahead of me in wide arcs, looking for furniture. When I found Tasty's desk, it didn't take long to locate the desk lamp and cast some light into the room.

I was still moving very slowly, listening and trying to keep my breathing quiet. I was terrified of being found in the room. But so far, so good. I could still hear Milo's music and nothing else.

The lamp created a pool of intense light on the desk that shaded the rest of the room in an orange-purple glow, like a London night sky. There were filing cabinets all along the wall facing the window. The first few I tried weren't locked. Opening them quietly was not easy, especially when I knew that Milo and Lily were through the wall. I could only hope they were up to something more exciting.

The files in the open cabinets were what I expected: invoices and bills for cleaning products, stationery, the furnace equipment, heating, telephones etc. It all looked legitimate. The second open cabinet had clients' names, next of kin details, invoices and expenses related to them and payment details. Their dates of arrival were noted alongside their leaving dates. This was where I started to notice something a little odd. Several of the names in this cabinet were still active, accounts were still being drawn up; to all intents and purposes they hadn't left, but I knew this couldn't be right because I'd checked. The only client in the home was the old lady. There was no one else. The only male client I'd ever known had died months ago.

I stood by the open cabinet and rested my hands on the metal edges, bending forwards and letting the blood rush back to my head. I felt very alone. How could this level of fraud go unnoticed? She hadn't even bothered to lock the filing cabinets.

Once I'd got myself back under control, I slid the drawer shut, walked back to Tasty's desk and sat in her swivel chair to think. Either I had to copy these names and dates down, or I had to photograph them, or I had to just call in the police and hope they'd follow it through. There was also the matter of the locked filing cabinets. If several of these clients were meant to still be living here, what had happened to them? Where had they gone? I put my hands firmly on my knees and turned the chair from left to right, searching the room, trying to gain back some sense of control.

Of course. It was the most logical place. In the desk itself was another set of drawers. I remembered

Fran used to keep the office filing keys in the top drawer of her desk. The drawers were locked.

I looked about the desk. She could carry them around with her – that would be the safest option – but people don't think like that. Tasty didn't strike me as a woman terrified of discovery; come to think of it, her dress sense was more like a display of wealth than anything else. Those bloody heels probably cost a fortune.

No. Like the way people hide keys under doorsteps, or mats or flowerpots and that, I was certain that Tasty would hide her keys somewhere on her desk. Possibly in a desk tidy. No. Or underneath it. Yes. A small metal key was hidden beneath the pen holder to the right of her computer.

One key.

The first place I tried turned out to be the right place. It opened the desk drawers. I was just getting ready to leaf through when the music from next door stopped abruptly. I switched off the desk lamp and sat as still as possible. I didn't think I'd been banging about, but …

After several minutes of waiting – I couldn't tell because I couldn't see my watch, it could have three, it could have been twenty – I realised the music had not stopped on my account. I hadn't heard Milo's door or footsteps. In fact, I'd heard nothing.

Carefully, I switched the lamp back on and got back to the top drawer. As predicted, there were another two keys, probably for the locked filing cabinets.

I got slowly to my feet and tiptoed back to the cabinets, slipping the keys into locks until I'd married them correctly.

Inside the first two drawers of the first locked

cabinet were reports and brochures updated to reflect each report's findings. I couldn't see why these had been locked. As far as I could see, they confirmed everything the previous files had stated. Health and safety checks, regulations, all of it matched the numbers of clients Tasty was claiming for and only ever suggested standard improvements, like new carpets or a review of the ventilation system. I knew I was probably missing something here. I did notice that the same name cropped up a few times, signing off the reports, but it wasn't always the same.

Inside the second three drawers I found something that baffled me at first. Filed in months, the lower three drawers contained scheduling information, spreadsheets with lists of names and conditions of health. Phrases like, 'Heart – good condition, awaiting order' were common. When there was a marked deterioration in health, the columns read, 'immediate dispatch only'.

I opened the second locked cabinet hoping to find something to make sense of all this. It was clear something very wrong was going on.

Inside this cabinet things were made clearer still. Though there were no names, only dates, inside these drawers were files of orders, invoices, despatch dates and so on of hundreds and hundreds of different body parts. And I don't just mean hearts, I mean bits of skin and teeth and even hair and nails.

The company they dealt with was called OrganoMed.

I put the files back in the drawers, locked them and sat back down at Tasty's desk. Working while I thought, I replaced all the keys and switched off the light. Then I folded my arms on the desk and let my head rest against them. Typically, Tasty had one of those desks with a leather inlay; cold at first, the leather gradually heated to my body temperature, soothing me. I didn't know what to think. All these months I'd been working for people who not only cheated ordinary folk of their money, but went on to desecrate the bodies of their loved ones, sold off piece by piece, the evidence burned in that bloody incinerator. I couldn't bear to imagine what they would have done with Fran. What they might do to the old woman. And how much did they all know? Was I the only one not in on it? Suddenly so many things made sense. An old man like me, with a sick wife, was just who you wanted to employ. I'd gone all these months without even thinking about how quiet it was, how few clients they seemed to have and how many visitors.

A loud thud from next door knocked me back to attention. It was followed by loud laughter, Lily's. Whatever I did next, I had to try and get out of here. These people were not the people I thought they were. The place was run by monsters. Who knew what they would do to me if they found me here, stealing keys and snooping into files?

I waited for the laughter to die down, reopened the curtains and felt my way to the door. It was easier to move about the room now, lights coming in from outside. I must have been in there for hours. I'd have to hurry. Dawn was drawing on.

I put my ear to the door and listened for a few moments. I couldn't hear anything. There was nothing for it, I'd have to make a run for it.

I turned the lock, opened the door and stepped through into the corridor, pulling the door closed as quietly as possible. There was no time to waste. I could hear Lily and Milo's voices. If it was later than I thought, Lily would be through that door any minute.

I rushed past Milo's door and into the kitchen, the door making a nasty clicking sound – I pushed it before the handle was fully turned. I didn't quite leap, but I moved faster than I had in a long time getting in behind that kitchen door.

This time I had been too noisy. I could hear Milo's door open, Lily talking at his door. Footsteps would soon follow. There was just no time. I dropped Lily's keys onto her jacket – it would take too long to replace them in the pocket – and ran through the canteen into the big armchair and sank into it, pulling my feet up off the floor. It was too light now to risk leaving my feet on the floor, in case they could see them under the chair.

My feet had just lifted as the kitchen door opened wide, banging against the wall. The force of it shook Lily's keys loose and they fell loudly to the floor.

There was silence for a moment. The door hadn't yet closed. Whoever it was was standing there at the kitchen door. Why weren't they moving? Had they heard something?

Then I caught it. Gently, under her breath, Lily was crying. She sniffed a couple of times and then scraped the jacket off the counter, swiping the keys from the floor, and left, letting the kitchen door slam behind her.

I let trapped air sigh out of my throat. But midway through the sigh, Lily was back. Pushing the door hard again, her coat was thrown down somewhere as loud echoing retches filled the kitchen. Lily was throwing up in the sink. When she was finished, she ran the taps, spat a few times, picked up her coat again and left.

This time I waited for a few minutes, waiting for someone else to come in. No one did. The day room was now full of morning light. I could read the wall clock with no trouble. Five o'clock. In an hour I could legitimately get up and go back to work. In the meantime, I decided I would sit in the chair and plan what I was going to say to the police.

I went out through the kitchen door at six o'clock. I had my mobile in the shed.

When I finally got through to the police, all my preparation was for nothing. I couldn't order my thoughts and it all came out in a jumble.

'Yes, how can I help?' the voice said.

'I'd like to report Home Comforts Care on Mare Street.'

'The care home?'

'Yes.' I waited nervously. I could hear the officer on the line tapping at a keyboard.

'Your name, sir?'

'Stephen Green. I'm the caretaker here. I've seen it all. Please, you have to come quickly. I don't know what they'll do when they find me out. Please.'

'Okay.' The officer's voice was very calm. 'What do you want to report?'

'You need to go there, get a warrant. They're doing terrible things, cutting people up, selling body parts. They have a morgue and an incinerator.' It all rushed out of me, the whole list of horrors. 'And there are photographs, such terrible photographs – real people treated like dummies.'

'Calm down, sir. What exactly are you accusing the home of?'

'Fraud and maltreatment and murder. There's only one client in the home, but there are loads in the files.

You need to get into the office files.'

The officer sighed. 'These are very serious allegations, Mr Green. Do you have evidence?'

'That's why I need you to come. Please. You need a warrant to check the files and you should bring a doctor.' I started to cough. It was all getting too much.

'All right, Mr Green, take it easy. We will follow up your call.'

'Today? You need to come as soon as possible.'

'Allegations of this magnitude have to be looked into as soon as possible, Mr Green.'

I gave my address and the call ended with a crime reference number.

I felt completely exhausted, faint. I slumped into the chair in the shed, allowing my eyes to close. I was terrified and relieved and realised I'd need something to get me home. I put the kettle on and sat for a few moments in my chair, drinking coffee and looking out over the garden. I should have run.

The heat of the mug and warmth of the coffee were comforting. Without realising it, I must have drifted off. I woke with a start. Squirrels were running over the roof of the shed. It was nine o'clock.

Though I felt better for the nap, I was still a little groggy and I'd wasted a lot of time. I left the unfinished coffee on the work surface and grabbed my bag, Fran's picture safely inside. I had one more thing to do before I left. Just one important goodbye.

I went back in through the kitchen door. I didn't see much need for pretence any longer – I'd given my name when I reported them – so I just got straight in the lift and went on up to the first floor and the old woman's room. She was sleeping. I walked over to her bed, bent down and gently kissed her forehead.

She didn't wake up.

'I've done my best,' I whispered. 'I've done my best.'

I gently touched her cheek, hoping I'd done enough, and left. She didn't even stir.

The corridor was empty. I would soon be back outside the home and on my way to my real home.

I went back down in the lift, zipping up my jacket for the cold. I was almost at the entrance hall when Sour-grapes called me back.

'Steve,' she said. 'Mrs Tace would like a word with you in her office.'

'Can't stop, Sarah, I'm afraid,' I said. 'Got to get on.'

'You'll come to Mrs Tace's office, Steve.'

Well, I thought, no harm in it really. What could happen?

I was such an old fool.

Tasty was sitting on her desk, the doctor on her swivel chair behind her. She picked up her telephone and dialled a number she'd jotted on a yellow sticky.

'Hello, inspector, it's Mrs Tace calling you back. I've got the doctor for you.'

She handed the phone to the doctor.

'Sorry for all this bother, inspector,' the doctor said. 'Occasionally, we have a client like this. It's unusual for us, but, well, you can't always tell how dementia will progress. I'm afraid Mr Green has started to have some rather wild delusions.'

He paused.

'Yes, yes, of course. I think Mrs Tace has faxed through our recent inspection report?' Another pause. 'Quite right. If you send someone over later today, you can come and see the client. I'm sorry to say, you won't get a lot of sense from him.' I heard the inspector's voice speak for a few moments, but couldn't make out the words. 'Fine. Anytime this afternoon is fine. It's my home check-up day, so I'll be here with Mrs Tace should you need to ask any questions. ... Excellent. ... Yes. ... Goodbye.' The doctor put the phone down.

They all stared at me and I stared back.

Tasty nodded at Sour-grapes and before I could think to do anything, I felt a sharp jab in my upper arm.

That is the last thing I remember before this bed. I am in a room at the home, my arm is connected to a drip.

They say it comes to us all. They sit on the edge of your bed and nod and smile and talk loudly and slow.

You tell them everything, everything you've seen, all the details. They sigh and shake their heads, but nothing happens.

They pat your arm. They wave goodbye at the door. They do their best not to look you in the eye.

Woman – IV

I remembered something the other day. Nothing grand, but a little flicker of something.

The male nurse was washing me, if you can really call it that. He had a bowl of lukewarm water and he wiped me down with a cloth, shoving its edges in between folds of flesh, carefully avoiding the area around the stoma that is definitely infected now. Not seriously, I hear them saying. They have to swab it down with medicated wipes and I'll be on antibiotics if they don't do it more often, but, you see, they do try.

He wasn't paying very much attention to me. It has been a while since anyone washed me, so of course the cloth was coming away darkened with a smear of flaking dead skin, just like the dirt that collects beneath uncleaned fingernails.

As he wiped, rubbing the cloth thoroughly in the water between each stroke, the sunlight shone through his dark hair. He kept pushing it back behind his ears, but out it would spring again, thick with a lick of a curl.

His hands are long and thin, the skin curiously pale beneath their olive gleam. His eyes are wide-set and elegant beside his charming angular nose. The width and height of his cheekbones give him a square, broad face that tapers slightly towards the chin. His mouth is a little cherry, lost inside a big frame. I find him especially attractive when he doesn't talk, when he is absorbed as he was then. The moment he engages with my presence, his features twist and revolt me, but like that, pushing back his hair, sliding the wet cloth between my shoulder blades and along my inner thighs, he is beautiful.

The memory came from a tickle of unintentional touch. The ragged end of the cloth trailed beneath his hand as he moved from my hip to the bowl. Its edges glanced over my pubic hairs, gently disturbing their languor. I had been looking behind him, out of the window, but this sensation made me turn towards him. The hairs on his arm formed a halo of colour against the sun. His arm was so long and bony, the fingers dextrous, broad-knuckled, their nails round and flat. I felt something stir, a tiny grain of desire turn and grow. My thighs twitched slightly, pleasure arching down my back towards my groin.

He didn't seem to notice. He began to hum under his breath. They were foreign words, a tune with the trilling wail of a different culture. And it was then I remembered making love to a man called Anton. A tiny name without a face that heightened my longing for movement. The desire reminded me that masturbation was one of those things I used to indulge in. A book in one hand, my crotch in the other, like one of those eighteenth-century paintings depicting the dangers involved in giving women access to novels. I can see one painting in particular.

Did I study painting, perhaps? The woman is lying in a park with trees and a country house in the distance. She wears a pink dress with white lace trimmings, the skirt cut from a line below the bust. The sleeves trail over her hands. She holds a book with her left hand and her right casually rests between her thighs, the cloth of the dress rucked slightly underneath it. I used to think I was like her.

It's an accomplishment, this memory. I have remembered a secret part of myself that cannot be taken away because I never revealed it. There is strength in that.

It is growing hot. It changes the sound of things. I don't remember noticing this before, but heat puffs up the air, widening noises, softening them almost, like clouds of warm breath. But for the occasional shout, a squeal of delight from a child, a car horn, and of course the beat of music from open-topped cars, the street sounds muffled and slow, as if I'm hearing it underwater. Perhaps the people have gone. Summer means holidays.

My arms ache terribly. I don't remember having medicine in days and it makes everything seem dry. I'm thirsty and my head pounds.

Joe came a couple of days ago, or at least it seems like only a few days ago. It was hot then too. His sister wasn't there. She was at a party, the other Mrs Eames said.

I like it when the nurses say her name. I wonder how many Mrs Eameses there are. Names are funny like that, cloning people indiscriminately. This Mrs Eames spent most of the visit by the window, clawing at the shirt sticking to her chest. The heat had made her hair damp against her head, so she opened the window and put a chair in front of it, letting the breeze blow over her. She just wilted there, distracted and exhausted, her bony limbs collapsed over the chair. She renounced all responsibility for the visit. She let Joe do it by himself. I suppose being there was enough: she could now tick me off her list. I let my eyes linger over her scrawny chest, thinking about the energy she seemed to invest in life, and then I forgot her. She didn't even seem to observe Joe and me. It was most unlike her. When she finally did stir, jolting upright, to take Joe and collect Amy from the party, she explained it all. 'I'm so sorry I've been so tired today,' she said. 'You see, I came, really, just to let you know I'm pregnant again.' She smiled weakly. 'Something for us all to look forward to.'

I can't say I will, though, look forward to it that is. I pitied her. Looking at her there, one hand on her stomach, now noticeably swollen, her other arm calling out to Joe, I felt a moment of connection: she is what others make of her. Joe moved in under her wing and I watched them leave. He gave a little wave at the door and then they were gone. She had forgotten to close the window and as the day drew on it grew colder. The blowing wind made the room feel like an empty shell.

But, back, before all that, it was as if Joe had come to visit me on his own and he brought something important. With his mother collapsed in her chair, Joe pulled a creased photograph from a pocket in his combats.

'I've got you a present, Granny. It's a picture of you.'

He leant over the bed and held the photograph over my eyes. I had to frown to bring it into focus. It was easier to see as he pulled away. I think I used to have reading glasses.

The photograph was a sepia shot of a young woman, her hair set elegantly back from her forehead, looking up into the face of a young man. They were holding hands. The woman was pulling down on the man's arm so that her upper body could twist into his. She wore a knee-length dress with puffy sleeves and she was smiling, her cheeks full and high with happiness and youth. Underneath her chin, between her shoulders and his neck, there was a glint of sunlight. They stood in front of a tree in what looked like someone's back garden.

I couldn't honestly say if this woman was me. I could see she was excited. The man whose face she smiled up into was wearing a loose-fitting suit, his free hand in the pocket of his trousers. He looked out at the camera, his expression composed, ready for its gaze. He was proprietary somehow, proud, and handsome in an awkward way. He had the air of a boy trying to be a man.

'That's you,' Joe said pointing at the woman, 'and that's Grandpa.'

Surely I would remember such a handsome man, but I don't. I feel the glint of sunshine warming them, I feel the rustle of the leaves in the trees behind them, but their faces are blank, masks with dark holes for eyes.

I smiled at Joe.

'You can keep it,' he said, propping it up on the side table. Then he launched into a long monologue about his latest video game and playing football at school.

The photograph isn't there any more. Maybe the wind from the open window blew it to the floor, I don't know. I think someone took it away. I want to see it again. I've been dreaming of a sunny day in the garden of that photograph. The light shimmers through the moving leaves of the tree, making mottled patterns over the bare skin across my shins. I reach up and grasp one side of a rope swing. I run my fingers around its thick, grey knots, and twist down onto the swing, my skirt flaring out around the knee. I kick out at the ground, starting myself off. Then I move through the air, from the shadow into the light and back. The wind pushes against my face so that my hair falls from its combs, the curls blowing into and away from my face with the movement of the swing. When I lie back, I sway over the thin patch of grass where people's feet have worn mud across its growth. I shut my eyes and fly backwards and forwards, my stomach struggling to keep pace, making sickness and excitement meet around my waist.

I think I am alone. It feels so blissful hanging in the air. It is carefree solitude, no need to play up to anyone, no need to save face. I dance guiltless on the wind, back and forth and back again.

Then, suddenly, I feel a shadow draw in. Though my eyes are still shut everything feels darker. Something stands between me and the sun. It startles me. I open my eyes and see a man by the swing, standing just to the right so that my legs almost touch his cheek when I move forwards. I look at the man, searching for some connection, trying to work out why he is in the garden, whose friend he is. I lose momentum, my feet kicking out with less vigour at each swing, in order to look at him more carefully. I seek out the expression on his face, but the eyes beneath the flopping fringe are blank. I stare into the blackness of his empty face and wake up screaming.

I've had that dream more than once. One time I was so afraid it took me a while to remember where I was. Looking from one wall to another, hoping for something familiar, there was nothing but blank space. I held my mouth open, the scream long since silent but its feeling no less real. I squeezed my eyes tight shut again, pushing pressure into my face, forcing blood at my panic, until the door clicked. It was the woman from the 'day room'. I had no trouble recollecting her.

'I'm sorry to disturb you,' she said, slipping in behind the door like a fugitive. 'I heard a noise and I wondered if everything was all right.'

She smiled at me, timidly tiptoeing towards the bed.

'You remember me, don't you?' she paused, frowning slightly, peering at me over the edges of her glasses. 'I met you in the day room, when we were visiting my father-in-law. Do you remember? I thought I'd met you before.'

I tried to smile at her, but I was wary. None of my other visitors had sneaked in like this. Spotty always led the way, her brash remarks forming some kind of bond with reality. This woman's visit felt surreal. She was so intent on looking at me that she seemed to bend towards me, her face much larger than her frame. It was unnerving.

'You can't talk then,' she said, retracting her head a little. She opened the clasp of her handbag and took out a yellow cleaning cloth. She removed her glasses and wiped them as she spoke. 'I'm sorry about that. I would like to be able to talk to you. You are just so familiar, you see.' She placed the glasses back on her nose, twisting the wire a little behind her ears. 'I could swear I knew you. Your face seems so ...' She frowned again. 'Well, I'm a little senile myself, I suppose. No reason to rely on the old grey cells these days.'

She walked closer to the bed. She was well kept. Her hair cut in a careful bob, its edges dried inwards so that the tips couldn't hit her shoulders and flick upwards. She was dressed smartly in a fitted trouser suit. And yet, despite all these efforts at glamour, there was a casual, disinterested feel to her appearance, as if she did this for someone else. Her shoes were flat slip-ons, comfortable and somehow unsuited to the outfit. There was the tiniest line of beige sock visible between the ends of her trousers and beginnings of her shoes. It made the outfit look borrowed, or perhaps barely worn best.

She was staring at me, her whole face drawn into one extravagant expression of confusion: brows knit, lips folding in, nostrils tight, eyes narrow.

'Who do you remind me of, I wonder?'

I stared back up at her.

'Funny how we all grow so alike.' She looked down at her hands as she spoke, slowly stroking the skin that hung loose over her knuckles. 'There is a tiny window of time, our middle age perhaps, when we really look like distinct individuals, but at either end we merge into one another, don't we? Our skin is either too plump and smooth with youth or too tired, discoloured and loose.' She sighed and looked for a moment at the window. I could see bright squares of light reflected in her glasses. Sighing again, she turned back to me, her face warming into a smile. She leaned in over the bed.

'You look just like my father-in-law did. Hollowed out like a rabbit in headlights.' She shook her head. 'It's probably for the best he's passed away. He wasn't half the man he used to be. Barely recognisable.'

She raised her eyebrows and let the corners of her mouth fall in defeat.

'Well, you seem all right. I thought I heard a kind of groaning noise. I probably imagined it.' She paused. 'I expect my husband is beginning to wonder where I am. He gets so embarrassed when I wander off.' She sighed.

'So this is it. The last time we'll come here.' She looked up from the bed and along each of the walls, taking in the ugly curtains and lino. 'It's a pretty miserable place. Still, we can't complain. I did offer to have Bill at home with us, but my husband wouldn't hear of it. It's the price you pay, I suppose, handing the responsibility over.'

Her eyes, looking towards the back wall, had shifted focus to a point far beyond the room. Then, as if the cogs of her mind had slowly turned around the wheel of whatever thoughts she was following, she turned her head and looked back down at me with a renewed sense of purpose.

'So,' she smiled at me again, 'as it's our last visit, this is goodbye. I hope you won't mind me popping in for a moment. I expect you can never have enough visitors.'

I tried to make my eyes plead at her. Damn it, for the first time in a long while I truly wished I was capable of more.

She frowned again.

'You know,' she said, 'if I didn't know she was gone already, I'd say you were a dead ringer for my old friend Katherine. I knew you reminded me of someone. Yes, it's quite uncanny.'

She reached out and touched the edge of the bed,

smoothing down the sheets as if it were essential she sort them out. Her eyes followed her hand, thinking of something else.

'She was a dear friend, Katherine.'

She tugged at the sheet until it was perfectly flattened and tucked tight around the mattress. I could imagine her making beds with hospital corners. Her neatness seemed so studied, as if she'd painstakingly learnt to be precise. Her considered gaze returned to me again.

'Can I do something for you? Would you like some water?'

I smiled my squinty, barely moving smile again and she filled a glass with water, held one arm behind my head, nudging me upright, and one hand around the glass, pouring the water slowly into my mouth. She had to climb onto the bed to do it. She smelt faintly of mothballs, her arms around me so gently.

They won't let anyone do this. I could choke, or so they say. The bit that blocks off my airway isn't working properly, apparently. The water might run into my lungs. This woman couldn't know that they put the water there for the visitors, or if she did know, she didn't seem to care, and I must say the water felt good sliding down my throat, cool and soft around the tube.

She eased my head and neck back onto the pillow.

'There,' she said, 'better?'

She made me want to cry. I felt my face grow hot, blotches of colour flushing to my cheeks. Outside the room we heard the lift doors shunt open. A trolley was being pushed out over the bump between the lift and the tiled floor, things rattling on its metal surface. The woman looked up, suddenly nervous. I didn't want her to go.

'I'd best be off,' she said, turning back to me and smiling with her head cocked a little to one side. She opened her handbag again and came away with that same yellow cloth. She rubbed her glasses, replaced the cloth, shut the clasp of her handbag and stood up. She tiptoed to the door, peered through the keyhole and, reassured of a clear exit, turned back, smiled, held up a hand and said, 'Goodbye, dear. Good luck.'

I watched her close the door behind her. I was jealous of Katherine. I wished the lady could be my friend.

Since her visit, I've been thinking about her father-in-law and whatever I have felt about dying out of spite shrivels and curls like plastic in a fire. When faced with death, I still want life, however precarious or infirm. That word sums it up: infirm. I try to work out who I am, but it's like building a house on the sand. The foundations slide and tear the walls apart, roof tiles crashing around me.

I think that's why they removed the photograph. They don't want me to have solid evidence to build on. They remove everything personal that gets left in the room. But it doesn't matter. I dwell on the photograph more in its absence. I turn it about in my head and if they aren't careful it will become a memory anyway, even if only a fake one. Burn the neural pathways too often and the image will feel real, it will thicken with the burden of time. They really are an ignorant lot, Spotty and the other one. I'm quiet but I'm not stupid. It's infuriating that people think they mean one and the same thing. They think because I don't speak, I don't hear. In a way it is a small mercy. They talk over me, their words scraps of the puzzle that makes up this place.

The nurses woke me the other day. I was dreaming about walking up some stairs to a flat. I could hear someone moving above me on the doorstep, shifting from foot to foot, and just as they were about to come into the light, Spotty pulled open my right eyelid, and then my left.

'Her pupils seem to be dilating.'

I let my eyelids fall closed, deciding to pretend to remain asleep, though I'm not sure it would have been very convincing if they had thought about it. They must have assumed I was unconscious.

With my eyes shut I could hear Spotty scratching a pen on paper.

'Seven days, no obvious side effects. Let's check through the list.'

Cold fingers pulled back the sheets.

'What am I looking for?' It was the male nurse.

'Let's see,' Spotty paused, ruffling papers, 'Hair loss, discoloration of skin, impeded healing – so let's get another look at her stoma and the swelling around her nose – malodorous discharge, increased drowsiness – though we can't really account for that.'

The male nurse started to untie my nightdress. It does up with little bows along each side, making it easier to clean me and empty my bags. He pressed his fingers into my skin, kneading at wasted muscles, feeling for something.

'When are they coming in?'

'Some time tomorrow. I've got everything ready. All her possessions are in a little box. The mother kicked up a real fuss about the photograph. Something about sentimental significance. If they cared that much, you'd think they would notice.'

'You cannot blame them,' the male nurse said,

prising my legs apart. The breath from his lungs tickled my thighs. 'They trust us.'

He ran a finger across my pubis.

'Look at this,' he said, 'fallen out.'

'God,' Spotty said, 'you'd better check the rest of her.'

'Looks weird, eh? Like plucked chicken force fed on GM corn.'

Spotty laughed. 'You're sick, you know?'

'No sicker than woman who visits mother-in-law behind husband's back.'

He ran his hands underneath my armpits.

'None here either,' he said.

'And her head?'

'Looks all right.' He combed a hand through my hair. It felt satisfying, like working out knots. 'Fuck,' he said, 'is coming out.'

'Right,' Spotty said, making more scribbles with her pen. 'You'd better check the stoma. I think we're going to have to keep her case open longer.'

My case? The male nurse ripped the plaster from the skin around the stoma. It made a sound like Velcro, unnatural and sharp.

'You'd better look,' he said.

I could feel them both leaning in. The orange light I'd seen filtered through the skin of my eyelids was blackened by their shadows.

'We'll have to get the doctor in,' Spotty said. 'Take her off the drug immediately.'

'Doctor won't like it,' the male nurse said.

'There's nothing he can do. Does he want her healthy or not?' She sighed. 'You'd better clean that up.'

The male nurse moved away. I heard him looking for something on their metal trolley. Then he was back, an antiseptic wipe stinging around my stoma.

'Who are they seeing tomorrow?' he said, pressing the cloth hard against my skin.

'No one. She doesn't want the kids to see.' Spotty sighed. 'Anyway, does it matter? The funeral home will have someone if necessary. It's just another old lady.'

They worked in silence then for a time, cleaning me up, dressing my wounds. And the drip bag was changed, a new cooler liquid flowing up my veins. I no longer had any hair. No hair at all. I felt cold, even when the male nurse had tied my nightie back on and put back the covers. I was so totally naked and exposed. And they had taken my photograph. They'd put it in a box with other things and Joe would come and collect it. Would I see him then? I looked forward to his visits. Perhaps I would be able to communicate with the doctor. Surely he would want to find out how I felt and wait patiently for me to blink at him? I could trust the doctor, couldn't I?

Milos – IV

I don't know how Ana and I fell apart. How things went wrong. The mother of my Jelena turning against me. It's true she pisses me off. She has a narrow view of the world, living day to day, with no real ambition. She does not understand me. But still I love her. Nothing can change that. Hate and love for another can live together in one person. I will never desert her, not fully, and she knows that. She hangs around the edges of my life, waiting for me to turn back to her. She has Jelena. She holds the promise of a real family, of me as a loving father, and the pull is too great.

I will go back one day. This waiting, this collating, the dream of a real career, of pictures in magazines, newspapers, of exhibitions, this is what holds me back. I do not want to go back and do hack work that gets nowhere beyond the capital city. This is where international recognition is possible. Ana thinks it's a joke, that I sacrifice happiness for a pipedream. That I live here in this warren of a care home selling my soul for nothing. It doesn't matter how much I talk about reincarnation, about drugs and cosmetics tested and approved, for Ana, I am a grave robber; I am guilty of seeing old people as the other, like the other of race or nation, like the other of war. It doesn't matter that for me they are dead already, that for me it is not murder but euthanasia, not cruel but kind to rid them of their empty loveless lives and put their bodies to better use. She says I play God. Says I represent the kind of people who started the war, that I am a machine of greed. And after all this, still she wants me back. She wants me back to poke and needle, to nag and mould and remonstrate and love.

I cannot hope to understand her.

The promises and tricks I use on Ana are easily repeated on Lily. It is not that I lie exactly, more that I evade certain topics. I tell her that Ana is being difficult about divorce. I tell her that it will take time. She'll have to be patient. And there is Jelena. I have to have custody of Jelena. When I say that, I always try to look distant, upset, and Lily seems to accept it. She will wait for me. She is more naïve than she thinks. Every day she seems more at ease. When she goes for a shit, she no longer closes the door.

In the meantime, I change the focus of my photographs. I make the time and place clear. It's not easy to get access to the records, but I shoot them when I can. Soon I will have enough evidence to safeguard my escape. And as I gather the evidence, I keep adding to my personal collection. I keep fucking Lily and calling my wife and sending home extra money made from the tissue trade. There is a rhyming kind of reason guiding my life.

The strange thing about my new photographs is that they require me to do much more sneaking around and somehow that seems to walk me straight into Steve. I find him mopping the corridor just outside of Alexa's office, or sweeping the stairs leading down to the morgue and furnace. He looks pale, withdrawn almost. He still whistles, but it sounds different, as if he has started it midway through the tune. You turn a corner and the whistling hits you. Was he whistling before? It's hard to say, hard to pin down.

We do not smoke together any more.

'I have to go slower,' he told me. 'My back, you see. Can't take breaks like before.'

This seems reasonable enough, but something about the shifting of his eyes makes me wonder what is really going on, why he avoids me. Maybe it's as simple as knowing about Lily. Though I would have thought he might wink at me for that. I've seen him ogling the *Sun* on the fire escape, drinking from his flask. He's an old-fashioned, working Englishman who likes blondes with big tits. Can't say I blame him. Steve is a good man. It's a shame we don't smoke together any more. Especially now the weather is getting so hot – breaks seem the best part of the day, I'm sad not to share them. The air on your face, the smell of the garden, fresh coffee, anything to take away the heavy gelid atmosphere inside the home, where the heat makes everything stink. When visitors come, they crank up the radiators and there is no escaping the stench of urine and decay. I smelt it on my mother the last time I went home, a faint hint of it on her breath. It made me want to weep, like I could smell her insides dying.

Today the heat is stifling. Alexa called a meeting to inform us that the old woman will go soon. As she spoke, she had to keep flapping her hand around her face. There was a fly buzzing round her office, landing on her hair, tickling her forehead, probably attracted to all that salt. I am fed up of this place. I will be happy if this old woman is my last. I'm tired of it all. Tired of Lily, so often there, making me more lonely than when I am alone. Tired of Sarah, cleverly offloading work on me with a knowing smile. And tired of Alexa, pushing out her breasts at me, unaware that I am fucking her daughter. I've made my own labyrinth, every woman a wrong turn, a dead end that blocks my way out, and I've become Rip van Winkle, bound to turn into an old man upon whom they will prey, tearing my guts out for OrganoMed. Shit, I have a sick mind. Ana is right about all this. Ana, what have I done?

I go alone to the garden door of the kitchen. Alone I lean against the frame and smoke. Thick, heavy gusts of tobacco rushing down my throat, into my lungs and out through my lips and nostrils like a man in a film. I can imagine how it would look, smoke meeting and curling above my upper lip, like three joining tornados, mysterious and ugly all at the same time. It's unsatisfying smoking in the heat. I have always preferred to smoke in cold weather – in the heat one's addiction is so much balder. Hi, I am a smoker, see me polluting in the sunshine. It's no good, everything seems burnt and twisted today. It has been so hot recently that the grass has gone yellow and brown patches of earth have appeared, even though no one ever walks in the garden but Steve.

There is a hose ban. I remember last year Steve would stay late to set off sprinklers after dark. Not this year. Maybe he stays late, I don't know, but not in the garden. From the window in my room, the garden remains empty of all but a build-up of dry, fallen petals that make the flowerbeds look like city gutters. It could be his back.

The noise from the road is faint, a gentle breathing of traffic with the odd car playing loud music whose bass fades in first and last, long before and after the notes or lyrics. There is occasional birdsong from dry branches of trees and bushes. It is so hot the air seems to muffle sound. I am glad of the shade the home provides. I would not want to tend a garden in this weather. I can barely lift my arm to smoke.

Sarah says Steve has been nosing around. She caught him with his head round the old woman's door only last week. It is suspicious that with all those rooms to choose from, he found an occupied one. He could have been checking every room. Empty bed after empty bed might make you suspicious. I didn't think he was the type for investigations, but something could have set him off. Whether it's his back or his curiosity, the quality of his work has suffered. As well as the shrivelled garden, the corridors are so tacky that the soles of your shoes stick for tiny moments to the ugly lino, and cobwebs are building up in the day room. The weather has caused freakish multitudes of flies that go unchecked through the home, buzzing their way into everything. Steve has done nothing to combat the flies.

Sarah says it is only a matter of time. Alexa won't put up with it for much longer.

I had a dreadful dream last night. The famous picture of the old woman, masked in her wheelchair, hovered in front of me. She was staring at me, black dots gleaming out through the holes in her mask, freezing me, my limbs stiff and useless, able to do nothing but look back. Almost without realising it, my eyes still fixed on those two black points, she seemed to glide to her feet, the black dots of her eyes getting closer and closer as she walked like swans swim, all movement under the surface out of sight, towards me. When I could smell her breath on my face, she peeled off the mask, and before her face was revealed I knew from the taste of the air from her lungs that this was my mother. With the mask came strings of flesh pulling off her skin like melted cheese. I woke and did not sleep again. I was too hot, too disturbed, and lay restlessly waiting for this stifling day to break with the dawn.

Taking the last drag on my cigarette, I decide to take the rest of the afternoon off. I can check up on the old people later. I will go into my room and sort photographs, waiting for the cool of evening to make moving palatable. In front of my work, at least, I can feel something of life is worthwhile.

Two weeks later, the weather is unrepentant. It's seven in the morning but already a fly hits against the glass of the window again and again, missing the open air that holds no relieving breeze. I am lying on my bed, tangled in a single white sheet that has knotted itself around my lower half. I have been awake for hours, thinking.

Yesterday, they got rid of Steve. He found out, Sarah said. He called the police. So they pretended he was a client with dementia and delusions and stuck a needle in him. They've got him in a bed upstairs. He is the new old man.

The policeman came in the afternoon. He found that what the doctor and Alexa said was true. He went away satisfied.

I think Sarah must have talked to Alexa about me

being friends with Steve. They haven't asked me to do ward rounds for him. Not yet, anyway. I'm not sure I could do it. Steve. Nice man, Steve, is in a bed somewhere above me. If he felt alone before, it will be nothing to the days spent with only a window for company. There isn't even a TV up there. That's what the day room is for. That is what we tell visitors.

It casts a whole new light on life here. Especially in the heat. He'll get terrible bedsores. I don't even have the urge to photograph him. It's what they say about farming, isn't it? If you name your animals, it's always harder to kill them. You have to remain unattached.

Though I haven't been asked to go up there yet, Steve's change in circumstances has left another job vacant; the cleaning has been added to my schedule. I am meant to share that responsibility with Sarah, but she gave me a hard, sharp look. It was clear I had no choice but to do her share. I did my first mop last night. It's easier in the cool, but I couldn't really see and now the floor is tackier than before. I didn't try the floor-polishing machine. Steve said it was tricky to handle, especially in hot weather. You almost have to lift it to steer. I can't imagine how he used to do it. He was tougher than he looked, old Steve. Smarter too. Just not smart enough.

I twist and pull until the sheet unsticks itself and I lie naked on the bed. I can picture Sarah's face when she called him in. My distaste for her has turned to distinct dislike. I detest her. She is a sly cunt. I wonder if I should go to the police, present my photographs as evidence, hang the risk. They couldn't claim I had dementia. They could say I was a party to what goes on here, but they couldn't lay all the blame on me. They'd have to come and search the files.

The fly finally finds the gap between window and sill and escapes out into the garden.

I don't want to go to prison, though. If it weren't for Steve, I couldn't care less about the old people they lock in here. No one cares about them. That is the whole point. At least here they are put to some use. No, if I want to escape like the fly, I need to threaten Alexa with incriminating photographs so she will fear me and let me alone. Maybe then I'll be able to put on an exhibition in some foreign gallery. Berlin is a good place to go now. Everyone talks about it. There will be no connection to this place and still the home will make me a famous photographer. I won't have to put up with living here much longer. They've planned a transfer for the old woman next week. If I can get pictures of the doctor, Sarah and Alexa performing surgery in the morgue, of men from OrganoMed, I'll be home free.

We are doing the transfer this afternoon – a new old woman for Katarina. It's a relentless business – 'managing the growing elderly population'. Lily says that. Probably Alexa's phrase. Lily will come over later when the old woman is in pieces and ready for trade. She will keep me company, if you can call it that. She cares even less than me, I think. It's not a happy thought. Part of me already hates her, in the way you can hate something that you desire and cannot escape. Our lovemaking grows harder, angrier, but she sees it as wild passion, not my desire to pummel, consume and destroy her. I fuck her with lustful frenzy, wishing for some manga-inspired eruption of my penis through her head, her mouth, her chest, cum and blood mixing in a climax that penetrates all these new orifices and leaves her a skewered, lifeless puppet; a fuck colander. But the silence of these thoughts means she imagines contented fulfilment and slowly over all these weeks she is growing plump with it.

I try to stop myself thinking these things. It does no good. I just have to keep on. Everything is carefully downloaded from the computer into albums, and digitally stored in all mediums available. I just have to get through today and tonight and in the morning I will quietly add the final files to a small bag already packed and I will leave. I will not say goodbye. I will just leave a letter on Alexa's desk, telling her not to try to find me. The letter will contain a photograph of her in the morgue. They will have to find a new live-in nurse to continue their dirty work.

It's early morning, too early for anyone else to be here yet – the kitchen, the whole of the home will be empty – so I get up and go to make coffee in my boxer shorts. When I leave here, I will miss the silent looming of such a large space. It's unlikely I will get it again, not soon. I open the back door and smoke, hot ash falling onto my naked torso, burning a few sparse dark hairs. When the coffee sounds I come back inside, smoke another cigarette, sipping scalding liquid between drags – all of me immersed in the heat of fag, coffee and sun. The caffeine and nicotine twist my anxiety about, leaving deep, fluttering knots in my stomach. I will not eat breakfast today.

Back in my room to dress, there are more flies. I pull on my scrubs to the sound of insect head-banging. They drive at the window several times in a row before pausing, each at different times rubbing their front legs like dogs licking wounds, and then get back to smacking their bodies against the glass again. When I am dressed I go and open the window wider, shooing them out into the back garden and away.

Upstairs, the old woman is barely lucid. I go into her room, pretending she is still our only client. I have been careful to avoid all contact with Steve. I go past his door assuring myself that it still stands empty. I will not look.

The old woman is a mess. Hair that was once died honey blonde now scratches coarse grey lines in a tangled mess on the pillow, like a bottlebrush. It has only just grown back since she reacted to some drug the doctor and Sarah tried on her. She has both gained and lost weight. Her muscles are wasted, but she is fatter, her flesh pooled at her sides, her breasts hanging under her armpits, the nipples almost touching midway along her upper arms. The infection around her stoma has cleared, but the skin is still rough and flaky. It looks like the cradle cap of a newborn. As I lift each limb and clean her back and front, I note the crimson bedsores, the calluses. I did this. I neglected her. I don't have the heart to photograph her now. It is a strange misgiving to have after all this time, but when I close my eyes I see the image of my mother from the dream, her flesh like melted cheese. And when I don't see my mother, I see Steve. I am glad this will be my last client.

It isn't that I feel regret, or guilt, or disgust, but instead an absence of feeling, and this deadness inside is hard and hungry, sucking at every shred of meaning. I am hollowing out, as if all my photographs have stolen my soul and not the souls of my subjects. Every shot has drained me, trapped me into a series of captured, frozen moments that I am unable to flick between – pieces of myself spread out, framed by white borders so that fragments can no longer bleed into each other. I am unaccountably afraid and fearless all at once because fear is not about the outside any more. It is what is within that terrifies me and threatens to unmask me.

For distraction, I sing, humming over forgotten lyrics. I am so caught in the tune that I clean her thoroughly for once. My hands work their way between her folds without thought. I do not notice the unfolding of time until the doctor interrupts me, opening the door with a firm, masculine hand. Sarah and Alexa are with him.

'For God's sake, Milo, cover her up. I know it's hot, but really, she can't take this sort of exposure.'

His outburst jolts me from my soothing world of song. I have been working on her for over an hour. She is definitely clean by now. I put the sponge back on the trolley and start to tie her nightdress back around her. She has opened her eyes. Probably woken by the sound of Alexa's heels.

'It's too late now, man. I need to get a look at her.' He leans in over her bed. 'Any progress?'

I undo the ties again and start to unwind the bandages from her face. Her nose has healed, though the break has left an unsightly bump, so even with reduced swelling her face looks botched, her eyes, nose and mouth jumbled into position, pulled from different places to create this Picasso of a woman: she is masked even without the bandage.

'Mmm-hmm,' he says, 'and the stoma?'

I pull up a flap of her nightdress. He snaps a glove over his right hand and prods at her, pulling at the dressing around the stoma.

'This all looks perfectly in order. Let's check

the internals.'

Alexa and Sarah say nothing. We all watch him as he starts to act out a bedside manner.

'If you feel any pain,' he says to the old woman, 'close your eyes. Alexa here will notify me.'

He turns round to Alexa and winks at her. Stony-faced, she obliges, moving closer to the head of the bed. I do not understand this little game. It seems unnecessarily cruel. The doctor starts to run his hand all over the old woman, tapping, pushing up beneath her ribcage, smiling down at Sarah, who is standing further away by the door.

The game ends with the examination. He starts to talk to Alexa as if the old woman had suddenly disappeared. Because I am not normally at these examinations, I wonder if he is always like this, pretending to be a proper doctor, pretending to care.

'Good,' he says. 'Well, Alexa, you'll be pleased to know I think she's doing fine. Everything's in order.'

As he continues to talk about prognostics and blood type, my mind drifts to the old woman on the bed. Her eyes are still open, looking pleadingly up at the doctor. I turn to look out of the window. I cannot help the smile that creeps across my face. Behind me, the doctor continues, bending down low over the old woman, talking directly at her. I do not hear what he says. I do not care. Instead, I see a young woman with a pushchair on the street below. A little blonde-haired girl is walking beside her, one hand clasped around the pushchair, pretending to steer. Even from here you can see she is headstrong. I miss my Jelena.

'Milo? Are you listening?'

I turn. It was Sarah who spoke. Something about her tone always cuts into my consciousness. It seems I have missed something important the doctor wanted to say.

'Bring her down for one o'clock, will you?' he says, pulling off the glove, talking at my chin. He is now standing in the doorway at the brink of the corridor. He passes the glove to Sarah, who tosses it onto my trolley. 'Okay?' he adds.

I nod. They all traipse out and I hear the doctor continue to talk to Alexa.

'We can have an early lunch. Will that suit you?'

Outside, the little girl has gone. I turn to the old woman. She has shut her eyes. It is hard to get used to her face unbandaged, but there is no point now in putting it all back. Roughly, I pull the sheets properly under her arms, collect my trolley and head out. The doctor's talk of lunch has made me hungry.

In the morgue, everything goes as planned. Shooting from my hip, I capture Alexa, the doctor and Sarah. As luck would have it we are all in there today. I capture the moment of each organ's removal as it is lifted out of the woman's living body.

'What the hell is wrong with you today, Milo? I can't hold this up forever.'

A series of decisive, defining, unequivocal moments photograph themselves. I am distracted. I am busy buying my freedom. When the time comes to bike the organs over, the speed of the ride is a release. Adrenaline finds a natural outpouring and our secret swap is also photographed, as if by someone else. The day is passing like a dream.

I return to the home, my helmet stored where moments before I had the old woman's organs, feeling the rush of air through my hair. Not caring about the dirt and dust blown into my curls. Just wanting a feeling of freedom, like an adolescent on a joy ride. I can only imagine what real freedom will feel like. No more home, no more Lily, no more thinking about Steve, no more cleaning old people's shit.

Back down in the morgue, the doctor and Alexa have left Sarah to get on with the final removal of tissue and the tidying-up of what remains. I'm glad I won't see any so-called relatives tomorrow. I'm fed up with their stupidity, no longer interested in their posing, guilty grief. I haven't even asked what Steve's son has made of recent events. I can only imagine that the man is a bastard, or weak-willed at least. I remember Steve saying something that suggested it was the girlfriend who held the reins. A bastard and an American bitch. They fit the demographic of this place: distant, uncaring, selfish consumers.

I help Sarah clean up the pieces. Any life left has gone with the organs and washing the body down is more like handling a carcass than a cadaver. Her tissue will be scattered across the world. It isn't such a bad end. They'll do it to Steve too. I hope, for his sake, it is sooner rather than later.

I do not take further pictures in the morgue. My artistic interest has dwindled and I do not care to incriminate Sarah further. Even though she's a bitch, she's nice enough as colleagues go. It's just work, after all. What job does not exploit someone? I have not changed my feelings about that. I have not turned sentimental. Simply, Sarah, the doctor, Alexa and I, we live by the rule of nature, red in tooth and claw. We have accepted the shit beneath our feet. We knock others in the muck to keep the smell from our own nostrils, but we don't forget it is there. Such living is an art. It is what I hope my work can show: civilisation as a cracking, temporary crust under which molten lava flows.

Together with Sarah, we lift the old woman onto a metal tray. The morgue is our filing cabinet of death. Sarah shuts the drawer with a loud clang. She thinks I will help her lift the old woman out tomorrow, return her to her room for viewing. Storing her overnight in the cooler keeps decay from setting in. She will seem fresher for those troupes of greedy mourners, come to scavenge inheritance. But I will not be here tomorrow.

'Well, that's it for now,' Sarah says, a soft, smacking pop sounding as she pulls off her gloves. 'Fancy a cuppa?'

I joke frown at her, collecting her gloves in a bag I will throw into the furnace.

'Coffee for you, of course?'

'Sure,' I say. 'I will just get rid of waste.'

The bag contains bits of skin and swabs soaked with the old woman's blood, our gloves, needles, everything we used. Sarah waits for me while I walk through to the incinerator, opening the hatch and chucking in the bag, then my own gloves thrown behind. All DNA burned. Once the rest of her is cremated, the only evidence of the woman's existence will be in my photographs.

We take off our scrubs by the door, dropping them into another sack that will be burned later, our own trousers beneath, but me with no undershirt and Sarah only in her bra and vest. Just outside the heavy doors of the morgue are hooks on which our other clothes hang. Sarah, as always, pretends not to look at my pigeon chest. We put on our shirts and travel back up to the ground floor in the lift, walking silently down the corridor to the kitchen.

'She was quite young, you know?' Sarah says,

slumping against a counter.

I put on the kettle and set the coffee on the stove.

'Can I bum a fag?'

This surprises me. I've only seen her smoke once, at my Christmas party. I'd assumed she was against it, wrinkling her nose at the smell of me and Steve. I thought she'd only smoked to entice Drago – what a joke. I hand her my cigarette packet, which she taps against one palm, expertly knocking a single fag into the open. She takes it, slides the pack along the counter towards me, and lights it, not bothering to open the back door.

'When did you start smoking?' I ask. She shrugs, does not reply.

'Sometimes I wonder if I'll end up here myself, you know?' Sarah laughs. It's a strange sound. She is not given to frivolity. She is normally a bitter cow. 'Apparently,' she continues, 'they got info on this one and knocked her cold outside her own front door. There was nothing wrong with her at all. Not before she got here.'

'Why do you ask where they come from?' I want to know. I've not known her so candid before.

She holds the fag from her lips and ponders my question. Before she speaks, she pushes her greasy fringe from her eyes, jerking her head slightly.

'Curiosity, I suppose.'

I take a cigarette, still standing by the stove. Steve is gone and no one gives a shit about smoking indoors any more. I flick ash on the floor.

'You should leave,' I say.

She nods.

'Maybe, maybe. But what else will I do?' It's not a proper question. She does not expect me to answer.

We smoke quietly for a while, waiting for the

kettle to boil, for the coffee to percolate through.

'What about you?' she asks.

'We'll see,' I say.

'You're becoming one of the family,' she laughs again, only this time it's her usual bitchy, pointed laughter, like the tinkling of fallen shards of glass.

I ignore her.

'Quite the family man,' she adds, twisting her head on one side. There is something ominous about the statement, like she knows something. 'Been in to see Steve yet?'

Before I can react, the kettle clicks. I shake my head to her last question and get on with making her tea. It's a useful distraction. Such conversation is pointless. I will be gone tomorrow. I drop a teabag in a mug, pour the boiling water onto it and hand it over like that. Sarah helps herself to milk and adds three teaspoons of sugar before dumping out the teabag. She uses the tap in the sink to put out her fag and drops the soggy butt in the bin, blowing out the last of the smoke from her lungs as she does it. I will not miss her.

'He's doing okay.' She takes a pack of custard creams from the cupboard. 'Biccie?' she asks.

I shake my head. The coffee is ready. I can't wait for it.

She munches on a biscuit, her lips smacking loudly, crumbs dropping onto her top, littering the floor. I hold my coffee, too hot yet to drink.

'She's looking a bit plump these days, eh?' she says, taking another biscuit. Is she talking about the old woman? 'Lily.' She nods the word out into her tea.

Really, there is nothing to say to this.

She taps her nose using the forefinger of the hand

that clasps at her half-eaten biscuit.

'Mum's the word.' She winks, shoves the rest of the biscuit in her mouth and slurps down the last of the tea. 'Got to go,' she says, dumping her mug in the sink and patting my arse as she leaves the room. 'Have fun.'

My cigarette finished, coffee steaming in my hand, I am left pondering the import of Sarah's words, knowing I have to get back to my room, copy the last of the photographs and get ready once and for all to leave this home. Was she trying to suggest she'd have made a better prospect?

Preparing to leave takes up most of the afternoon. Though it is still light, the purple hue of evening is making everything hazy, unfocused. My leaving bag is pulled out onto the middle of the bedroom floor. I am putting in the last few files when there is a knock at my door. I get up, pushing the bag under the bed, but Lily is too quick for me. She has just let herself in. I feel the colour slightly draining from my face, but she seems not to notice me kicking the bag further under. I push my hair back from my face with both hands, elbows making ugly triangular barriers to her oncoming embrace.

She stops halfway through the bedroom door, her smile fading slightly.

'Hey you,' she says.

'Hi,' I say. She doesn't look good. Her clothes are too tight and for one odd moment she looks very like her mother. They say all women end up like their mothers. Oscar Wilde said it, I think. It makes the thought of being with her more frightening than ever.

As my arms drop down to my sides, she walks towards me. She stretches her arms out, touches my face with her fingertips and pulls me into a tight embrace. I do not kiss her back, but let my arms fall around her, loose so I am holding and not holding her at the same time. When she finishes kissing me, she looks up, through her hair as always, but this time she is timid rather than coy.

'Shall I cook this evening?' she asks. 'I want to treat you.'

'Have they gone?' I do not want her cooking in the kitchen when Alexa is still here.

'Not yet. But, baby, couldn't we tell her tonight?' Her eyes have opened inwards almost, shimmering like desperate imitation jewels.

'Not tonight, Lily,' I say, stroking her hair, trying for comforting finality.

'But Milo, when?' She pulls back from me slightly, but still I have her in the compass of my arms. My grip tightens.

'Soon, soon,' I say. 'Just need to prepare ground. No one likes to be first to step on ice.' My excuses aren't good enough tonight. She pulls away fully, wrenching free of me.

'I can't wait any longer, Milo. Even Mother thinks I'm getting fat.'

'What are you talking about?' But I know, I know already. Sarah's wink flashes through my mind again and a feeling of terrible sickness presses the air from my lungs. I gawp, desperate to breathe but unable to, my mouth just flapping uselessly open.

'I'm pregnant.' She says it with defiance, her hands slipping open-fingered over her belly, drawing attention to it, protecting its taut fecundity.

We stand there, her glaring pleadingly at me.

I don't know how to move, what to say. It is the worst possible news she could give and I feel so foolish, so stupid not to have known, not have seen it coming. It feels like the whole world is collapsing around me, shifting into ugly, twisted shapes that threaten and mock and dissolve into a whirling mass of solitude, where an ever-present sense of her face and our child, clasped in her stomach, only makes me more alone. I cannot do this again.

'It's yours.' She says it needlessly, filling the floor between us with words.

'What will you do?'

'What will I do? Fucking hell, Milo, this is our baby, yours too. What do you mean, what will I do?' She drops her head, running both her hands, once, twice, around her stomach, making me feel the size and weight of it. Continuing to stroke, she glares back at me. 'This is our chance, Milo. You and me living together, making a family.'

It is like looking at a madwoman.

'You are so young' – I manage to splutter the words out, already wishing I could take them back, but too late more spill from my tongue – 'what about future?'

'I only want to be with you, Milo. I thought you knew that.'

A strange wistful smile creeps over her face, her hands still moving, caressing the strange flesh within.

'Can't do it, Lily,' I say. Her rubbing doesn't stop. 'I can't do it.'

Her smile deepens.

'Why not?' she asks. 'You say you love me. You're getting a divorce. Why can't we have this baby, together? Why can't we be happy, Milo?'

I feel cornered. All I have is the truth to turn to.

'I'm not getting divorced.'

It's almost as if she doesn't hear me at first. She

keeps on touching herself, staring at herself.

'I don't want another child,' I say, trying to make things clear.

The smile drops from her face, her hands freeze over her belly.

'It's too late.' She says it quietly, but a quiver floods over her jaw and lifts the left side of her upper lip into a snarl. 'It's too fucking late, Milos.' She pronounces my name badly, but in full, like this gives her some kind of hold over me. 'I'm having this baby and there's nothing you can do about it. I'm going to go and tell Mum now. I'm going to tell her everything.'

'Fine,' I say. It is a strange relief. The bag by my foot is ready. I can walk out early. Pictures from an earlier delivery will have to be enough. I laugh. 'Fine. Go on.' The letter for Alexa is ready. Lily won't make any difference. They will have to let me go. 'What will Mummy do?'

But she doesn't rush out of the room. She comes towards me again, takes my hand and presses it with hers onto her stomach.

'It will be a sister or a brother for Jelena, Milo.'

I pull my hand away.

'We can all live together, you, me, Jelena and the baby.'

'You planned this,' I say, 'didn't you? You fucking planned it.'

She reaches a hand out towards my chest, stroking it down my torso towards and over my belt, down towards my crotch. I brush her away.

'You can take pictures of me as I get more pregnant. I'll be your muse. You'll never have to go back. You'll stay here and become a famous photographer.'

She is talking more to herself than to me, repeating everything she must have gone over so many times in her head.

'You love children. You are a good father.'

She keeps moving in to touch me, her fingers like weed trying to drown me into her.

'No, Lily.' She keeps at me. 'Lily!'

Her hands drop. Tears are forming in her eyes and when she opens her mouth to scream at me, saliva stretches and pools across her lips and teeth.

'You bastard. You fucking bastard!' In one flurried, angry rush, she runs at me and kicks me hard in my shin, arms flailing at me, hitting out. The pain is excruciating, crippling. I try to grab at her as I buckle over and fall back onto the bed, but I can't get a fix on her. Even so, my fall seems to unbalance her and she staggers backwards. Looking down, she sees my bag, zips left open, still protruding slightly from under the bed.

'Lily,' I say, and this time I am pleading with her. 'Lily.'

She grabs my bag quickly and runs from the bedroom. I try to follow her, but I have to limp and hop; my shin is bleeding, a huge swelling already forming over the bone. She reaches the door to the corridor, pulls it open and slams it behind her.

'Lily!'

'I'm making us supper,' she screeches back at me.

The commotion has brought Alexa from her office. She follows the sound of her daughter's voice. I hear her clipping past my door, then the mumbling of voices. I have to follow them. I drag myself to the door and lunge out into the corridor. Hopping and limping, using the walls to support me, I make my way to the kitchen.

'Don't let him in,' Lily shouts. 'Don't let the bastard in here.'

'Lily, what's going on?' Alexa is trying to reason with her.

'Just fucking keep him out, Mum, okay?'

Alexa looks at me, my face, my leg. I must look terrible. And strangely, in this moment, as in all the times when you imagine drama will strangle your mind, I feel unusually calm, my brain races ahead of itself, logical, resigned, searching for new ways to move forward, almost standing outside of itself, seeing the pale, thin man leant against the kitchen doorway, watching two women, one busy with the oven.

Lily, undeterred by Alexa or me, has shoved the whole of my bag into the commercial-sized oven. Still she has to shove and tear and realign, but she gets it in there. She doesn't bother with the gas, she has my lighter in her hand – and it is in this moment that I remember I haven't seen her smoke in some time, had taken her casual don't-feel-like-its as one further caprice. She flicks it on and holds it against the photo albums, the old T-shirts and all those files of data, lighting one piece after another until the flames are too hot and she has to pull away.

'Lily, what are you doing?'

Ignoring Alexa, I try to get to my bag, but there isn't enough room for me to get past without touching Lily and she pushes me back. The smell is unbearable, thick yellow-black smoke choking us. The fire alarm is shrieking, deafening. Alexa yells something at me I cannot hear. And then, surprisingly, I remember my letter. It's still in my room, by the computer. If I can get it, then I can still leave. That one photograph will be enough. Alexa has rushed to the fire extinguisher, yelling at Lily to get out, to go through the back door into the garden. I cannot see them any more. I am trying to lurch my way back to my room. If I can only get there.

But Lily is there first. She pushes past me. She must have run through the canteen into the day room and in a wide loop. She is carrying a heavy pan in her hands. She is too far ahead. I cannot see her. I just hope she doesn't see my letter.

When I get to the doorway, Lily is standing above my computer, her arms raised. I cannot see my letter. The movement I make, swaying against the door, makes her turn around.

'I'm destroying it all, Milo. I'm going to smash it all.'

She turns back to the computer and brings the pan crashing into the screen. Splinters of glass skate across the room, sparks from inside the computer screen crack and flare. She drops the pan. She pushes the remains of the computer onto the floor in one heavy sweep, her whole body behind its weight, scratching her arms on broken glass. As I watch it smack to the floor, wires pooling, I catch sight of my letter fluttering down beside it. I don't care about the computer. All the files, the hard drive, were all in the burning bag. My only hope is in that letter. Everything else is already lost.

Lily, frenzied, her arms streaked with blood, her face blackened by the kitchen fire, is looking about wildly. She sees me staring, catches the trajectory of my glance and seizes the letter. She tears at the envelope, ripping it open, letting pieces of the note and photograph scatter onto the floor. She won't let me reach them, but snatches at them, shoving every torn fragment down the front of her T-shirt. She strides towards me. Pushing her face as close as she can without touching, she spit whispers at me, 'Fuck off, Milo. Fuck off home.'

Woman – V

When I open my eyes, everything swims. It is as if a film has grown between me and the world. It's both milky-white and pink, a mixture of smoke and blood. Tiny dots of light prick in through these blinds and if I focus very hard I can make out parts of objects: a leaf on a tree outside the window, the corner of the window frame.

My dreams are very vivid now. There are voices drifting in the space between my ears. One minute I am Ann, flying in her wheelchair, rushing down a hill, the wind whipping my old hair in my face. The chair becomes a seat and then I'm driving a car. Ann is beside me, Claire in the back. Claire is strapped down tight, but Ann isn't wearing her seatbelt. I feel light-headed, giddy, the car picking up momentum down the hill. Ahead I see a bend in the road, approaching faster and faster and then a shaft of sunlight falls into the room and my sleep shifts. I hold a mirror to my own face, but my reflection shimmers. A series of faces shift from one to another like an endless flick book, flipping sets of features into one another so that the eyes appear to grow closer and then apart, the ears move forwards and backwards, the nose breaks and heals, nostrils shifting in shape, the flicking picking up in speed through faces of all ages, races, sexes. I recognise none of them, all the time waiting, hoping for the face upon which the flickering will stop. And then a breeze creeps through a crack in the window, rippling the mirror that has become a lake, and swimming within it is Joe, his eyes deep and round, pointing to the bottom where a woman in a white nightdress floats up from a heavy stone, her legs chained down. One thin wisp of hair drifts madly upwards from her head, swaying lithe and dark like a water snake. He points again and I see words carved in the stone. 'That's Grandpa,' Joe says, looking at the stone, 'and that's you, Granny.' I look away, but my feet become entangled in the woman's chains, the cotton of her nightgown snapping at me, dragging me down.

When the doctor came, he was accompanied by a whole troupe. The nurses were there, along with a short woman in heels. I heard them clipping along the corridor to my room.

They came and formed a circle round the bed, judges to examine the evidence.

'Any progress?' the doctor asked. His voice was like liquid gold. I would say chocolate, but chocolate is too sticky, too unrefined. This was a warm but clean sound, calm, comforting and educated.

The male nurse started with the bandage over my nose. He unhooked the plaster.

'Mmm-hmm,' the doctor purred. 'And the stoma?'

Once again my nightdress was untied and the plaster ripped, more gently, from around the stoma.

'This all looks perfectly in order.' He snapped a glove over his right hand. The fingers were broad and hairy. He prodded the stoma, his hand giving off a sturdy heat. 'I see the hair is growing back. Let's check the internals.'

He looked up at me and smiled.

'If you feel any pain,' he said, talking directly to me, 'close your eyes. Alexa here will notify me.'

The short woman shuffled closer up the bed. She looked like she'd put her clothes on in the bath, they pressed in on her, every seam biting into her torso, breaking her into a series of mounds and rolls. She was petite and porcine, a woman on the edge of fat. Even her feet were bursting over her high-heeled shoes and she moved awkwardly, as if everything was stiff and held in. Her face was freckled and rosy, but dusted in a shiny bronze haze. As she walked, her dark hair moved all as one, set stiffly with mousse or hairspray. It looked dyed. She didn't bother to smile, but I didn't care about her. They'd sent for the doctor and I had been right. He wanted to know how I felt.

The doctor started to press his hands in around my stomach and under my ribcage. Nothing hurt and I was careful not to blink, just in case Alexa got the message wrong. I liked the doctor's hands and didn't want him to stop. He was so warm and firm. Surely, after he'd finished my physical examination he would want to talk. I would be able, somehow, to explain all the confusion.

'Good,' he said. 'Well, Alexa, you'll be pleased to know I think she's doing fine.'

Why, I wondered, would Alexa care?

'Everything's in order,' the doctor continued. 'We won't know for certain, of course, but her pulse is normal, blood pressure well within the expected range and her health records give a good prognostic of sound tissue. All lucrative stuff.'

He nodded at the nurses, smiling at them through one side of his mouth as he continued to speak to Alexa.

'This is a job well done. At sixty-three, we should have no trouble with the market.' He consulted his notes. 'Lived alone too, I see, and O blood type. All very good. I shall look forward to seeing her,' he looked down again, pausing as he lifted a couple of pages, 'in three hours' time?'

The nurses nodded and Alexa smiled. I could see why she hadn't before. Her teeth were narrow and crooked.

'How are we feeling?' he asked me, his voice raised in pitch and tone. He no longer seemed as kind, but he was addressing me. I would have to try.

I opened my mouth and tried to speak. Nothing but a groan would come out. He moved Alexa out of the way and stood right by my head. I thought he was trying to hear me, trying to help by moving closer, but he did not bend his ear to my face. Instead, he took my jaw in his left hand and pressed the gloved hand into my mouth, holding down my tongue. He peered down my throat.

'Excellent job.'

His fingers still on my tongue, he put his eyes level with mine.

'In the old days we would have cut out your tongue.' He smiled, a thin film of saliva stretching between his parted lips. He pulled out his fingers, letting my jaw shut of its own accord, and snapped off the glove, passing it at arm's length to Spotty, who took it between the edges of her forefinger and thumb.

'A sad, lonely old woman,' he said to Alexa. 'Is that all? Only I'd like to have lunch before returning to the morgue.'

Alexa checked back with Spotty, who shook her head. The doctor followed their gestures and looked pleased. 'Right,' he said, and they all followed him out of the room.

Acknowledgements

Thanks to all my family, friends and colleagues who have supported and encouraged me over the years. Particular thanks must go to: Caroline and Karen at Red Button Publishing for wanting to add *Home* to their list; the Arts Council for awarding me a grant in 2007 to finish the first draft of *Home*; Heidi James of Social Disease for believing in this project at its earliest stages and continuing to encourage me throughout the writing process – you've been invaluable in so many ways; Paul Blaney for all his excellent advice, support and editing skills; the person who took me round a care home and pointed out that most professionals caring for the elderly work tirelessly to improve the lives of those in their care; Sue and Geoff Perrott for giving me lunch and talking to me about the coach business; Katherine Jones for offering me the rare privilege of working with a highly skilled and emotive artist; and of course, my husband, Daniel, who always has my back.

About the Author

Rebekah Lattin-Rawstrone is a writer, editor and creative writing teacher. *Home* is Rebekah's first novel. A chapbook of her short stories, *Glitches*, was published by Acorn Books in 2014, and she is currently working on her second novel, a series of picture books for the under-fives, and a blog in which she reviews a new novel every week.

About the Artist

Katherine Jones is a painter and printmaker. She has won numerous awards and residencies, including a residency at Eton College 2015, the Royal Academy London Original Print Fair Prize 2014, a residency at Winchester College 2014, the Birgit Skiöld Memorial Trust Award of Excellence for the National Art Library V&A Whitechapel Artists Book Fair 2010, and was a finalist for the Arts Foundation fellowship award in printmaking 2013.

www.katherine-jones.co.uk

About Red Button Publishing

Founded in 2012 by two industry insiders, Red Button aims to give a voice to talented writers who are often overlooked by the mainstream.

Our mission is to find books that are simply crying out to be published.

For more fantastic fiction visit

www.redbuttonpublishing.net

Lightning Source UK Ltd.
Milton Keynes UK
UKOW06f0325071115

262204UK00010B/91/P